NO SHADE IN THE DESERT

R.R. Mangold

NO SHADE IN THE DESERT

To my younger self.
Sixteen years old and crushing on every
Buffy the Vampire character.

Nervous tapping of pens on notepads filled the room. Reporters scratched their scalps and fidgeted in the scratchy tweed chairs of the press room for the United Nations. Press releases by political leaders are rarely given in the middle of the night. Tonight, being a valid exception. Six world leaders were assassinated simultaneously four hours prior. Making nothing about this press meeting common.

The world has been anxiously demanding statements from every nation involved. The news stations speculate on every theory. Countries were blaming each other and threatening war. Military leaders are having their armies prep for a battle. Not knowing who the enemy is. The Secretary General of the United Nations claims to have knowledge that will stop all the governments involved from acting against each other.

Steel double doors open to the left of the stage, but no one enters. Reporters shift in their seats and halt conversations. The air went stagnant. Recording devices were lifted into the air and notepads at the ready. TV Cameras hum from the back of the room. The Secretary General requested the announcement should be broadcast live around the world. Whatever he needed to say, he only wanted to say it once.

A man appeared in the doorway. The Air was sucked from the room as he glided onto the center of the stage. The crowd expected someone else. This mysterious man wore a fitted black suit with a white Victorian collared shirt. His long silver hair floated behind his shoulders, catching the light like spiderwebs in moonlight. Silver rings adorned every finger.

He was pale, but not sickly looking. Up close you could see red veins pulsing under his skin. Mouths in the audience were agape at the sight of him. The usually aggressive reporters sunk into submission when his dark red eyes flicked over them. Despite their unnatural color they soothed the reporters. Filling them with a false sense of safety.

It was the tall dark-skinned woman behind him that caused every breath in the room to hitch. Her presence incited fear. The sides of her head were covered in swirling tattoos, leaving a row of braids down the center of her head that hung to her tail bone. The United Nations Headquarters building has a strict no weapon policy. It appears, not even the bravest security guard attempted to disarm her. Two short swords with obsidian blades crossed against her back. The dark red of her eyes was enhanced with smudged eye liner that matched the glossy black of her lips.

One corner of the man's lip twitched upwards when he reached the podium. Pleased that the audience was ready to hang on to his every word.

"Good evening humans." Spoken with a smooth tone of someone that could not be bothered. With an English accent that could seduce anyone. Reporters teetered on the edge of excitement and fear with the immediate confirmation that the man standing before them is in fact something different. Something inhuman. "For hundreds of years I have worked diligently to keep my species and others out of the light. Never involving ourselves in human politics. Enforcing our own laws to keep you oblivious and safe. The look on your faces tells me we were successful."

The fierce woman behind him let out a single chuckle to herself. Her firm biceps were on display as she stood with both arms linked on her lower back. A soldier at the ready to take down the entire room if necessary. His energy rolled over the room like intimidating waves. No one dared to ask a question.

"Earlier today a rogue group operated outside my directions to take it upon themselves and remove six world leaders from the game board." Camera flashes lit up his face. Even with his hair so silver his skin was youthful. Porcelain in appearance. "It appears to be the beginning of a plan that has been festering for some time."

The reporters began to shuffle in their seats, but he lifted a single hand that calmed them. A spell of dominance that could not be resisted.

Hiding in the back row was a young man with the top button undone of his shirt. It was untucked, as if the reporter got dressed while walking to the press room. I suppose most of them had, considering it was the middle of the night for New York. He yelled without lifting from his seat, "The assassins claim to be vampires. Are you really vampires?"

The last word was stuck in his throat and had to be unlogged with an audible gulp. Quiet murmurs filled the crowd. Shocked, one of them was brave enough to ask the question they all desired to. It brought a crooked smile to the man behind the podium. His elongated canines caught everyone's attention as they gleamed under the studio lights. He touched the tip of his tongue to one fang. Letting it linger while cameras flashed again.

The woman behind him hisses at the commotion. Again, the room is still. Heartbeats race in rhythm as they wait for his answer.

"Yes," he motions behind him. "We are vampires. I am Adonis Creon, reigning King of the Vampires and Commander of Shade."

Voices blended into each other over the clicking shutters and gasps. The tall glass of intimidation standing behind the King hissed again. Her fangs are on full display. The reporters froze to silence.

King Adonis pointed with a sharp black nail at a female reporter raising a shaking hand. Her entire body shook as she stood.

"Your majesty? Um King Adonis Creon, would you mind explaining what Shade is?" The moment she was back in her chair every neck in the room flicked towards the podium. Recording devices lifted above their heads. Never have reporters been so eager. This was the story of a lifetime. There has never been a more shocking discovery: Vampires exist, and they are governed by a King, a King who leads a secretive order.

"Shade has operated behind the scenes since the beginning of vampires. Shade is the reason you have not seen us, heard of us, and have no evidence of vampire related deaths. Shade keeps order. Shade is responsible for keeping vampires in line. Shade acts as bounty hunters, judges, and executioners." His eyes flashed brighter red, before darkening again. "As well as crisis clean up."

King Adonis motioned to the woman next to him. She squared her shoulders and brought her arms to cross her chest. He continued, "Meet Lieutenant Imani, who will lead a task force within Shade. She is committed to hunting down and eradicating the vampires behind today's attacks. Shade's reach knows no jurisdiction of human terms. And I expect complete cooperation from the United Nations and all other nations, regardless of membership. Our forces may have been invisible before but make no mistake—we are everywhere. From this moment on, our existence is no longer a secret, though it was unveiled under unfortunate circumstances. I will personally collaborate with global leaders to develop a plan for the integration of enhanced species into human life."

Two alarmed voices spoke at the same time.

"Enhanced? How were vampires created?"

"Species? Is there more out there than vampires?"

Imani and King Adonis shared a smirk at each other. He pulled the microphone closer to his face. Long black nails clacking the metal base.

"Since we are being exposed forcefully, I might as well take the werewolves with us." A cold smile filled his face.

The room erupted into chaos.

THIRTY YEARS LATER

Twelve anxious men in muted suits stood in a line rocking on their heels and clenching their jaws to keep from drooling. A camera crew shuffling around them in the driveway. The sun had not retreated behind the Hollywood hills mansion. Painting the sky with thick brush strokes of pink and orange. Before the line of desperate men waiting to be chosen walks a Goddess. A Goddess in comparison to them. Her body may be long and lean, but she could throw any of them across the yard without breaking a sweat.

A camera operator pans from her metal stiletto heels, follows the high slit of her black dress, before resting on her sharp features for a long beat. Filling the TV screen with a stunning woman that appears to have stopped aging in her twenties. Over the horizon a beam of sunlight shines across her face breaking through her thick dark lashes. The iris of her eyes illuminates bright red. The color of fresh blood. The favorite color amongst most vampires. Which is what she is. A vampire. She slides sunglasses up the narrow bridge of her nose for protection. One flawed result of their creation would be a sensitivity to UV rays. It only takes a few minutes for their eyes to burn out of their skulls.

Hundreds of miles away, desert dust settled throughout a sleepy town of Vaughn, New Mexico.

"You should go on this show." Said with a belch. A beefy hand with harry knuckles and cheese stuck to the fingertips pointed at the TV above the bar. Alex's eyes followed the direction. She cringed at the thought of a vampire on a reality TV show. Never did she imagine it would be commonplace to see a vampire parade herself around for entertainment. She finished the liquid in her glass before turning towards the man.

"You should lay off the cheese fries, Frank." Alex nodded towards his gut. Her relationship to frank consisted of one or two sentences a day. He learned fast Alex would not answer any questions about being a vampire. She learned how to ignore his drunk rambling. Most of the time. She found the sight of a vampire on a reality dating show annoying enough to break her silence.

This establishment was nothing special, but her options are limited. Jackalope is the only bar within a thirty-mile radius that carries blood liquor. Alex being the only one in town that drinks it. One of the main reasons she chose this Podunk town. No vampires around.

"All I am saying miss sassy vamp, is that if you put on a dress and some lipstick you could be the next Vampire Bachelorette." Frank reached across for the full pint of beer waiting for him. Alex grunted and rolled her eyes. "Maybe you would be less grumpy if you had a man to warm your bed and hold your hand."

"Pass." Her phone vibrated in her pocket. "I like my cold sheets; they match my cold heart."

He chuckled into his glass. Alex slid her phone out of her pocket and nodded to the bartender. He pulled an unmarked bottle from under the bar. The glass was so dark that the only indication it wasn't empty was the sloshing sound it made as he moved it. He flicked golden locks from his eyes and glanced around the bar. It was just after sundown on a Tuesday. The only patrons are the usual bar rats. Frank, who had his liquid dinner here every night. A young couple that moved here recently to start an alpaca farm. Everything about them screamed "I'm a hipster from Brooklyn". Land around Vaughn was half the price of Santa Fe. Alex did not like it that people were starting to notice the appeals of not living in a big city. Although she was no different than the rest of them, seeking seclusion and freedom.

When Alex moved here two years ago, she was the first vampire most of the town's folk had met. Vampires have always been city dwellers. They found it easier to blend into a crowd. Predominately living in large mansions or high-rise buildings. Using the money they have hoarded to buy nightclubs, casinos, and other businesses that operate at night.

Turning new vampires is highly regulated by Shade and punishable by death. Unless the vampire petitions a Shade agent who then gets permission from the King himself. It's time-consuming and only done after a commitment vow has been made. A commitment stronger than a marriage between humans. Vowing to love each other till death means a lot more when you are hard to kill. Alex has never made such a vow. Although she came close once. Just once in all her centuries alive.

In a time when there were more ships than cars, exploration was the focus for sovereign nations. Cities popped up across the world, the vampire population was diluted. An early European war was used to cover up the targeted attacks on vampire hives.

Vampires were scattered and tend to mimic moths to a flame. Staying in hives for convenience. A concept of community living and found family. Alex has had her fill with vampires and has no desire to share her space with them. The thought of working with them also caused twists in her stomach. She spent a century hunting down vampire criminals and removing their heads. Developing tracking skills that she has no issue letting go idle. Or at least she would if the local law enforcement could do their jobs.

Thirty years ago, she delivered the head of the final remaining vampire believed to be responsible for the UN attacks. Throwing it at the feet of Imani and Adonis before walking out of Shade Command Center. Never looking back. It took years to decide where to settle down. Moving around to random cities and towns. Making sure to leave no impression she was even there. Not wanting it to be easy for anyone from her past to find her.

The rural areas are not ideal. Harder for a vampire to hide their feedings. If they choose to feed on humans. One would be surprised how easy it is to find a human willing to sacrifice blood for the experience. Vampires are exotic and dangerous. Much like getting a tattoo, the scars left on their neck are worth the pain to some.

Rural areas increase the chance of a wolf pack being nearby. The war between vampires and werewolves has been over for quite some time, but the two groups are not intertwined. They have found ways to live alongside each other and keep out of each other's business. Agreeing to protect the laws of Shade based solely on the fact that they are both supernatural beings.

All these inconveniences of rural living are worth it to Alex. It means staying far from a vampire hive and Shade. She has seen enough of them to last many lifetimes.

Alex leaned her phone against the freshly filled whiskey glass. The smokey liquor scent was tainted by a coppery tang. Humans cannot smell it, but any vampire would pick up on the distinctly human blood mixed into her glass.

On the phone screen was a live feed from a camera. It was mounted on a tree with the occasional leaf moving in view from the wind. The words "Motion detected" were blinking on the bottom of the feed. A car has stopped in the center in a patch of dirt made from years of driving over the same path. A man with hair longer than Alex's and a neck nearly twice as thick was opening the passenger side door.

Bingo. Alex thought as a young woman stepped out. She willfully held his hand with an eager grin on her face. In the low light of the fading sun, it was difficult to tell if the woman was still human, but something about the eagerness in her steps and the flowing white gown suggested Alex only had minutes to get to her.

Alex pulled a crumpled twenty from her pocket and tossed it on the counter. She stood up retrieving her helmet from the stool next to her.

"Thanks for the drink, David." Tossing back the last of the liquor. David lifted a hand. He has known her since her first week in Vaughn but remains timid in her presence. He had no issue taking her money but would never invite her to a cookout.

"Alex." He cleared his throat. "That was my last bottle." She looked down at the live feed on her phone. The man had his hand on the woman's lower back and was guiding her away from the car. A large barn was in the background. A warm glow squeezed through the gap under the wide barn door.

Alex pulled out a man's leather wallet. She tossed three more twenties on the counter. "This should cover the taxes." David nodded and took the money from the counter with a smirk.

Ordering liquor that caters to vampires is taboo in these small towns. In the city there are bars with walls full of blood liquor options. David only agrees to order her favorite because she offered to pay the taxes and does not argue when he overcharges her per glass. Money has never been something Alex has had to worry about. A vampire can accumulate much wealth over the course of their long lives, and Alex was raised by one of the oldest.

The sun was below the horizon now. Letting the stars come to life above. She fastened the helmet against the back of her '67 Triumph Bonneville Motorcycle. It was not necessary to wear it at night. There are no UV rays to burn her eyes, and the threat of injury or death was nonexistent. It would be very difficult to fall off and decapitate yourself. The true reason vampires prefer the night. The sunlight will quite literally burn the eyeballs from their skulls. A common form of torture within Shade. Eyes never grow back. Even for a vampire. They become overly sensitive when they are turned. Changing shades of red based on emotion and stress. Like vampire mood rings.

Alex followed the main road out of town until she needed to switch to a dirt road rarely traveled. The trees were thin. She ditched the motorcycle a mile away to make a stealthy approach. Her footsteps were silent as she sprinted towards the source of her camera feed. The scent of floral soap and what she guessed was cherry ChapStick caused her to stop mid stride walking through a thin patch of Cottonwood trees. Alex crouched low and cocked her head towards the faint sounds fifty yards away. She had to listen past the hoot of a barn owl and the scrape of a lizard belly on a rock. Multiple sets of feet and shifting fabric whispered through the air. The sounds began to paint a picture in her mind. Gaps in her vision filled by what she could smell.

The young woman on the camera feed matched the

description of a missing person from Albuquerque. Her mother had been calling every nearby police station begging for a huge search. They ignored her when the young woman's internet search history was filled with evidence that she left willingly. The cops lack of enthusiasm to find her being the reason it was handed to Alex in the first place.

The forming of harems was outlawed by Shade in 1935. That didn't stop stubborn vampires from using their power to lure vulnerable women that have no understanding of what it truly means to be a vampire. What it means to fear the sun and live without a soul. To cramp and ache with solid food. To miss fried bread and stewed meats. To watch many of your friends grow old and die. Loneliness and pain have become Alex's closest friends.

Alex is tired of making connections. Tired of having lovers. She came to Vaughn for peace, but the local sheriff has asked for her aid on a few cases over the past two years. If they involve something supernatural. Sherriff Jules's only other choice is contacting the local Shade office and inviting them into her jurisdiction.

Alex reluctantly made a deal to assist on cases if it keeps Shade out of her backyard. Which is precisely why Alex is currently climbing a converted barn at night, looking for a missing woman.

Modern elements have been added to the barn that was previously used for hay storage. Including a skylight. Alex lays on her stomach and crawled to the glass. Gritting her teeth when the rough roof catches on her favorite leather jacket. She holds back a groan.

Small cases like this are easy for Alex. She barely

has to do any work to solve them. Alex spent centuries tracking down some of the world's slipperiest criminals. Finding a missing woman that has turned up less than fifty miles away from where she is from is a piece of cake. All it took was one hour with the woman's laptop. Alex had found that this missing woman spent a lot of time in chat rooms making friends with people claiming to be vampires. To be honest most of them were frauds. Taking advantage of the fetishes that have become so popular in many social circles. But one chat stood out to Alex. He was claiming to be sired directly by King Adonis himself. Calling himself the Prince of Night. A laughable title that does not exist.

Alex could name every vampire that has come from the King's line, as she knows firsthand exactly how selective the King is with whom he chooses to turn. She did not recognize the name that the vampire was using in the chat room. His claims of being heir to the throne lit a fire within that made this case feel personal. Also, Alex would have been aware if one of her fellow brothers or sisters was in fact living a mere ten miles away.

Two days ago, she tracked his car to this barn. He was prepping the space. Sweeping red dirt that blew in. Covering the wood floor with a layer only seen when the sunlight was low in the sky. Alex could have captured him then, but her main task was finding the woman. Decades ago, a case like this would require her to hide in the shadows for days. Now she can set up a camera while continuing to drink her thoughts away.

Below her, in the center of the barn the young

woman is sitting on a wooden chair in her white cotton dress. Her fists are nervously gripping the fabric on her lap. Alex's eyes scan the barn trying to spot the vampire who lured her here. Heat grew in her when she noted multiple scents in the air. She has been focusing on the scent from the woman now sitting in the chair. But there are three other distinct vampire scents. She may be walking into a hive. Are they planning on sharing the missing woman as a long-term blood source? Or do they plan on making her like them?

Alex adjusts her angle. Making sure not to put weight on the glass. The man walks into the center of the barn. The space was partially renovated. No longer suitable to house animals. Cabinets waiting to be installed leaned against a far wall. There were two doors off the main rom. One was open and she could see the edge of a sink cabinet. Behind the closed door was a strong heartbeat. Anxious with a quick pattern. He hummed a song she didn't recognize. It was deep and soothing like a lullaby.

The man appeared from the room. He has changed into loose trousers held on with a tie and a billowing tunic. He is really putting on a show for her. Trying to look from another era. One with more simple clothing and traditional gender roles that had her gaging. He looked to be in his late twenties. Not far from his actual age. Alex smirks to herself. *Idiot.* She has always been able to tell how old a vampire is by their scent. A rare skill she inherited from Adonis.

Trailing behind him are two young women. Younger than the one in the chair if she had to guess. The one walking with a bounce in her step could still be in high school. Or rather, she was in high school when this bastard turned her. The two women are holding hands and clutching bouquets of wildflowers.

Alex carefully got to her feet. Legs wide on either side of the skylight. Silently, Alex unsheathes the two serrated knives that were strapped on her hips. Over the years she wielded swords, bows, various axes, and plenty of guns. These long knives were a retirement gift from Adonis. With her full name engraved in Greek on the hilt.

The man took one step closer to the chair. The warm desert air stilled.

Alex knelt, then pushed up into the air. The movement smooth, as if wings sprouted from her back to slow her descent. She tucked her legs into a sharp point and went crashing down through the skylight. The glass bouncing off her thick denim pants. A shard nicked her chin. The pain didn't even register as adrenaline pulsed through her. Landing behind the chair with slightly bent knees and a wicked smile.

The woman leaped from the chair and screamed into the arms of the two vampire females. They cower together against the barn wall. Obviously not trained fighters. The male vampire lifted his fists and growled. Fangs on full display.

"Am I interrupting something?" Alex tilts her head to look over his shoulder. "Unsanctioned turnings? A harem perhaps?"

"I don't follow Shade's overbearing rules. I follow the old ways. The way we are meant to live." His voice echoes deeply off the bare barn walls. Alex flips a knife in her hand. The fear in his eyes created a thrilling chill up her back. The moment he recognizes her. He steps against the females hiding behind him. Making himself a shield. But Alex only smiles bigger. She is not here for them. She is only here for his head.

"Damien, is it?" Calling him the name from the chat room. She takes a slow breath. He flinches when her nostrils flare. "I am the old ways."

With a firm kick she launches the chair into his body. It cracks into pieces. Before he can gather himself from the impact, Alex is already in the air. Clearing several feet in a single jump. He uses his speed to duck before a swipe of her blade catches his face. Screams and whimpers blend with the sounds of fighting. The human is huddled against the wall with the two vampire women. Their terror enhances the aromas oozing from them. Nervous sweat mixing with jasmine lotion. It is going to take some smooth talking to convince them she is not the enemy. Not something to be feared. First, she needs to cut the head off the vampire that moments ago was vowing to be an eternal husband. A concept that has never been desirable to Alex. When vampires wed it is a commitment among immortals. A vow that can only be broken by death.

Alex kept her distance and circled Damien. It has been a long time since she has had a good fight. Although he has the skill of your average bar brawler, she wanted to draw out the fight.

Damien's hand wiped blood from his cheek. The cut is already beginning to stitch together. "You bitch. Can't you mind your business and get the fuck out."

She stopped walking and squared her shoulders.

Gripping the knife handles tight. Contemplating if she wants to use a blade or her bare hands to sever his head.

"You brought this to my home asshole." Alex pointed at his chest with the tip of a knife. "Now kneel and accept your punishment."

He scoffed.

"Bite me." He spat at her boots.

Alex looked down at the wet stain a few inches from where she stood. That would have been another reason to kill him if it had landed on her Verillas biker boots.

"No thanks." She glanced at the human whimpering behind him. "I prefer something sweeter. More feminine." Alex had no intention of biting the woman, but she wanted to test Damien. His face softened for a moment, and she knew he had failed any chance of redemption.

"Take her. Just let me and my wives go. I won't take anymore, I promise." He opened his fists so that his palms were on display to Alex.

The two vampire women gripped each other tight leaving the human to shiver from fear besides them.

"Ten seconds ago, you were ready to fight for her. Now you are willing to give her up." Alex brought her blades into a fighting stance. "I don't want your human. I don't want your promises. I want your head."

He managed to dodge her first few strikes. Moving like a dancer. The kind that spends most of their time spinning around the floor on a large square of cardboard. His white tunic became stained red around slashes from her blades. Alex lifted her left arm with the intention of catching his shoulder. He blocked it with both hands in a firm grip on her wrist. The knife in her right hand plunged into his gut. Damien staggered back. Taking the knife with him. The human woman shrieked as blood dripped from his gut. Staining the rustic wood floor.

Damien gagged on blood before spitting onto the dirt floor. Alex grinned and he mirrored her expression with a smile full of blood-stained teeth. He grabbed the hilt of the knife and pulled an inch. He grunted with pain. Alex took the time to examine her nails. The serrated edge ripped him inside. She faked a yawn.

"Kneel." Alex switched her remaining blade to her right hand.

"Fuck you." He pulled the knife from his stomach with a painful scream. Bright blood poured from the wound. Pooling at his feet. A vampire could survive the injury, but it would take a full day, and they would need fresh blood. Alex had no intention of letting him have either.

She lunged towards him. He shifted out of her way and bellowed with every twist of his core. Using her own knife, now dripping with blood, to block her blows. He was keeping up despite the gash in his gut. Alex admired his determination. Not enough to let him go, but enough that she was holding back.

Movement from the corner of her eye acted as a reminder this fight had an audience. The two vampires were holding onto the human and slowly moving towards the barn door. Hoping to slip away during the fight. The female vampire pulled the woman along like she was leftovers from a restaurant.

Alex decided it was time to end this dance. She

slashed his arm. The knife fell to the ground with his hand still gripped around it. Then she grabbed his remaining arm and yanked it behind his back. Pressing a knee to his spine she forced him to kneel. Pressing her blade against his throat. He swallowed against the sharp edge and a trickle of blood dripped from the contact.

"At least I will die by the hands of Adonis's protégé. An honor not known to many." Damien groaned. Alex leaned down until her lips were a breath away from his ear.

"More than you would think."

She gripped his hair and sliced the blade forcefully against his throat. The women screamed as she held up his dripping severed head.

66 Please. I beg you. Stop crying." Alex wrapped Damien's head in the discarded denim jacket she found in the room where Damien had changed his clothes. She was in the process of using a sleeve to wipe the blood from her blades before returning them to their places on her hips. The missing woman was a sobbing mess. Sitting crossed legged on the barn wood floor with her white dress tucked under her. The fabric splattered with blood. Alex would have found the image of her alluring. A beautiful woman covered in blood. However, she was in shock. Rocking on her ass and crying into her hands. Alex hates crying.

"I- I- I can't." The woman cried. Alex had no tissues to offer her and did not want her fluids touching her clothes. Tears and snot ran down her face ruining her wedding day makeup.

Moments ago, she sent a text to Sherriff Jules with the coordinates of the barn and a message that said, "come get your missing woman".

Her phone vibrated in her pocket. She put her knife away and pressed the phone to her ear. "You're welcome", she answered.

"Was she alive?" Jules asked as a car door shut in the background.

"Alive? Yes. Traumatized? Also, yes. I sent you the coordinates."

Jules was silent for a moment as she sends a text to her deputy. Alex could hear her snapping her fingers to get someone's attention. Jules was always attempting to do three things at once. Alex pictured her balancing her phone in one hand, a coffee cup that has been re-heated twice in the other, all while climbing into her Jeep.

"I am on my way." Alex heard Jule's deputy on the radio in the background requesting an ambulance from the operator.

Alex was kneeling at the feet of the two female vampires. They were tied together and leaning against the wall. Their red eyes were shooting daggers at her. With a wink she kissed the air in their direction. They hissed like feral cats. Their sounds had the human whimpering behind her. She was weak and Alex had no reason to tie her up with rope she found in the barn. Judging by the shaken expression on the woman's face, she was just now realizing what situation she put herself in. The glamorizing of vampires has diluted people's fear. They should be afraid. At no point was this woman safe with Damien or his wives. They could just as easily have had her for dinner instead of turning her into one of them.

Alex turned her back to them and focused on Jules waiting on the phone for more information.

"I am sorry to tell you this, but you will have to contact Shade for clean up."

"Fuck. Why?" Jules groaned into the phone.

"The asshole who lured the human had already turned two others. They don't appear to be completely corrupted yet, more like lovesick idiots. I think they hate me." Alex flashed them a smile and they both hissed through their fangs. "Shade will want them placed into a hive."

Alex could feel the Sheriffs eye roll as she sighed. "What if you take them in? Create your own hive. Teach them how to feed properly." Jules pleaded. "We could leave Shade out of it."

Much to Adonis's disappointment, Alex is the only one from his lineage that does not have a hive under their control. She tried once. In Boston MA. It was her first assignment in America and Adonis received a tip that a vampire was trading liquor for blood. Prohibition was at its peak. Causing a frenzy for alcohol that powerful people were more than happy to take advantage of. One vampire found a way to benefit himself greatly.

When Alex arrived in Boston, she found a group of eight vampires working for him. He kept them with full supplies of blood, and they used their stealth to deliver the liquor to underground bars. It was a good system, and he was becoming very wealthy in addition to the blood he collected. But it was not sanctioned by

Shade. His punishment would be death. Alex severed his head without him seeing her face. She was a shadow in an alley that moved on him quickly.

Narrow steps led off an alley. They went down to a door where she scented eight vampires behind it. The fresh copper aroma of blood had her stiffen before she opened the door. Her guts twisted with hunger. Alex had been tracking the vampire for two days. Whose head now dangled by his hair in her grip. She was persistent and took no time to rest or feed.

She barged in and was ready for them to fight once they noticed what she held. Thirteen eyes gaped at her with surprise. One vampire had a black hole where an eyeball should be.

The vampires did not move from where they sat. Scattered around the room with various barrels, bottles, and crates. One vampire had a look of relief, not shock. Her eyes glinted scarlet in the light from a hanging bulb in the center of the room.

"You killed him." She said far more enthusiastically than Alex expected.

Alex looked down at the head. His hair was slick with grease, and she had to tighten her grip to keep it from slipping out. "It appears so."

The vampire that spoke had medium brown skin. With tight finger curls framing scallops around her face. "Good." She smirked and placed a hand on her hip. Her dress was a dark green satin and hung low on her hips. Hips that were full and swayed when she took two steps towards Alex.

Her empty hand hovered over a curved knife tucked into a belt under a tweed jacket. Men's clothing helped Alex be invisible as she moved around the city. Paired with short hair styles, from a distance she could be mistaken for a teenage boy. This allowed her to go places women cannot. Misogynistic principles heavily divide society even now.

Judging the way this female vampire is approaching her; Alex assumed her goal was to seduce her. Thinking she was a man. Alex matched her smirk.

"You can put those tits away. As glorious as they are. Seducing me wont effect the judgement by Shade." This would prove to be an inaccurate statement. Alex was in fact seduced by Anita. Every night for sixty-four years, seven months, and twenty-one days. Those tits will lead to her begging Adonis to keep her stationed in Boston. Claiming the vampires there needed to be monitored. They did not.

Alex always suspected Adonis allowed it because he was thrilled to finally see her in a relationship. Allowing herself to have attachment outside of him and the assignment Shade gave.

Alex, Anita, and the other seven vampires moved into a gilded mansion on Park Ave. Hosting parties where Anita would entertain the guests with her songbird voice. She wore beaded dresses, paid for by Alex, and hid her face behind veils while on stage. She became known as the Veiled Dove. Enticing the room with a siren song that had them emptying their wallets at card tables.

Alex protected the eight vampires like they were family. She denied they had formed a Hive for as long as she could. Until Anita suggested bringing three humans that volunteered to be fed upon into their home.

The humans having nowhere else to go were happy to remain in the mansion. Serving drinks and food to the patrons during parties.

Their hive pampered their humans with decadent food and wine. Gave them plush beds and clothing fit for royalty. Twice a week Anita and Alex would call one into their room and feast together. Each of them latching onto a thigh while draining enough blood to keep them sated, but not kill the human. They would stare at each other longingly. Jealous of the skin being gripped. Until Alex could not spare another second. She would pounce like a lioness on Anita. Tasting the blood on her tongue. Often forgetting a human lay on the bed next to them. Unconscious from the blood loss.

Anita and Alex would use the energy surge from the fresh blood to pleasure each other for hours. Oblivious to when the human woke up and left the room. Alex was probably busy with her mouth devouring Anita's center. Lapping up every drop of bliss.

"Alex! Are you even listening to me?" Jules screamed into the phone. She shook the memories out of her head. The sobbing brought her back to the barn she was standing in.

"I am not really the hive type." Alex walked towards the barn door. She could hear the police sirens. Five miles away if she had to guess. "Give the two vampires to Shade and get this woman in therapy. Maybe take away her internet privileges."

"I can't exactly take away a person's internet access." Again, Alex could sense the eye roll.

She looked down at the woman and motioned for her to stay put. "Too bad. She's an idiot." The woman sobbed louder as Alex dropped the head on the floor. "I am leaving you a present by the door." She walked away leaving the bloody mess of the barn behind her.

She jumped to retrieve the camera mounted on the tree. Alex turned it off and tucked it into the pocket of her leather jacket.

"Don't leave. I am almost there."

"What was that? I think your phone is cutting out." Alex sped up into a jog towards her motorcycle.

"Alex. I need to talk to you." Jules was agitated. Her voice sounded like she was whispering into a cupped hand around the phone. "I would rather talk to you in person."

"You know where to find me Jules." Alex heard the police cars turn onto the dirt road. She sprinted. "Your pigs don't want me at their crime scene."

Reaching her motorcycle, she took the key from her jeans pocket and pushed it in the ignition. Jules would be arriving at the barn any minute now and Alex was already a mile away. Eager to put distance between herself and the swarms of law enforcement.

"I would like to find you not at the bottom of a bottle. I need to speak to you with a clear head." Jules said between barking orders at her deputy.

"How about you worry about the head I left you and not mine." Alex smiled when she heard a man's voice in the background shriek in horror. He must have opened the bloody denim jacket. "Later Jules."

Alex went to hang up, but the Sherriff had her pause.

"Alex, wait." She whispered. "Thank you."

The words stung. They were a kind reminder that she was hiding things from Shade. From Adonis.

That she was walking a fine line easily translated as betrayal. Alex was banking on guilt to protect her. That the last mission she completed for Shade caused Adonis so much guilt he did not try to persuade her against retirement. Perhaps asking her to deliver Anita's severed head was more costly than he expected. It cost Shade their best hunter. It cost Imani her best Agent. But greatest of all, it cost Adonis his favorite daughter.

B*uzz*
Alex rolled over and contemplated throwing her phone into a cholla tree. The metal truck bed bruised her back as her legs hung over the edge.

Buzz

She sat up with a groan. Next to her lay two empty bottles of whiskey and a drained blood bag. A perfect cocktail to knock her into a muted sleep. The only way she can block out all the memories that parrot themselves as dreams.

It was half past six in the morning. Alex was in the back of her truck out in the middle of the desert. It was easy to find a place to be alone in Guadelupe County. Another bonus for living here. When she reached for her phone, the sun moved above the horizon.

"Fuck." She said to herself with a leap over the

side of the truck bed. The driver's side door slammed behind her with a creaky thud. Could she afford a brand-new truck with all the bells and whistles? Yes, she could. Alex prefers the stench of old cigarettes and desert dirt. She has no intention of parting with her '84 Toyota truck. She slid her dark aviator sunglasses off the visor and put them over her face. After a moment she opened her eyes wide enough to read the buzzing phone screen. Finally able to read the message without the threat of the sun in her eyes.

It was a message from Jules.

Shade just left.

Alex let out a sigh of relief. She was worried a Shade agent would show up at her door and opted to hide in the desert all night. Her truck turned on with two turns of the key.

Who did they send?

She typed in response.

Alex sat in her vibrating truck watching the dots on her phone. Depending on the name Jules gives, she was either driving home or driving a hundred miles away.

A vamp named Rodrick Brooks.
He was skeptical when I said it
was called in by an anonymous
person. I suggested another
vampire had beef with Damien.
Killed him and moved on. Shade
has no reason to suspect you.

The name was familiar, but they had never worked a case together. If Adonis wanted to bring her in, he would send someone she knew personally. Alex put the truck in drive and headed home. Her phone buzzed again.

I still need to talk to you. Alone.

She typed out her response while driving with one hand. Nearly dropping her phone as she took the turn onto the main road too fast.

You can come this afternoon.
Bring lunch. No bacon.

Her phone buzzed quickly.

I hate you.

No, you don't.

Alex tossed her phone onto the seat. It did not buzz again. She smirked to herself. Jules was one of the good ones. She might even go as far as to call Jules a friend. Although she would never admit it. Life in Vaughn is not for making friendships. She is here to be bored and suffer alone. Punishment she awarded herself for being blind to those close to her in the past.

A three-year-old Alex bounced on the knee of a white-haired man with red eyes. She nibbled on a ball of Lokma. The honey sticking to her fingers. It was a reward for perfect bait. Leading to his loyal followers and himself being well fed for days.

"Papa," Alex looked up with her wide hazel eyes, "How do I know I am doing the right thing?"

He stroked her long dark hair and tugged her face forward. With her back to him, he gathered strands of her hair and began to braid it. "What moves you forward?" the question was rhetorical; he did not expect a three-year-old to have an answer. But he would repeat the question to her many times over the next century.

With her palm Alex wiped a streak through the steam kissing the mirror. Eye contact with herself begged a question, what moves you forward? She said aloud to herself, "Nothing."

Her olive skin was not dark enough to hide the enhanced color of her blood. When she flexed her dark red veins pulsed under her skin. A trait mostly visible immediately after a vampire consumes blood. A vampire's blood was never blue. Forever red. A powerful life force that needed to be replenished to keep up strength and other abilities.

Her hair was longer than usual. Cut at a sharp angle from the back of her head following her jaw. Slightly longer on the right side. She wondered if Anita would have liked it. Anita had always been the feminine one in their relationship. With a love for luxury clothing and adding color to her face with makeup. Anita's darker skin helped her hide being a vampire easier. Needing only to cover the red of her eyes.

Alex often wished she had met Anita when she was still human. She would have loved to memorize the color of her eyes. All vampires lose their original color when they are turned. They become irises of electrified blood. Her eyes were green. Or at least she believes they were green. Her human memories are hazy.

A car turned onto her driveway. She tilted her head back and sniffed the air. It was Jules. There was a distinct smell of burnt coffee and pine deodorant. Alex threw on a faded band t-shirt. Not bothering with a bra. She tugged on men's boxer briefs and walked into the living room.

Every window was covered in her adobe style house. She had a large TV mounted on the wall and a dark purple velvet sofa. Papers and a laptop filled the coffee table. She could hear Jules walking up her steps. Belt jingling with her baton, gun, radio, and comically large key chain. Alex opened the door before she could knock. Jules held up a mini cooler and glared at her.

"Oh, good my lunch is here." She grinned and licked the tip of a fang. Jules pushed her way in.

"Yea yea. Here's some blood bags for you."

Alex tilted her head. Her eyes trailed Jules muscular form as she walked into the living room. Jules had broad shoulders and arms that could squeeze someone until their ribs popped without breaking a sweat.

Her hair was slicked back into a low bun. "Blood bags? How do *you* know I didn't mean *you* were my lunch?" Alex teased.

Jules scoffed and planted herself on the far end of the sofa. Alex put the three blood bags in the fridge. She dropped a fifty-dollar bill in the empty cooler when Jules was not looking and handed it back to her. Choosing to sit on the arm of the chair with her legs on the cushion.

"Jesus, Alex. Can you put some clothes on."

Alex looked down at her shirt sticking to her damp body and boxer briefs. "Does it make you tingle inside to see me like this Jules?" She raised an eyebrow and lifted her arms in a stretch. The shirt lifted above her belly button.

"My wife told you to stop flirting like that Alex. You may be a vampire, but she is Latina. I have no doubt she could make you disappear." Jules adverted her gaze away. Alex threw her head back and laughed. She flipped her body off the couch and sprinted to the bedroom.

"Start talking while I cover up my sinful body." She dug around the floor for jeans that met her standard of clean. Settling on a pair of grey wash Levis with holes in the knees. They smelled slightly like whiskey and gun powder from the last time she went target shooting.

"Do you know the werewolf pack in Encino?" Alex hummed a response. "Well, their Alpha has been contacting departments in the area looking for missing wolves. He keeps getting pushbacks. I don't know much about looking for wolves. I was hoping you could assist."

She returned to the room. Now fully dressed and took up the seat on the other end of the sofa. Balancing an ancle over one knee.

"Why are you so bent on getting me alone? Your department has seen us together for two years. They know I do your dirty work." Jules tugged at her shirt collar. The rim was dark from years of sweating in the desert. Alex pulled up an app on her phone and turned on the air conditioner. Extreme heat or cold doesn't bother her, and she rarely had human company. Well, she never had human company. Jules is the only one she has allowed into her house.

"I want an outside eye to find a connection between the missing wolves. Before I get Shade involved or the FBI. I need to know if they are related." A quiet breeze moved through the room from the AC mounted in a window. Jules eased deeper into the couch. Letting the cool breeze roll over her body.

"Does the Alpha want Shade involved?" Alex asked.

"Yes and no. They want their wolves found, but don't want to owe Shade any favors. I don't understand the politics of it all, but what I gather Shade lets the wolves pretty much govern themselves. I gather that's how the werewolves want it."

Alex stared at her unmoving. She could divulge her curiosities and tell her what she knew of the relationship between Shade and wolves, but Alex was a secretive asshole. The werewolves were around longer than vampires. Once the top of the food chain. It took centuries for them to manage their own transitions.

They used to roam on nights of the full moon. Free to hunt and mate. Then the world became more populated, and bodies were found torn to shreds.

Now werewolves lock themselves up willingly when not in a safe place to roam. They travel to sacred locations as a privilege where they can roam free during the transition. The females using that time to get pregnant and ensure the wolf blood line. Shade keeps land open for them. Protected from unwanted humans. One of the many things agreed upon in the treaty.

Jules has no clue New Mexico hosts one of these sacred areas.

Alex cleared her throat. "You don't trust the skills of your detectives?"

"Not all the cases are in my jurisdiction." Her hazel eyes met the dark red of Alex's. "I need to keep this off the records. For now."

"I see." Alex looked at her fingernails. "You need help from your favorite sexy morally grey vampire to do your dirty work."

"I never said you were sexy." Jules said flatly.

A low chuckle rumbled from Alex. "But I am your favorite."

Jules grabbed the mini cooler and stood up. "You are literally the only vampire I know." She began to walk to the door and stopped with her hand on the silver knob. "Will you help?"

Alex turned her body towards Jules. Helping with cases has kept her plenty busy. Lately it seems the only time she leaves her house is to get a drink or to help Sherrif Jules.

Alex nodded. "Of course."

Jules groaned as she walked back out into the sun. There was not a single cloud above. Causing the desert landscape to feel endless. Alex stayed inside the house and watched Jules get into her Jeep.

"I will email over the files. Let me know what you find." She rolled down the window and waived as the car moved. Alex saluted like a jackass. Making sure to stand at attention. Jules flipped her off in response.

A storm rolled in early in the evening. Alex watched the cacti swell from her porch. Filling up from the rare rainfall. She matched the thunder with a swipe of a Cretan Oilstone over her knife. Rain washed away the red dirt from her truck and pinged on the steel roof of the carport protecting her motorcycle. Next to her sat a crystal glass of blood. It sustained her in strength only. Every day was a battle of willpower not to drink directly from the vein. It kept her alive without any of the benefits of fresh blood.

Alex tilted her head and paused her hand grasping the stone. The laptop inside was dinging with alerts. Tossing back the rest of the blood, she stood. She placed the knife and stone haphazardly on the dining table next to the laptop. Multiple emails came through from Jules's private email. The subjects were:

- Paul Grady - Registered werewolf – Encino NM –April 2
- Alejando Jimenez – Suspected werewolf – Pastura NM – March 26
- Jolene McKean – Registered werewolf – Santa Rosa NM – March 12
- Colby Jenkins – Registered werewolf – Albuquerque NM – February 27

She studied the four subjects without opening the emails. She did not recall hearing any of their names on local news. Either law enforcement did not think missing supernatural's are important or someone was covering it up. It could be either. Once vampires and werewolves were revealed to the world, signs went up all over the place restricting access. "Human Only" establishments became a normal thing. Shade tried to endorse a bill in the US that would protect them under current discrimination laws, but in the end, congress decided predators do not deserve protection. That is what vampires and werewolves were seen as. Predators and nothing else.

A fair assessment if you would have met Alex in her early decades as a vampire. Trained by adonis herself to stalk and consume. Choosing targets that wouldn't be missed or according to Adonis, don't deserve to live. Draining a human completely could sustain Alex for nearly two months. The temptation is not too strong in Vaughn. Alex has no desire to bite anyone in this town. And little desire to roam the nearest city for a willing donor.

Alex opened the email for the most recent missing person. A man in a nearby town, Encino. Paul Grady was a known werewolf, which meant she needed to start with his pack. Rule out a serial kidnapper by discovering if anyone in the pack wanted him gone. People go missing all the time. Werewolves are more complicated people. They have animalistic desires. Paul probably followed the scent of a deer and got lost. Or mated with a wolf in a cave and they are settling in. Alex knew those options were inaccurate assumptions, but it made her chuckle to picture a wolf in mated bliss, hung up in a cave with a non-werewolf wolf.

She skimmed over the other emails and decided to take the case one wolf at a time.

The rain outside concluded its thrashing. The desert was blanketed with silence. Soon it will be dark. Alex decided to visit the pack when she had full advantage. No sun to blind her and at full strength from a belly filled with blood.

She left her large knives behind and tucked a gun into the waistband in the back of her pants. Alex covered it with a jacket that made her look like a dad couching a youth baseball team. The sleeves were grey leather. Contrasts to the black body that appeared to be wool. Too hot for Spring in the desert, but Alex was not bothered.

She drove away in her truck with only her phone, wallet, gun, and a pack to visit.

The GPS on her phone said it took fifteen minutes to drive to Encino. Alex made it there in eight. After passing the city limits sign, she pulled over. Leaning with her head out of the window she sniffed the air. There are a few things vampires and werewolves have in common. They both have heightened senses. Although admittedly they would win over a vampire's sense of smell during a full moon. The one night the odds are increased in their favor. They could kill anything in their wolf form. A reminder to keep your friends close and your enemies closer. Which is why Shade vowed to protect them.

Shade held their pack leaders accountable to have every member locked up in iron chains during a full moon. Those old enough to turn. The shift to werewolf is like puberty. They have rituals and ceremonies. Parts of their culture that have remained a secret to outsiders. Even to Shade.

There was a time when Alex wanted to spy on the wolf packs and see what went on in secret. But that would go against a treaty signed by the previous King. One that Adonis has no intention of breaking.

Alex drove slowly through the town. Town being a loose term. It was a dozen scattered houses on a strip of highway. The rain had stopped and gave each surface a fresh start. In the distance she smelt the musk of multiple werewolf bodies. She turned down a dirt road and into the dark desert landscape. Puddles of water sat in patches on the ground, the earth being too dry to absorb it. Imagine being so thirsty you could not drink. Alex chuckled to herself at the thought. She continued to follow the stench of wet fur. Even in their human form their scent resembled a wolf.

Out in the middle of nowhere were small buildings with rounded roofs. A large bonfire was blazing in the center. Cars and trucks lined the road. She continued driving until she reached the end of the road and a large metal gate. It connected to a fence of corrugated steel. High enough to keep a human out.

She turned off the truck and tucked the key under the sun visor. Before she could open the door, a shadow caught her eye. There was movement behind the truck. Alex watched another shadow join it in the reflection of the rear-view mirror. The truck door creaked open. She made sure the gun was secured in her waistband and stepped out with her hands up.

"Come on out pups, I come in peace." She spoke into the darkness. Rustling in the dirt had her spinning to find large man with two braids staring down at her. He had a full foot in height over her and it was exaggerated by heavy work boots. His features were sharp. His lips plump, held in a flat straight line. She would consider him handsome if she was into that sort of thing. He sniffed in her direction, and it made her cringe. She wondered if she was that creepy when smelling people.

Alex felt another man approaching behind her. He was trying to keep his steps light, but her hearing caught the slight shuffle of dirt as he moved. She stayed facing the tall man before her. Giving them the false security that they could get a jump on her.

"We have no scheduled visits with Shade." There was a deep rasp in his voice. Like he was screaming for hours at a concert. Or howling at the moon perhaps. "State your business, vampire."

Alex glanced over her shoulder. The man behind her was much younger. His hair was cut short, and his skin was not as tan as the man before her. She could smell the fear leaking from his pores.

"Why is your pup so scared?" Alex flicked her chin at the young man. The larger man clenched his fists and narrowed his eyes.

"We don't get many vampires out here." He squared his shoulders. "Again, state your business."

"I need to speak to your alpha."

Alex found it annoying to keep her neck cranked at an angle to look at him. He must be close to seven feet. Instead, she took a step back. Letting him have a small win in territory dominance. He smiled as if reading her thoughts.

"No."

"No? That's it. No?" She placed a hand on her hip, making sure her jacket kept the gun covered. "You are not curious why I need to speak to your alpha."

"No."

"I am not trying to cause trouble in your little doggy club." He barred his teeth at her, holding in the urge to growl. "I was sent to help on orders from Sherriff Gefahr in Vaughn." Referring to Jules by her last name felt unnatural.

"The Sheriff employs vampires?" He scoffed. "That seems unlikely."

"I am on no one's pay roll. This is just a favor for Jules. I have dog in this fight." She grinned. Her poor choice of words was intentional. It only made him grin. Alex appreciated someone with a sense of humor.

His shoulders relaxed "First names with the Sherriff. Are you sure you don't work for Shade?"

Alex placed a hand on her hip. "The Sherriff would not accept my help if I worked for Shade. I think she distrusts law enforcement as much as I do."

He hummed in agreeance. His dark eyes scanned her under the moonlight. She was waiting for him to demand her weapons, but he just nodded to the young man standing behind her.

"Tell Thor I am escorting in a vampire." He barked.

"Yes sir." The young man burst into a sprint. Leaping over the gate in a single stride. He pulled out his phone and tapped the screen. The gate began to slide open. Shaking while it was pulled by a cable.

"Pup in training?" Alex pointed in the direction of where the man ran. The man just nodded once in response. "I am Alex."

"Turn around Alex." He grunted. "Spread your arms out.

The gate was nearly all the way open. She considered bolting past him towards the bonfire. Judging by the air, there were over a dozen wolves living on this commune.

"Do you have a name?" Alex teased. "I don't spread for just anyone."

He rolled his eyes. There was a hint of beer in his breath, and she wondered if her visit interrupted his night off. Night off from being brooding and intimidating. Who needs a look-out tower when you are built like one.

"James. Now turn around." He twirled his finger in the air.

"Nice to meet you, James. If you touch me, I will break your hands off." His eyes went wide. "This will be a quick visit. I just need to speak with your Alpha, and I will be on my way."

James took a step towards Alex. "Give me your gun."

"No." Alex hissed through her fangs. "I am not walking into a fucking wolves den unarmed." It did not need to be said out loud that the bullets in her gun were tipped in silver. Like all living things, werewolves can be killed by decapitation. For a werewolf, a silver bullet to the heart is just as effective.

"If you attack the alpha, the pack will tear you to shreds." This time he did growl. "Understand."

Alex turned on her heels and walked towards the open gate leaving her truck behind. "Understood, James. Now take me to your Alpha."

Oh, the drama. The commune was built for the houses to mimic light from the moon. With a large clearing in the center and a couple larger structures behind the houses. Torches were lit in a half circle in the middle. People watched from the other side of the windows. Hiding their faces behind curtains when she looked in their direction. Alex attempted to soften her face as she approached. Trying to look like a friendly vampire and not a complete bitch.

James remained one step in front of her. His large shoulders barely moving as he walked. He had the presence of someone wearing football pads, except it was all muscle.

There was a large building in the back of the commune that smelled like crayons and juice. A school if Alex had to guess. This was a rare experience for an outsider. Most will never get a glimpse into the commune of a werewolf pack. Her instincts were to roam and search. To unearth their secrets, but she kept her eyes trained forward.

The Alpha sat in an Adirondack with a fire blazing before him. Built inside a recycled oil drum. They can usually be found being sold by locals at markets in Santa Fe. The fire was low, as if it was fighting against the moisture in the air left from the rain.

Standing behind the alpha were six people. One was the young wolf from the gate. Two of the males were human. Judging by the lack of fur smell on them. Their arms were crossed tensely across their chests. One of the men pulled a camping chair out and unfolded it with shaky hands. He motioned for her to sit and took his spot back behind the Alpha.

She leaned back in the chair and crossed an ancle over one knee. The silence was deafening. Only a cricket was brave enough to break it.

Alex had the urge to reach for her flask before remembering she had left it in the truck. "So-"

"You say you are not with Shade, vampire." The Alpha cut her off.

"Not for thirty years." Up close she could see the necklaces hanging around his neck. Multiple layers of stone beads, but no silver. Silver being one of the things New Mexico is known for. One would think a werewolf would want to stay as far from silver as they could. In fact, a smart pack took ownership of the land and had a hand in all silver trade in the area. Maintaining control over the thing that could kill them. "I am not here in an official capacity. Just as a favor to Sherriff Gefahr."

"Her name is Alex." James said over her head. She could feel his eyes drilling into the back of her head. Along with all the wolves watching. If she were to flinch towards the gun, he would pounce like a dog on a ball.

"Do you have a name? Or do I call you Alpha like your pups?" The people behind him shifted. Either they don't like being called pups, or they don't appreciate the in-formalness of her speech.

"You may call me Thor."

"THOR." She said far too loud. "Like the God of thunder?"

"No." He sighed. "Not like the God of thunder."

Alex held in a laugh. "Ok, Thor," She smiled, "I am here about Paul Grady. He went missing on April 2nd." Thor looked her up and down. There was a knife tucked into her boot that he clearly noticed. It was not silver, but she could do enough damage with it. James seemed to notice how calm Alex was. She was not a woman who would feel fear surrounded by a group that was once the enemy. A war only known through legends passed from vampire to vampire. Only Adonis and a few others remember life before the treaty.

"Why would the Sherrif send a vampire instead of coming herself?" His thick black hair brushed above his shoulders with a slight breeze.

"Something about jurisdiction." He stayed silent. Waiting for her to elaborate. "Because I am good at what I do."

"And what exactly, do you do Alex?" Thor clasped his hands together on his lap.

Alex went over the many answers in her head. *Kill*

vampires, kill werewolves, kill people occasionally. Drink a lot to avoid thinking about Anita. She settled on "Find people. I was a tracker for Shade before I retired."

"You look too young to be retired, but I guess one cannot tell how old a vampire truly is." His smile was warm. A sharp contrast to the faces behind him. They were ready to tear her apart for speaking to their Alpha. "Does this mean you are tracking Paul?"

"And other missing werewolves that might be related." She dropped her leg, and the movement had James's shift an inch closer. She ignored the sign of mistrust. "Tell me about the last day he was seen."

The Alpha cleared his throat. "Paul visits the pack about once a week. He brings papers and magazines for us old folks who refuse to get the internet."

"Is that how you knew he was missing? He didn't show up."

"His brother got a text from his boss that he didn't show up for work." The fire cracked and she felt James flinch behind her. "I contacted his landlord. He's a friend of mine and I had him check his apartment. There was no blood or other signs of a fight. I had him send me photos."

Thor lifted his hand and a man next to him placed a cellphone in his palm. Alex waited patiently as he narrowed his eyes at the screen before handing it to her.

She scrolled through the photos. It was a studio apartment with a red brick wall that was broken up by a large window. The blankets and sheets on the bed were tussled.

"Was he the type to make his bed in the morning?"

"Fuck no." The man next to Thor chuckled.

Thor raised a hand to calm the snickering. "He was not known for being tidy, but he was known for being kind. He made friends everywhere he went."

"How about enemies? Did he make any of those?" Alex tapped her fingers on her thigh. The alpha answered without hesitation.

"No. Paul had no enemies. He was bright and hopeful. He was a real-" Thor paused and looked around at the faces. Alex just noticed how somber they were. Paul was truly missed amongst them. He had a commune full of people that love him. She wondered who would notice if she went missing. Who would gather to say kind words? If anyone would look for her.

"Golden retriever type." A young woman's voice broke the silence.

"Were you his girlfriend?"

She laughed, "Oh, God no. We both attended pack school here."

"The only relationship Pauly had was with his Xbox." More in the circle laughed until Thor hand up a hand to silence them.

He waited until those standing around them were silent. Behind her was the faint sound of James grinding his teeth. Thor huffed out a breath before speaking.

"What they are trying to say is, Paul was not in a relationship. And my pack searched his apartment. There were no scents belonging to anyone else in his apartment. They even patrolled his neighborhood for two days trying to find a trail. I asked the local police to get a warrant for nearby camera footage, but they had no reason to believe he was taken. As of now they are claiming him as a runaway."

"Would he run away?" Alex asked.

"We have no reason to believe he would."

The lights from the houses around them have been off for a few minutes. Thor has stopped feeding the fire and was letting it die. Behind her, James shifted his feet. His knees tired from being locked.

Alex stood and stuck out a hand towards the Alpha. Thor matched her strong grip. She let his large grasp dominate hers. This was his territory and the last thing she needed was to embarrass him by breaking bones with a simple squeeze.

James walked her back to her truck. He paused outside the driver's door with words hanging on his lips. She raised her brows, "Got something to say?"

He let out a deep sigh. "Why are you doing this?"

"What? Driving this piece of shit? Cause I like old things." She slapped her palm on the steering wheel.

"Looking for a missing wolf. Vampires only care about other vampires." He flattened his full lips into a line. She looked at his face in the moonlight. In the distance there was just enough light for her to make out a person linking arms with the Alpha and walking him towards a larger house in the back of the commune.

"Jules, Sherriff Gafahr has my back. By helping her I am helping myself." She turned the key twice until the engine ignited. "So, I only care about one vampire. Me."

She shifted into reverse and drove until the road was wide enough to turn around. Alex had cared about other vampires once. She cared greatly for Adonis. Part of her always will. Without him she would have been nothing. He pulled her from the stiff arms of her dead mother and raised her. She was human then. Surrounded by ancient vampires. Used to lure humans into traps. Pretending to be a lost child in Athens. Then in Croia and Naples. She came into adulthood in Portugal. Where Adonis gave her the choice. Leave their hive and be free. Or become his immortal daughter and begin training.

Alex often wonders what she would have become if she chose to walk away. If she had lived a short human life. Then she thinks of her time with Anita and wouldn't trade the sixty-four years, seven months, and twenty-one days for anything.

Alex's memory was strong. She wrote down everything she learned from the Alpha. Adding extra lines on behavior she observed. As well as the description of Paul's personality. She decided to trust the pack and not waste her time checking his apartment for clues.

The only conclusive link in the millions of notes Alex had written about was that they were all werewolves. The similarities ended there. They lived in four separate cities. Their ages ranged from twenty-three to forty-two. Jolene and Paul were from the same pack. Although Jolene's most recent address is in Santa Rosa. An hour away from the pack commune.

Alex pinned important documents to a cork board next to the TV. The news channel was muted. On the bottom of the screen words ran by on a red banner.

*United Nations scheduled a hearing for May 24th –
USA military will discuss recruiting supernatural's
for their extra abilities and strengths – NATO in support of recruitment.*

Alex wondered if she would be receiving a phone
call from a recruiter. Having a soldier that is very
hard to kill would be convenient for any army. One
that cut her ties with Shade and is roaming as a free
agent would be at the top of the list.

Adonis would be against any supernatural joining
the military. He has always kept Shade operatives
out of politics and war. Allowing the subject to get
as far as being discussed with global leaders now, did
not sound like him. Yet, her curiosity was not strong
enough to contact him. It had been years since she
had spoken to him, and even with him being the closest thing to a parent she has, there was no desire to see
his face again. It may have been Imani that gave her
last mission orders, but it was Adonis who sanctioned
everything Imani did. It was his nails in Anita's cof-
fin. He put the blade in Alex's hand. He taught her
skills only valuable for hunting and killing.

She threw a small dagger into the corkboard im-
pelling a word written under Paul Grady's name.
Toast. The newest bar to open in Vaughn and the
current place of employment for Paul. With an annoying name and equally annoying clientele. Started by a hipster couple that couldn't afford to live in
Albuquerque. They did not carry blood liquor. What
they had was enough flavored bitters lining the wall
to confuse patrons that it was more of an apothecary
than a bar.

Alex went to the fridge and bit a small hole in the

corner of a blood bag. She poured half the cold contents into a metal flask and tucked it into the pocket of her leather jacket.

The sun has already dipped below the desert edge. Leaving behind a trail of thin tangerine-colored clouds. Alex ran her fingers through her hair and noted the faint fur smell in the distance. She recognized it but chose to ignore it. For now. With a smirk on her face, she started her motorcycle and headed down the road.

Toast was once a western tavern until the walls inside were painted black and filled with mismatched art. Pieces that were found at estate sales or thrift stores. No two frames are the same. There are oil paintings of people on horses next to neon velvet paintings from the nineties. It was tacky and Alex hated it. She hated the fear pouring off the bartender even more. Jules had warned Alex when this place opened that the owners were not vampire friendly. They boasted to their real estate agent about moving away from cities because vampires are known to flock there.

A petite redhead with hair spun into two small buns at the sides of her head stared wide eyed. She paused her chopping with a knife stuck in a wedge of cheese. Alex crossed the room that was lit with red hanging globe lights. Eyes racked down her back as she took up an empty chair. Flicking the hair out of her face and grinning large enough to show her fangs.

"Um-" the woman began to say before a man stepped in front of her. He had broad shoulders and a pudgy belly, ready to burst from a short sleeve plaid shirt. Tattoos of birds and trees covered his arms. He braced himself on the bar. Hiding the woman with his body. It was an act of dominance that Alex had to hold in a laugh witnessing. She could break him in half and begin to drink that woman dry before he realized what was happening.

He cleared his throat. "We don't have blood liquor here." A fact she already knew. Alex tossed four twenties on the bar counter.

"I'll take a double of Uncle Nearest." Money is the one language spoken by all. It has bought secrets, discretion, and freedom. Money vampires hoarded in ancient tombs around the world. Filling the pockets with more than was necessary to live off. They were a slow growing population of predators that chose to let the prey believe they held power. Humans believed it was their intelligence and ingenuity that put them in charge of the world over other species. When in fact humans are right where vampires need them. Distracted, ignorant, and plentiful.

The man picked up a crystal glass. He dropped a single round ice cube inside before pouring a healthy serving size of amber liquor over the top. The muscles in his jaw tightened as he slid it over to Alex. Moving his hand back quickly as if he was afraid to be touched. Alex pulled the flask from her pocket and filled the glass to the top with dark red blood. His eyes turned to saucers. The corners of her mouth twitched at the rapid increase of his heartbeat. "Thanks, Jasper."

"My names not Jasper." He gulped.

"You look like a Jasper." She tossed back the entire glass of whiskey and blood. A drop escaped. Creating a trail from the corner of her mouth to her chin. She swiped a finger over it and sucked it into her mouth. The man was frozen. She tapped her nails on the glass. He filled it halfway. Again, she filled the rest with blood but sloshed it in front of her while glancing around. The woman finished the cheese plate she was making and was bringing it to a couple sitting in a dark booth. The scent of fur wafted by once more. It was faint. Coming in from under the main entrance.

"Tell me, not-Jasper, how long have you worked here." Alex adjusted her posture with a foot on the stool next to her. She leaned on her propped-up knee. Attempting to ease the tension with casual posture.

He crossed his arms over his thick chest. "Since it opened. I own it." She could have sworn he made his voice deeper.

"So, Paul Grady worked for you?"

This made him flinch. "Did you do something to Paul?"

The red headed woman stayed in the furthest corner behind the bar. She kept looking at her watch and was fidgeting with her apron.

"I am looking for Paul." She took a slow sip of her whiskey with her eyes trained on him. She was listening for changes in his breath. In his heartbeat. Watching his skin closely to see if beads of sweat form. More sweat than what's normal for a human scared of vampires.

He seems to be fearful, as he should be. Alex did not sense he was nervous because he had something to hide. His soft frame and eyes did not fit the profile of an evil kidnapper.

"Why is a vampire looking for Paul?"

"He left his phone and pants at my house." Alex

answered over the rim of her glass. He choked at the response. "Just kidding, Jasper. I was asked by the Sheriff to look for him. Now tell me about the last time you saw him."

The bartender looked around before taking a single step towards Alex. The curve of his stomach pressing against the bar. He scrubbed at the back of his neck. Contemplating if Alex was the enemy or not. Whether he should even talk to her. Or if she was toying with him like a mouse. Buying time before she bites his neck open on the bar.

"It was over two weeks ago I think." Not-Jasper had a lumberjack's body. Large muscles under a soft layer of fat. He was clearly trying to puff up his chest, but there was not a scary bone in his body. He was a giant teddy bear. A friendly giant. Unlike the wolf she scented outside the bar. She ignored the aroma and focused on not-Jasper.

"According to the police report, Paul went missing shortly after leaving your bar. Did he say where he was going?" The tone of authority latched onto her voice so naturally. Decades of demanding answers and interrogating suspects for Shade coming to the surface. He was a fragile human. Alex had to remind herself to be gentile and not grab him by the throat. Most vampires will not spill secrets if you hold a knife to their gentiles. Knowing it would heal. She suspects it's different for humans. This bartender might be large in stature, but she could hear the fear in his voice. A small tremble at the end of each sentence.

"He was coming back here. It was a big night for

him. I let him cut his shift short so he could go home and prepare." His voice lowered an octane on the last word.

"Prepare for what?"

The bartender looked over at the woman who was now hanging her apron on a hook before retrieving her purse from under the bar. He gave her a pleading look. She shook her head in response.

"I can't wait any longer. I have plans in Santa Rosa at 8pm." She rushed past Alex towards the door. He waved her away with the back of his hand. As the door opened three dark figures loomed outside. The werewolf scent hit her like a brick. She rolled her eyes as Thor walked in followed by two men. One she recognized as James. They headed towards a dark booth in the back. It had a candle illuminating the red glass holder. It cast a shape that resembled a rose in the center.

"He was preparing for a big date." The bartender stepped away from her. "Excuse me for a moment."

Alex turned her back to the wolves and kept her focus on the bartender. He brought menus to the table of snooping men. She pretended to be interested in the specialty cocktail menu. Scrunching her nose at the drink names that sounded more like perfume. *Lavender Gin Fizz*. Sounds terrible. Sounds like something Anita would have ordered.

The bartender returned and started making three drinks. Alex tapped her empty glass. She only had enough blood in her flask for one more blend. He filled her glass before starting the drink orders from the wolves. She wondered if the bartender knew what they were. He had no hesitation when greeting them. In fact, his heartbeat gives the indication that he is thrilled to have customers.

Alex cleared her throat. "Who was the big date with?"

She watched him pour gin and olive juice into a shaker. The cracking ice sound had her cringe. Flashes of broken bones from centuries of fighting flooded her mind. One more thing she does not miss from her life before. When not tracking for Shade, Alex was Adoni's personal enforcer. His enemies never suspected the fight to come from short woman at his side who looks not a day over twenty-four.

Alex finished off her drink and inhaled deeply. He was distracted by making drinks and not answering her questions as fast as she would like.

"Traci. If you wait a minute, she will be here shortly." He poured the mixture into a martini glass. "Hopefully."

He took the martini and two beers to the wolf table. This time she did turn around only to find James was already watching her. He picked up the stick with three olives and crunched one between his teeth. His eyes never left her. A small threat behind them. It only made her want to taunt him. There was something about his stoic face that made her want to piss him off. The inner child that never grew up no matter how hard Adonis tried to mold her into a respectable Princess.

She can't help who she is. Alex loves to be feared, but there was a sick part of her that enjoys being hated even more. The bartender returned and filled her glass without her asking. For a bar that is not vampire friendly, he was making her feel welcome. Jackelope might have competition.

"So, Paul had a hot date with Traci the night he went missing. And he never showed up." Alex topped off the whiskey with the last of her blood.

"Pretty much." He grabbed a towel to polish glasses with. "He was chasing Traci for months trying to get a date. He was so stoked when she finally said yes. He saved money to take her to a real nice place, Flemmings Steakhouse. They have white tablecloths and a separate wine menu and all that shit."

"Has he ever disappeared before?"

Before he could answer a blond tornado ran into the bar. She was tall. Alex would have to look up to her. Her high ponytail swished as she threw her purse behind the bar and grabbed the hanging apron.

"I am so sorry. My sitter was late. I drove as fast as I could." She scurried over to us and greeted Alex with a friendly smile. Alex smiled back. Forgetting the sight of fangs can be jarring for some people. "Oh my. You're a vampire."

Alex tipped her glass in her direction. "You must be Traci."

Her eyes bulged comically, and she flicked her attention to the bartender.

"You are talking about me with a vampire." She shrieked.

Traci this is-" He gestured towards me then paused. "Alex."

"Alex." He repeated. "She is working with the police to find Paul."

Traci stiffened at the mention of his name. Her

mouth fell agape as she tried to figure out why a vampire was in their bar looking for Paul and if she was in trouble.

"I don't work with police." Alex took a sip. "I am helping Sheriff Gefahr."

Her doe eyes traveled between us. The wolves in the back of the bar were silent. Obnoxious eavesdropping pups. She bit her bottom lip. "You are looking for Paul?" Alex nodded. "What are you going to do if you find him?"

"Eat him." Alex said flatly. The bartender glared. Traci cupped her hand over her mouth. Alex could not help but smirk. She let the corners of her lips fall when she heard an aggravated sigh come from the table in the back. James was clearly listening to every word of their conversation and was not amused by her sarcasm.

"Come on. Do you think I would ask around to find him if I wanted to kill him? I have faster ways to get my dinner. If I find him, I will bring him to the Sherrif. No one else."

That last part was as much as a reassurance to them as it was for the snooping wolves. They would expect Paul to be brought to the pack, but her loyalties did not reside with them. There is only one person she trusts the slightest. An ex-body builder sheriff with a fiery wife.

"Now Traci, tell me about the last day you saw him. Don't leave out any details." Alex put on her most inviting smile. It stung to wear it.

"I was planning on changing into a cute red skater dress for the Date."

Alex palmed her face. "I don't mean the type of dress. Tell me about Paul's behavior. How long did it take you to notice he wasn't coming"

The bartender looked down at Traci and gave her the reassuring smile of an older brother. There was no relation between them, but he had big brother bear vibes. Traci finished tying the apron around her waist and grabbed a tray of cups from the dishwasher. She stacked them as she spoke.

"Paul was a goofball." The corners of her mouth tugged up for a moment. "He's always spinning big plans about moving to California and becoming an illustrator for Disney. Said he would drag me and my son along with him. I waited in my cute skater dress for him to show up after my shift ended. I sent him a text after fifteen minutes. There was no response."

The bartender returned to her side after checking on the other patrons. "I watched her wait outside and called him myself. It went straight to voicemail." He said.

"How long did you wait before contacting authorities?"

"We didn't." The bartender said. "Paul didn't show up to his shift the next day. I sent a text to his Pack. They were listed as his emergency contact. I am not sure who it even went to."

"I knew something bad happened." Traci pinched her eyes trying to hold in tears. "He's the nicest guy. I can't imagine someone wanting to hurt him."

Alex was out of blood and reached her limit of whiskey before her head became too fuzzy to concentrate. She stepped off the stool. Clothing rustled behind her from the table of wolves.

"Is there anyone you can think of that had a grudge against Paul or wanted something from him?" She directed the question at both of them. They shook their heads in unison. Alex sighed. "Anything else about the day he went missing you can think of?"

"I have a photo of what he was wearing when he left the bar. I gave it to the police already." Alex knew the photo she spoke of. It was printed with a cheap printer in the precinct and stapled to the missing person's file. She noticed the photo on Traci's phone was taken landscape and not cropped.

"Can you send me that?" Alex asked. Traci nodded.

lex stared down at her phone waiting for a photograph to come through. Traci did not have much insight into Paul's life outside of working at Toast, but she did have a picture of him the day before he went missing. They took a selfie together at work. Her phone dinged. She opened the message to find an adorable photo of them scrunched together. His face was slightly turned. Ready to plant a kiss on her cheek judging by the look of puppy love in his eyes. Her face beamed with a smile showing all her teeth. She zoomed in on the photo. There was a strip of tape with a cotton ball on his arm. Having a life that revolves around blood, Alex is familiar with how to bandage after a donation.

Her hive used to retrieve blood from their feeders if one of them was traveling. But there were no vampires other than Alex in Vaughn. Is there a vampire nearby collecting blood? She filed that question away as James came out of the bar.

He walked over to her where she leaned against her motorcycle. Tucking her phone in her back pocket.

"You, hovering over me, is distracting."

James had his dark hair in a low ponytail instead of the two braids she saw him in last. His shirt had a faded graphic of a woman riding a beer can like a bull. It fit tight to his muscles as he crossed his arms.

"You have not earned our trust yet." His gruff voice had no hint of stutter. James had no fear of being close to a vampire. She wondered if it was her small frame or experience that gave him this confidence.

"I don't need you to trust me." Alex squared her shoulders. "I need you to stay out of my way."

"Thor called the Sherrif to verify your story." Alex did not respond. Watching him like a stature. "She confirmed everything you said."

"Of course, she did." This was a waste of her time. Alex resisted rolling her eyes and wondered if this giant man was going to follow her for the entire case.

"The Sheriff also made us promise not to tell anyone you are here." His biceps flexed as he smiled. A smile that attempted to hold power over her. She scanned his body and contemplated how many strikes it would take to take him down. James narrowed his eyes on her. "Who are you hiding from?"

A car pulled up to the bar and she waited until the man was inside before replying. The Taos Hum filled the silence between them. A steady buzz that took Alex time to get used to. Jules said it was seismic activity, and most people never notice it. Alex found theories online that attributed it to underground military bases that are kept secret from the public. She wondered if the werewolves heard it too.

"I am not hiding. I just don't want to be bothered." Alex placed a hand on the handle of her motorcycle. The leather was cool now that the sun went down hours ago.

"Bothered? Sure. Tell me, why a vampire would be afraid of other vampires? You must be afraid of someone. Why else would you choose to live in a place like this." He opened his arms up to gesture to the one street town around them.

"Let's just say, I have had my fill of vampires." She flung a leg over her bike and inserted the key. "I have had my fill of werewolves too. As soon as I find the missing wolves for Jules, you won't see me again. Tell your Alpha to give me space or I will eat his pups when I find them."

James flipped her off playfully. She smirked at him in the side mirror. She could tell he was aggravated by her cockiness. Hated her aggressiveness. It did not matter to Alex if she was liked. She needed him to admit she would do a better job tracking them down than he could.

Alex left a trail of dust in her wake as she sped down the road towards home.

She sat on her couch and scanned the police reports pinned to her wall. Alex tossed a knife in the air and caught it with the hilt. She was seriously lacking clues. A small-town bartender, who happens to be a werewolf, goes missing. He was not tied to any criminals as far as she could tell. He did not have money that would make him a target. The young wolf didn't even have a completed college degree. Hell, he could barely get a date. What made him special? What made him worth taking?

She looked at the wolf's name just before Paul's that went missing. Alejando Jimenez. There are no notes on his file. He was undocumented. Has no known family in the US and was not a member of a pack. Alejandro was reported missing when his landlord went to collect rent. They put his date missing as March 26th, but it could have been weeks earlier.

Alex focused on the third name. Jolene McKean. A twenty-seven-year-old that was raised in Thors pack but has not spent much time there recently. She has been living in Santa Rosa with her fiancé while working at a hair salon. Alex had a vision of a wolf hair salon. Alex wondered what would happen if you dyed a werewolf's fur? Would their hair remain that color when they returned to human form?

Werewolves had it so simple. They had increased strength and senses but can hide in plain sight. Only one night a month do they need to restrain themselves. It used to be done with chains and dungeons. Nowadays most choose sedatives. Enjoying a peaceful slumber in wolf form. She assumes the reason they allow humans to live on the commune is solely to protect them while they are sedated. They would protect them from bigoted humans, but it would be easy for Alex to take them down and wipe out the entire pack. If she wanted. The war between their species has been over for a long time. She would have no reason to remove the pack. Unless provoked.

Alex glanced at the time. It was 10pm. She could be in Santa Rosa in less than forty minutes on her bike. That might be too late to visit Jolene's fiancé. She thought about waiting until the sun came up. That plan fizzled quickly as her desire to operate at night won the battle against respecting the fiancé's personal time. She grabbed a gun with silver tipped bullets, a wad of cash, and a flask filled with blood bourbon. The essentials. Alex guzzled down a few ounces of whiskey from the bottle before leaving her house.

She needed to keep working on the case. Letting her mind go idle meant the memories would start creeping in. Focusing on the job only held them at bay for a while before Anita's face filled every corner of her thoughts. Sober, the memories hit her in waves, relentless reminders of just how alone she truly was. It was her choice, but the loneliness still stung, like an open wound she couldn't help but pick at. She clung to the pain, using it as a form of self-inflicted punishment, refusing to let it heal.

There are very few humans that would be happy to find a vampire on their doorstep. Choosing to show up at Jolene's house in the middle of the night and wake her fiancé from slumber was sure to insight fear. Their house was a narrow two story next to a park. The perfect image of a starter home.

The only sounds filling the air were moving trees and creaking swings. This manufactured neighborhood belonged somewhere with more rain and less scorpions. Each house was a carbon copy of its neighbor. Human scents lingered around her. A man must have walked his dog thirty minutes ago. His cologne and dog's scent still lingered in the air. The house to the west had an infant. She could hear the faint sucking of his late-night feeding. His mother was humming. For a brief moment it was comforting.

Alex had no memory of her birth mother and often wondered how her life might have changed if she'd been comforted and protected, rather than used as bait, a tool, or even a food source—before becoming a near-immortal dependent on blood.

The heartbeat on the other side of the door was too fast for someone who was asleep. The TV was on quietly with an episode of a home improvement show. Alex knocked. His footsteps were frantic and uneven as if he lost a slipper getting to the door. She took a step back and let him open the door wide.

"Jolene?" He bellowed. Alex waved a stiff hand once. She smiled without her teeth. "Who are you?" He took a step back. Eyes widening when he didn't recognize Alex. She was small in stature, but most people could feel her strength like an aura around her.

"Alex. I am here to ask you questions about Jolene."

"Do you know what time it is?" He searched behind her expecting men in masks to jump out. His hand creeped towards the baseball bat leaning against the wall next to the door frame.

"I prefer to do business at night."

"You don't look like a cop." She looked down at his single plaid slipper. Her eyes followed his ruffled sweatpants and oversized t-shirt. Ending on his brown eyes with dark swollen skin underneath. Results of many nights not sleeping. This man looked like he stepped out of hell. It has been over a month since Jolene went missing.

Alex decided to take a calm approach instead of scaring answers out of him. "Great observation. You must be Antwan. I was given your information from Sheriff Gefahr in Vaughn. True, I am not a cop, but I do have special skills that may help find her."

His shoulders dropped with a tilt of his head. "Special skills?"

Alex slowly stepped into the stream of light coming from behind him. She lifted her top lip until her fangs were on full display.

"Fuck." He grabbed the bat and gripped it in front of his chest with both hands. "You are not invited in."

Alex always finds this part amusing. She moved past him smoothly enough not to touch the door frame or his body. Fast enough he barely blinked twice before she was inside his house and sitting on a leather recliner. He spun around with the now empty porch behind him.

"I don't actually need your invitation." She pulled the flask from her jacket pocket and took a swig. "Movies got a lot of things wrong."

He pointed the end of the bat in her direction.

"Are you here to kill me?"

"I told you what I was here for." She capped the flask and returned it to her pocket. "Shut the door and sit down. I just need a few answers, and I will leave you to be depressed alone."

Alex held her fingers up like a scout. She was never a scout, but she did feed on a troop leader in the eighties.

Antwan did as she said. He kept the bat across his lap and wouldn't let his back touch the couch. His jaw was tense under his thick dark beard. The house smelled like dirty dishes and macaroni with cheese. There was a framed picture propped up on the coffee table. Jolene was in a blue bikini flashing her hand with a diamond ring on it. Behind her Antwon wrapped his arms around her waist with a roaring waterfall in the background.

It was so cute it made Alex's skin crawl.

"Tell me about the days leading up to her disappearance."

Antwan sucked in a slow breath of air. He closed his eyes when he began to speak.

"Jolene stays away from trouble. So, don't think she got caught up with the wrong people. We met two years ago when she was going to hair school in Albuquerque. We moved here so she could take a manager job at a salon." Opening his eyes Alex could see a softness in him. She imagines it attracted Jolene to him in the first place. The men in the Packs are more concerned about looking tough for their Alpha. They often never learn how to be soft.

He adjusted himself on the couch cushion. His heartbeat was still faster than a resting pace. Alex made sure to give him a toothless smile. "I work remotely. The day she went missing I was home all day. I know she made it to work because she posted a picture of her first client on her Instagram. She was proud of the way the color turned out. A purple pink blend. Jolene loves fun colors." He swallowed. "Then I just didn't hear from her. Her coworker said she left like usual and even got in her car. Around 5:15pm."

"Where is her car now?"

"Cops haven't found it." He gripped the bat. "If you ask me, the cops in Santa Rosa are all fucking bigots.

The second they found out she was a wolf they lost interest. One even made a joke that she was following a scent like a fucking dog."

Alex has made that joke in the past. But it was always to get a rile out of a wolf. They call her soulless. She calls them dogs. Then they fight. Nothing serious. Just a friendly bar brawl amongst supernaturals. She's an asshole, not a bigot.

"What about the day before? Was it a normal workday?"

Antwan glanced across the room at the wood dining table. Papers and pictures were scattered across it. He walked over and picked up a folded paper. Handing it to Alex he said, "Same as usual except this. She donated blood to one of those traveling vans. They gave her fifty bucks cash." He shrugged his shoulders. "Weddings are expensive."

Alex scanned the document quickly before shoving it in her pocket. Moments later she was at the door. Theories were already running through her head. Antwan reached for her arm but hesitated to touch her.

"Do you think she is still alive?" He took a step back. The bat hanging loose in his hand at his side. Alex thought of all the lies she could tell to make him feel better. She did think the missing wolves were alive. She suspected a situation much worse. If their kidnappings are related to something medical, it could only be the result of doctors running unsanctioned tests.

She prepared her mind to find something similar. If the van where Jolene donated blood is the same one Paul went to, it is her first big link. Alex must find their operation and destroy every trace of them.

"I have a strong feeling I will find her alive." Alex assured him and disappeared into the night.

Jackalope was closed when Alex returned to Vaughn. She would have to settle for the whiskey she had at home. She sipped on a smokey bourbon that was more blood than alcohol, and dove into files. The name on the flyer from Antwan was a fake. There was no Blundell Medicine registered in New Mexico. When she took her search nationally, she also came back empty handed.

"Two wolves go missing after donating blood." She said aloud to herself. "They were paid in cash. And of course there are no cameras in these small desert towns." Alex dug the tip of her knife into the coffee table. Next to her laptop. Adding to the puncture marks covering it from hours spent investigating over the years.

The van would have to keep the blood refrigerated. They would not want to travel far. She searched for hospitals or clinics with blood donation programs. Every turn was a strike out. Alex opened the flyer which she had previously scrunched into a ball in a fit of frustration. There must be a clue. It had a photo of a generic couple in the center holding up their arms. A bright red band aide in the cup of their elbows. With the words "Saving Lives One Donation At A Time" underneath. In the flattering, and completely fabricated, history of Blundell Medicine there was one word that stuck out. *Genetic*.

A light bulb illuminated. She cannot find a hospital or clinic that is responsible because it's run by a science lab. Labs have no patients and plenty of space for refrigeration.

Moments later Alex was deep in the state records. Searching for building permits and business licenses.

"Well, fuck me." She lifted the laptop like it was Simba on his birthday. "There you are."

GCGR, the Gibbard Center for Genetic Research, is based in San Diego, California, with an additional office in Albuquerque. Recently, they acquired property in Santa Rosa. While the building permits don't specify the primary purpose of the facility, they list the code 24-SP165, which a quick search revealed to mean genetic research.

Forty-five minutes of trying to find a backdoor into GCGR's website led to nothing. Alex was hoping to find details of employee records. Who might be assigned to a mobile blood clinic? All she found was a list of administrative people. Just in case, she sent an email to the head of security of the Albuquerque office. Alex made sure to clone the HR's IP address. Once the employee opened the email a program on her laptop will start to record their keystrokes. When she returns from her field trip to the Santa Rosa lab, there should be a detailed list of logins and passwords waiting for her.

She has always made a point to keep up with technology. Being around through the invention evolution of computers has its perks. Adonis always said, a worker that refuses to become skilled in all tools they have access to will never be at the top of their field.

Moving on from her laptop, she stood from the couch. The next task would have to be completed in person.

Alex gathered her gun, a wireless camera, and binoculars. She had her hand on the front door when she realized the sun was coming up. Reluctantly she left the supplies on the dining table. After plugging her phone into the charger, she stripped her clothes off. It is best to go at night. Alex could be walking into a room full of vampire hunters. They do exist. Evidence says the kidnappers are not vampire hunters, and their interest was in werewolf genetics. But she would not be surprised if they jumped at the opportunity to bag a vampire.

Her skin was the same temp as the cool sheets. She shut her eyes and forced sleep upon herself. Preserving her energy in a short coma. Vampires do not need much sleep, and when they do, it goes deep. Unraveling layers of their subconscious. She knew within minutes she would be in Anitas arms. Happy and satisfied after a long night of love making. Only to wake up with an empty bed and empty heart.

There were no trees to hide her motorcycle behind. Alex ditched it behind a sign for a wildlife education center that was up the road. Like most of the buildings in this area it appeared to have been neglected. She kept her steps light and silent as she walked towards the lab.

The sky still had a slight glow, and the stars were not yet shining. The sun had only been down for ten minutes. A tall metal fence surrounded the property. It did not appear strong enough to stop a car from plowing through but acted as a privacy shield. Meant to keep eyes out and create one entrance or exit. About thirty yards away there was a spot with a few dried bushes. Alex laid on her stomach. With binoculars she could read the names written on the guards' jackets. No other marking was visible on their uniforms. Vehicle tracks came from the direction of Santa Rosa and disappeared at the gate. The two guards sat in a small booth. It looked out of place. Dropped from the sky and placed near the wall. They were looking at phones in their hands. Despite being a guard station there was no monitor or any sign they had electricity. The light above them was connected to a solar panel on the roof. Alex wondered who was watching the camera feed if not them?

A breeze kicked up and she groaned.

"I thought I told you not to follow me?"

James stepped out of the darkness and got on his stomach next to her. He held his palm out flat. "Did you know Paul is my brother?"

Alex placed the binoculars in his hand. "Yea, I saw that on his file." She could knock him out with a quick punch to the temple. That would solve the problem of him showing up uninvited. If Alex hit him hard enough, she could be done surveilling by the time he woke up. The idea was tempting.

"Why haven't you questioned me? If you were really an expert, you would have started with his family." James said flatly.

Alex rolled her eyes. "I read everything I could find on you. Your life is quite boring."

"Living up to my responsibilities within the pack and my town is not boring."

She wanted to retort. To tease him. But she kept the resemblance of playful banter in her throat. He was a straight male, and she wanted to make sure there was no indication she was flirting. Although his pupils never dilated nor did his heart race when he saw her, she expects the feelings were mutual. He had no interest in her, sexually that is. He clearly wanted to observe her as she worked on this case.

The gate opened to allow a car to exit. A white sedan pulled up to the guard's booth. She only saw the shadow of a single figure in the car, the driver. Alex tilted her head to pick up a few words.

"I'm out……. not empty…. Mari… still there… should be out soon."

Alex looked at James as the car drove out of sight. She considered following it, but it seems there is one employee left in the lab. Just waiting to be questions. With force if necessary. James met her eyes in the dusk light. "Did you catch that?" She asked.

He shook his head. "Not really, but I can smell blood. It's faint. I think it's human."

"That's not that strange when you work in a genetics lab." Alex smelled the blood also. It was diluted with a chemical she couldn't recognize. It tricked her senses, making her unable to identify it further. But if she had to guess, it was not entirely human.

Alex stood up slowly. Thankfully the desert had very little light. She took a few steps towards the building. James grabbed her arm. She turned quickly with a blade to his neck and hissed through her fangs. His muscles went rigid. If she was a Shade agent still it would be her duty to knock him out and stop him from interfering with the case. He would have no authority. The curl of her lips softened as she remembered she also has no real authority.

"Jesus, fuck Alex. I am not trying to fight I just want to know your plan." Alex sheathed the knife at her thigh. "Did you just hiss at me?"

She was making up the plan on the fly. No longer having to run it by a team or notify a higher-ranking agent. Alex did not need a partner. She did not want a partner.

"My plan is to take out those guards. It sounds like there is one scientist left in the building. I am going to gently ask them a few questions." The moonlight reflected off her teeth as she grinned. Alex moved quietly toward the edge of the wall, determined to avoid confronting the guards head-on. She intended to come at them from the side. James moved with her. Somehow managing to be stealthy despite his giant frame.

"You can't just go around knocking out humans. You have no legal authority here. It would be a random vampire attack, and they would call Shade. I am pretty sure you are avoiding their involvement."

James touched her shoulder. He hovered over her and pointed towards the cameras mounted by the gate. "Can you make it over the wall?"

"Of course I can. I just thought it was boring to just jump over. I enjoy a fight. Even if it's over quickly." Alex huffed.

James stood next to her. He was twice her size in width and her head only came up to his chin. His hair was pulled tight into a low bun. He blended into the night with his dark jeans and black shirt. There was a strong scent of aloe and cedar on his skin. He must have tried to hide his scent.

"How long have you been following me?" Alex knocked his hand off her shoulder and scowled.

James ignored the question. "I will distract the guards and get the cameras to focus on me. How will you get inside the building? There are no windows, and the door requires a key code."

"I will find a way in." Alex sighed. "Fine, you can help. I will hop over the wall on the east side. You distract the guards. Give me two minutes to get into place."

"Just two minutes?" Before James could blink, Alex was gone. She ran silently over the desert dirt. Her feet barely touched the ground. When she arrived at the side wall she scanned the area. Made from cinderblocks stacked about ten feet high with a coil of razor wire at the top. *Childs play.*

She heard the mechanical whine of the camera turning. It was mounted twelve feet away on the corner of the wall. It moved away from her direction and towards the front gate where James was approaching. He was slurring his words and shouting about government conspiracies hiding in the desert. He even threw in garbage about an alien aircraft. It was perfect. The big dog is good for something after all, Alex thought.

Aiming her face to the sky, she inhaled deeply. There were no scents nearby other than the three near the gate. Feeling in the clear, Alex took a few leaps back before getting into the same position a runner would at the beginning of a race. She pushed off and leaped onto the wall, running up the side in two long strides before flipping over the top. Her cat-like landing was so perfect she was disappointed no one was there to witness it. There was a reason Imani sent her on so many missions. Her skill to be stealthy was hard to beat.

Before moving from her spot, she scanned around for more cameras or guards. There appeared to be no windows. The building was a concrete cube. Void of personality and signage. With no attempt to blend into the warm tones of the desert.

She looked for more guards before moving from where she landed. She saw no one, as she suspected. Either what was inside the lab was not of much value or they did not expect anyone to come digging around. Let alone someone who could jump a wall in a single bound. The few cameras mounted, and two gate guards are hardly a challenge. She crossed the courtyard towards the entrance to the building. Tucking her body behind three vehicles parked in front. A truck, jeep, and sedan were parked haphazardly in a makeshift parking lot.

She picked up a rock the size of her palm and aimed at the camera over the door. It hit its mark knocking the camera off until it hung from loose wires. Alex flattened her body against the building next to the door. The concrete was still warm from the desert sun cooking it all afternoon.

She braced herself and listened for footsteps. If there is a person on site watching the camera then the sudden loss of camera feed should smoke them out. Moments later the heavy metal door creaked open. A third guard walked out and looked up at the hanging camera. He held a gun at his side aimed at the ground.

Alex leaped out and kicked him in the chest. He fell inside the building, dropping his weapon out of reach when he slid. She followed swiftly behind. The door slammed shut behind them. They were in a brightly lit hall. Empty except for the two of them. His hand reached for a radio. She kicked it out of his grasp and reached behind herself to grab the gun tucked in to her waist. There was no need for casualties on a scouting mission. She struck him with the butt of the gun and caught his limp body before it hit the ground. There was a door open with the word Security to her right. She dragged him inside. On the monitors she could see James using his hands to enthrall the guards outside in a story. The obnoxious wolf does know how to create a diversion. He didn't even have to blow anything up.

There was not much on the main floor. A few offices. They were locked, but she could tell they were empty by looking through the large window each had from the main hallway. They didn't have much personalization. A computer, a filing cabinet, and fully stocked penholders. They appeared to have never been used. What she was looking for was a genetic lab. Nothing on this main floor could retrieve or test samples. Also, she smelled no blood or traces of werewolves coming from under the door to the offices.

However, the deeper down the hall she walked, the stronger the scent of blood became. At the back was an elevator standing like a steel monument. She winked at the camera when she entered. There were only two buttons. The number one and the Letter L. She pressed L and tucked the gun back in her waist as the elevator descended.

Before the elevator door could open, the scents became overwhelming. Blood. Both human and werewolf clear as day. Many chemicals she could not identify. And a sultry wave of roses. Rose water to be specific. It curled itself around her and pulled her in the direction of soft humming.

Standing in the doorway to a large science lab, Alex was not familiar with the cheerful pop tune being hummed. She hesitated to interrupt it. The woman's tone was warm and sultry. It instantly resonated within her. Her shape reminded Alex of sculptures from when she was young. A time when curves were worshiped by artists in all forms. The energy radiating from her did not match the sterile environment.

The workstations around her appeared to be unused. The surfaces bare and equipment tucked away. She had her note spread across two steel tables. A half-eaten sandwich neglected on a white plate. Alex could smell cucumber, cream cheese, and roasted peppers. She tried to block out the savory scent and focus on the sweet scent coming from the woman.

Alex leaned against the doorframe, watching as the

woman in the lab coat bent over the microscope. A slight bounce in her steps, and she hummed softly under her breath. Her glossy red nails danced over the dials with the grace of a pianist. A thick ponytail of dark hair cascaded past her shoulders, swaying gently as she worked. When she leaned in closer, one foot lifted behind her, just like a leading lady in an old movie caught in a kiss.

It had been a long time since Alex had experienced any physical contact, outside of fights. The sight of the woman made her ache inside. Her hand itched to reach out, to run her fingers through the thick strands of her hair. Though the woman's face was hidden behind goggles and a surgical mask, Alex was certain she was beautiful. She could tell by her scent, rose water, more intoxicating than Alex had ever known. She wanted to be bathe in it.

But Alex shook her head, forcing herself to refocus on why she was here. She thought of the desperate wolf above, keeping the guards occupied. She couldn't afford to let the allure of a beautiful woman distract her, no matter how much her mouth watered at the sight.

The woman moved the slide off the microscope and placed it on the steel counter. She pulled the mask down past her chin. Alex cleared her throat causing the woman to jump back. Knocking her stool over. Alex took confident steps towards her.

"Who are you?" The woman looked around and her eyes landed on the unlabeled red button on the wall fifteen feet away. Her voice cracked. "Who let you in here?"

Alex's eyes flicked to the red button and back to her.

"You are not fast enough to get to that button." Her leather jacket groaned as she crossed her arms over her chest. "Why don't you have a seat, and we can talk."

She stared at Alex. Her brows furled. "No. Get out." Her skin was a warm brown. The color of brown sugar right before it turns to caramel. She had a strong desire to lick it. Alex blinked the image out of her head and moved quickly to pick up the stool from the floor. The woman jumped back. Slamming into the counter. "What are you?"

"You know what I am." Alex righted the stool and sat atop one in another workstation. With enough space to give her a false sense of safety, Alex could easily reach her before she made it to the alarm on the wall. "Have a seat. If you answer my questions maybe I will answer yours."

She hesitated to take a step towards the stool and paused with a hand on the seat. "You're a vampire." Alex responded with a fang filled smile. "Are you here to kill me?"

"No."

"Are you going to bite me?" She eased her body on the stool. Alex was in fact not there to bite her. However, the sight of her full lips, dark lashes, and that fucking scent was making her question things. She considered going against Shades' rules on consent. Throwing this woman onto the table, ripping off her black leggings, and sinking her teeth into her thigh.

"Never on the first date." Alex smirked.

"Who are you?" The woman repeated ignoring Alex's aggressive flirting.

"Alex. Your friendly neighborhood vampire." The woman did not find that amusing. Alex straightened on the stool. "Let's just say, I am a tracker. I am looking for some missing people. Can you believe the trail led me here? Now, who are you?"

The woman finally removed the goggles from her face. Alex's chest tightened. Her eyes were so dark and big under naturally thick lashes. She had no makeup on. Not a surprise for someone that works in a lab. Alex wanted to reach out and touch her dewy soft skin. Cradle her cheek and force her to expose the curve of her neck. Again, Alex blinked the thoughts away and resisted the urge to reach for her flask.

"I am Dr. Nava. This is my genetic research lab, and I assure you there are no missing people here. I only deal with blood samples. Ethically donated samples."

Alex cocked her head. "What makes you think they are ethically donated? Do you collect them yourself?"

The woman glanced at her watch and to the red button on the wall. She let out a sigh.

"The samples are delivered here. Nothing nefarious is going on, I assure you. Someone would notice. We are one of the world's leading companies in pharmaceutical research." She adjusted on her stool. "Why do vampires have red eyes?"

Alex was taken back by the question. The woman said it so casually as if there wasn't a drop of fear in her. As if Alex was not a threat sitting less than ten feet from her.

"I don't know." She pinched the bridge of her nose and took a deep breath with her eyes closed. "I am the one asking questions."

Dr. Nava smiled. Actually, smiled at the vampire across from her. Like this was the start of a game she had a chance at winning. "I see no badge from local authorities or whatever you call the Vampire FBI."

"Shade." Alex said flatly.

"Yea, Shade. I see no sign you are working with them. The way I see it. You walked in here with the intentions of killing me but need information first. If that is the case, do it quickly. I'm bored."

"You pulse does not sound bored."

"Well, I am a scientist, and I have never met a vampire before. They don't tend to take PHD programs or work in scientific research. What you hear is excitement, not fear." She smiled again. Alex felt a tingle on her cheeks, grateful vampires couldn't blush. A sensation that has been lost for a long time. "I have so many questions."

Alex stood from her stool and prowled towards the Dr. She straightened her spine but didn't flinch from her approach. Alex leaned in close enough to place her hands on the steel counter on both of her sides. Dr. Nava was caged in. She did not flinch, but Alex noticed the way she held her breath. Alex made herself eye level with the Dr. Her eyes were dark pools. Unwavering with their intent to study the vampire up close.

"I will make you a deal." Alex cocked her head. The rose scent was intoxicating, and she was suddenly in need of a stiff drink. "If you answer my questions like a good girl, I'll let you ask me any question you like."

Alex watched her throat bob as she swallowed before she spoke. "Can I record it?"

"No."

"Can I have a blood sample?"

"No."

She didn't argue. Even though vampires live in the open now, they are extremely secretive. Dr. Nava opened her mouth to speak, and Alex's grip on the counter tightened. Her eyes locked onto the small silver ball resting on the woman's tongue, mesmerizing her. An overwhelming urge surged within Alex, a need to feel that tongue piercing, to taste her. It had been far too long since she'd felt anything. Other than disappointment in herself and annoyance for others.

With a sharp breath, Alex pushed herself away, taking a few steps back. The steel counter bore the dents of her fingers where she had held on too tightly.

The overwhelming scent of cleaner made her nose twitch. The lab was becoming claustrophobic. There was an animalistic urge withing her to ignore the case, throw the woman over her shoulders and run out the door. Then she remembered the promise she made to Jules and the dopey wolf waiting for answers on the surface.

"Not here. I hate labs. Plus, a security guard is about to exit the elevator. He is going to check on you. Tell him everything is fine because it is. Right?" She tilted her ear towards the hall. There was a gentle hum from the elevator descending.

"Right." She said with forced confidence.

Alex stepped towards the open door to the lab as

the elevator dinged. She stood with her back against the door. The elevator groaned open behind her. "We will finish this at your place.

Dr. Nava nodded. "Don't you need my address?"

"I will find you." Alex smirked. Her photographic memory recalled the name written on the outside of the lab. It would not be difficult to search for recent rentals in the area. Lucky for her the Santa Rosa records office has not changed their log in info from the last time she hacked in.

The guard was moving towards the lab. A cold sweat was soaking into his uniform. The musk strong enough to cover the rose water scent she was becoming too comfortable with. The guard hesitated before turning the corner. His hand wavered between a radio and the gun at his side. Alex moved next to him in a flash and removed both. She then placed the gun and radio next to the Dr. in the lab.

The guard locked her red eyes and froze. She placed a hand on his shoulder, slowly moving him until his back was against the door frame.

"You are safe. Dr. Nava is safe." She nodded as she spoke and tried to have the same cadence as Adonis when he controls people with his words. "I was not here. Right Dr. Nava?"

She shuffled to stand between us. "Yes. This meeting is classified and there should be no record of my guest. Official Gibbard business."

Alex grinned. Official Gibbard business. She thought the Dr. was adorable. A terrible liar, but adorable. His body relaxed and Alex removed her hand. In a blink she was steps away about to enter the elevator.

"See you later Dr." She waved with her fingers as the elevator door shut behind her.

Even being in the center of a small city, Alex could not forget she was in the desert. The air was hot, and sand has gathered in short piles at the corners of windowsills. She flipped the hair off her forehead and peered down.

Dr. Nava nervously walked by the window in her third-floor apartment. The building was newly built. It was designed to look like multicolored boxes stacked upon each other. Alex sipped on a blood bag with her legs dangling off the roof of the hardware store across the street. She has been there since the Dr. returned around midnight an hour ago.

After a divisive argument, Alex finally convinced James not to tag along. They exchanged phone numbers, and she even promised to keep him updated if she found any leads on his missing brother, though she wasn't sure why she made that promise. Earlier, when they stood by her motorcycle before parting ways, there was a faint sense that a friendship might be forming. Ignoring it, Alex called him a dog and sped off. He shouted back, calling her an asshole, but his tone was too playful, too friendly for her liking.

The Dr. stopped pacing and yawned. The light in the living room went off and was followed by a softer light flicking on in her bedroom. Alex jumped off the roof and crossed the street. There were no cars to dodge. Santa Rosa did not have a wild nightlife, and all the restaurants closed thirty minutes ago. There was no one to see her scale the side of the building and leap from balcony to balcony. Arriving on the third floor. Alex has found most people forget to lock their sliding doors. Dr. Nava was no exception.

Alex slid inside and closed the door behind her. The furniture in her apartment was void of personality. Alex was sure it was rented as a furnished apartment. The style screamed corporate takeover. She walked silently towards the bedroom. It was empty. The door to the bathroom was shut with the sound of running water behind it. Alex crawled onto the bed. Closing her eyes at the scent enveloping her. She lay on her side and bent an elbow to prop her head on her palm.

The door to the bathroom opened and Dr. Nava screamed.

"How the fuck did you get in here?" She pressed a hand to her chest. Still standing in the doorway.

"The door."

"Can you stop sneaking up on me?" She finally moved away from the bathroom. Her shorts had strings of Christmas lights on them. It made Alex smile to see someone wearing holiday themed clothes in Spring.

"No." Alex tapped the bed with her free hand. "Have a seat."

"I am not sitting that close to you." She folded her arms across her chest.

"I will not touch you." Alex smiled. Her fangs are on full display. "Unless you ask me to."

"Are all vampires such flirts?" She took two slow steps towards the bed and lowered herself onto the edge. Her eyes remained on Alex. Not wanting to put her back to her. She sat with her back against the headboard and her legs crossed.

"So," Alex cut to the point. "Dr. Nava what research are you doing for the GCGR?"

"Mariana. You are lying in my bed. Might as well call me by my first name." She cleared her throat. "I am looking for a genetic marker. A mutation."

"In werewolves?"

Mariana stiffened. Her project had her sign a strict NDA. She looked up to the ceiling. "Yes."

"To identify them?" Mariana shook her head. "To control them?" Alex focused on the steady beat of her pulse. Listening for an indication she was lying.

"I am not sure what their end goal is. I think they are more interested in their strength and healing capabilities. Gibbard has developed many pharmaceuticals that have made the investors wealthy. But nothing would create wealth like a pill to speed recovery or truly slow down aging."

This was nothing new to Alex. Back in the 1960s, a group of doctors had stumbled upon the existence of vampires by accidentally capturing two. They starved the vampires of blood until they were too weak to resist, then bound them in chains and began their brutal experiments. The doctors amputated limbs and carved away chunks of flesh, meticulously documenting how long it took for the vampires to regenerate. They kept the creatures alive with only a few drops of blood.

It was torture for the purpose of medical advancement.

Alex had been part of the team sent to rescue them. Those tortured vampires were Shade agents, and when they failed to report back from their mission, Imani knew something had gone horribly wrong. In a fit of rage, Alex and her fellow agents tore the doctors apart like rag dolls before setting the entire facility ablaze.

Mariana may present herself as kind-hearted, but Alex would never trust a scientist again, not after the first thing Mariana asked her for was a sample of blood. It echoed the same curiosity that led to those agents being tortured for science.

"Have you met any of the wolves that donated blood?" Alex narrowed her eyes.

Mariana shook her head. She made eye contact with Alex while fidgeting with the hem of her shorts. "How old are you?"

"Old. Very old." Alex smiled.

"You said you would answer my questions." She yawned.

Alex traced an embroidered flower with her finger. The bedspread was deep purple with stitched flowers. It was the only thing in the room that felt like it belonged to Mariana. "I said you could ask me questions. I never said I would answer them."

Mariana scowled. The Latina heritage within her becoming more prominent. If Alex was not a vampire, she would feel intimidated by the threat of pain behind her eyes.

Alex chuckled quietly. "I don't tell anyone my exact age, but I will tell you I am older than the United States."

This made Mariana's eyes widen. Alex could almost see the streams of questions flowing through her mind.

"Where-"

Alex held up a finger. "My turn. Why would the blood donation vans operate under a fake name?"

"Fake name? You mean Blundell Medicine?" She shook her head slowly. Her heartbeat was steady. "I was told to expect deliveries from them periodically. I had no reason to question the business name. You seem really suspicious of my science lab. Blood tests and genetic research are done all over the country. Why are you so concerned with this small operation?"

"How many people work in the lab?"

"Two for now, but it will be more. We just opened this location a few months ago. It's a new project."

"In the middle of the desert?" Alex cocked a brow.

Mariana lifted her hands with palms out. "I don't know why they picked this location. I was just grateful for the offer. Four years in this lab will pay off my school loans." She huffed. "They offered me a salary I couldn't refuse."

"They, being Gibbard?"

"Yes."

"To identify a mutation in werewolves."

"Yes." Her body was rigid, but her pulse quickened.

Alex scanned her body. She tilted her head and waited for Mariana to elaborate, but the words stayed in her mouth.

"You found it but haven't told them yet?" Alex was captivated by the subtle movement of Mariana's lips, knowing she was nervously playing with her tongue piercing. Back when Alex was dating centuries ago, tongue piercings weren't exactly common. It was one of the few things she'd never tried herself. The thought crossed her mind, what would it be like to cup the doctor's face and feel that piercing against her own tongue?

Mariana was silent. Alex continued, "You don't trust them either. Why?"

She looked around. Hands back on the hem of her shorts. "When I went into the main office in Albuquerque to sign paperwork, I saw something concerning. I was hired by Mr. Wheaton. He oversees the development of new pharmaceuticals. I was not told what drug I was working on, just to identify a mutation and test if I could stimulate a response in the mutation."

"A response?" Alex echoed. "You mean to trigger the transformation not relying on the full moon."

She nodded while a yawn bloomed. "Look I have been up for a long time. Are you almost done?"

"Almost. What did you see in the office that was concerning?"

"I really need this job." She fluffed her pillow and laid back.

"What did you see that was concerning, Dr. Nava?" Alex pushed.

She tugged the blanket under her legs until it was low enough to pull over herself. Alex noted how heavy her eyes were. Mariana's jaw clenched holding back another yawn. "I saw a note in Wheaton's handwriting. *Meeting with General Gain – bring suggestions to transport subjects to combat sites.* I was confused why Gibbard was discussing military things. Before I took this job, I researched the industry. There are many regulations that keep Werewolves and those like you out of the military. It felt off to see a General on the meeting schedule for a pharmaceutical company. Considering what they hired me for."

Mariana was fading fast. Exhaustion was winning. Alex rolled onto her back and stared at the ceiling.

"They want to weaponize werewolves and discover a way to control their transformations. I can't say I'm surprised." It was only a matter of time when someone treated werewolves like domesticated animals. It took less than one month after vampires being outed to the public for countries around the world trying to recruit them for their military service. It has always been against Shade's rules. We don't fight in wars. Even when we could end them quicker. We don't take sides. We stay out. A few of us broke the rules a handful of times. Helping people flee when they were in danger, but Adonis would reprimand us.

Wolves were never as desired to be soldiers as vampires. One, they are hard to convince to leave their packs. Two, they are only at full strength one night a month. Wars are not fought in one night based on the moon cycle.

Alex tucked her hands behind her head. Mariana's breathing was slow. Alex could tell she had fallen asleep. Without waking her, Alex got off the bed and turned off the lamp on the table. She walked into the main room of the apartment and over to the fridge. There was a small magnetic whiteboard with the start of a grocery list. Alex picked up the dry erase marker. She scribbled a note before leaving the way she came in.

Thanks, sleeping beauty.
    Alex

The sun hung high in the sky, baking the desert ground until it cracked. Waves of shimmering heat rose from the earth, distorting the horizon. Inside, Alex lay sprawled across her bed, having collapsed there hours ago. She'd downed half a bottle of whiskey, hoping it would drown out the nightmares that had been plaguing her. The lingering burn of the alcohol mixed with the heaviness of sleep weighed down her body, but the muffled buzzing from the living room cut through the haze, vibrating in her skull like a relentless mosquito. She groaned, tempted to throw the phone out the window.

Dragging herself up at a human pace, Alex trudged into the living room, her body sticky with sweat. She wore a black sports bra and boxer briefs, both stained with a mix of spilled whiskey and dried blood. The pungent scent clung to her skin, coppery and smokey. Her phone sat abandoned next to her laptop, buried under a mess of papers.

She snatched it up. "What?" she growled into the receiver.

"How fast can you get to Lake Sumner?" Jules' voice came through, breathless and urgent.

Alex's senses sharpened as she moved toward the bathroom. "That's about an hour away. What the hell are you doing all the way out there?"

"Just get your ass out here, Alex," Jules pleaded, her voice tight. "Please. I need your eyes on this."

The sound of the shower sputtering to life filled the room as Alex stripped off her clothes without hesitation. Her muscles tensed in anticipation.

"I'll be there as fast as I can," she said, tossing the phone aside and stepping into the steaming water, her mind already racing ahead. Eager and nervous of what Jules needed to show her.

Forty-five minutes later Alex roared up on her motorcycle. Lake Sumner is usually a peaceful remote reservoir surrounded by rocky red cliffs. The side swarming with cops is home to sandy beaches lined with low laying shrubs. The wind has created mini dunes in the sand that look like tan waves frozen in time.

There were two cops stopping traffic from entering the boat ramp, but they waved Alex in. Next to the sheriff's dusty jeep sat a coroner's van, its white exterior stark against the desert backdrop. Alex didn't need to see it to know what was ahead; the pungent stench of decaying flesh was thick in the air, mingling with the musky odor of wet fur, and sweat. The sweat was from the officers forced to wear a dark grey uniform even when the sun is blazing. She wrinkled her nose and muttered under her breath, "Fuck. Please don't be James's brother."

Alex pulled her bike up next to Jules's jeep, switched off her helmet, and replaced it with dark aviator sunglasses. The dry heat threatened the small cacti at the base of the Lake Sumner welcome sign. Alex has lived in the places most people would think of when they think of ancient times, but her mind always thinks of the desert. Mysterious carvings found in caves and vast landscapes that seem to be untouched. She thought of this as she followed the dozens of footprints towards Jules.

A group of cops loitered near the scene, their faces taut with unease, arms crossed as they exchanged quiet glances. They were trained to deal with death, but never expected to find it like this.

Jules stood alone at the end of the boat ramp, her silhouette framed by the glittering surface of Lake Sumner, the water shimmering under the harsh sunlight. Her hands were firmly planted on her hips.

The cops knew exactly what she was, but there was no need to flaunt her glowing red eyes, cool as they might look for a moment, they'd burn out of her skull in no time from the sun. They dispersed as she moved closer. Clearing a path from her to the Sherriff.

Alex strode down the ramp, her boots kicking up small clouds of dust, and stood over the body sprawled near the sheriff's feet. A twisted, grotesque sight greeted her: limbs contorted at unnatural angles, bones jutting beneath the skin, the corpse lying like a broken marionette. The stench of death making the whiskey sour in her stomach. She grimaced.

"Fuck," she muttered, scanning the body. The brown skin was streaked with blood, matted with uneven patches of fur that hadn't fully taken form. A bone jutted from the forearm snapped cleanly in half, its jagged edge glinting in the sun. Alex crouched, inhaling deeply. There was no trace of another scent, no humans, no supernatural beings. It was as if the body had been fighting itself.

"Fuck is right," Jules echoed, her voice low and tense. "The coroner estimates he's been dead less than twenty-four hours. We'll know more after the tests, but this-" She gestured to the twisted form at her feet, "this is not normal rigor mortis."

Alex's gaze shifted over the contorted limbs. "Last night wasn't a full moon."

"That was my first thought too," Jules said, running a hand through her smooth, tightly braided hair. The bun at the nape of her neck was a habit left over from her days in the National Guard. She glanced at Alex, eyes narrowing. "Have you ever seen anything like this before?"

The question hung in the dry desert air, the silence broken only by the faint rustle of the wind across the lifeless landscape and the low murmur of the cops still watching, wary of what might come next.

Alex held her face down. Her eyes were closed behind her glasses. She was hoping her sense of smell would pick up on something. She tilted her head and inhaled. The overwhelming fragrance of Axe Body

Spray filled her nose, and she frowned. There was a cop holding a camera behind her. His steps were timid as he tried to get closer to the body. Close to Alex. She turned and smiled big at him. His heart raced. "Back up piglet. All I smell is you."

"Stop calling my officers pigs." Jules snapped.

He waited for Jules to nod and stepped back. Alex narrowed her eyes on the pad of one of the dead wolves' paws. The cracking skin was black like a stamp that was pressed in ink. She slid a knife from her side holster and crouched near the body. Pinching the fur between his toes she cut off a piece. It was also tinted black at the ends. She brought the fur to her nose. Murmurs from cops whispered behind her. They were both fascinated and disgusted by her acts. It would take the lab in Vaughn an entire day to determine what this substance was, but Alex recognized the faint scent of fresh asphalt right away.

Ony one road near Lake Sumner had repairs recently. Alex tossed the fur on the ground by the body. She kept the information to herself. There were too many eyes on her and she was unsure who Jules trusted.

Alex stepped away from the body, giving the officer a wide birth. The officer took her place and began snapping photos with a large camera. Jules followed her until they were out of range for nearby human ears.

"What do you know about a small genetic lab that opened up in Santa Rosa a few months ago. Owned by Gibbard Center for Genetic Research." Alex asked.

"Nothing." Her head jerked in both directions as if

checking to see if anyone is listening. Jules pulled a cloth from her back pocket and dabbed her forehead. "Did you find a connection?"

"I am not sure yet. All I know is two of your missing wolves donated blood to a mobile clinic right before they went missing. I know the lab in Santa Rosa is receiving their donations and they are researching werewolf genetics." Alex paused to look back at the deformed body. A group of officers and coroners were discussing how to fit it into a body bag. None of them wanted to touch it. Alex could hear someone gagging from where she was.

"I could get a warrant to search the lab. See if they are there." Jules pulled a notepad out.

"Don't bother. I already checked." Alex grinned. "Spoke to a hot scientist. She is under the impression they want her to find a way to control the transformation in werewolves."

"Make them change when it's not a full moon." Alex nodded in response. "Hopefully we are able to collect a few clean fingerprints from the fingers on this body that are still human. I'm heading to the station to try and identify him now."

"I'll meet you there." Alex took a few steps towards her motorcycle. Jules caught her arm. Most people who touched Alex would be greeted with a punch to the face or a slash from a knife, but Alex didn't flinch at the contact from Jules.

"If this is tied to Gibbard you need to tread carefully. They are a multibillion-dollar company with deep connections." Jules whispered as Alex kicked a leg over her motorcycle.

Alex lowered her sunglasses for a moment. Her red eyes narrowed at Jules. "Careful is my middle name."

"You sure it's not Drunk?" Jules scoffed.

Alex started her motorcycle. "That too."

This could have been a phone call, but Alex enjoys making the police squirm when she walks in. Jules is still hopeful they will welcome the idea of a vampire helping on cases. They keep their mouths shut, knowing Jules could easily replace them with the scarcity of jobs in rural areas.

The stale air of a desert police station was guaranteed to smell of a few things. Sweat, burnt coffee, and sweet fry bread. A mix of warm sugar and over used oil blending together. It did not make Alex miss eating solid food.

She entered the police station in Vaughn towards the end of Jules's shift. She wanted to give her the afternoon to finish the reports for the body found.

In truth, Alex wanted to finish off a bottle of whiskey and a blood bag while watching the live stream of the cameras she had mounted. One across the street from Mariana's apartment, and another on the interior fence of the lab. Placed after she left the doctor's apartment. The mobile clinic did not show up all day.

Alex did not trust Mariana. There was something she was not telling her. *The absence of truth is a lie, even if you do not ask the right questions.* A lesson Adonis tried to teach her when she began her Shade training. Alex learned that the hard way. She never questioned Anita's intentions. She rarely worked alongside Anita for Shade. They reunited in their NYC penthouse when not traveling. She was blinded by love or lust. Never looking deeper. Overlooking the slightest hint of a lie.

A motorcycle helmet tucked under her arm and two knives sheathed at her thighs. None of the police officers tried to stop Alex as she walked past. A few even stepped out of her path. She flashed them a toothless smile as she walked into Jules's office. She could smell the fear in them. Keeping her fangs hidden was the nicest thing she could muster.

Mugs, large fossils, and a dusty name plate were spread around her desk atop stacks of papers. The papers fluttered as a silver fan circulated across the room.

"Reporting for duty boss." Alex dropped into the chair and flung her feet onto the only clear corner of the desk. Jule's scowled.

"Boss?" She snorted. "Right."

"Did you identify the body?" Alex asked.

The Sheriff stood up and shut the door. While passing Alex to return to her seat she tossed a file in her lap. "Male, mid-forties, Hispanic, confirmed werewolf."

"I deciphered that by his mangled body, and the fur." Alex scanned the document for any new information. Alex read aloud. "His fingerprints were not on file."

"Nope. But he does fit the description of one of the missing persons. Alejandro Jimenez. He was undocumented. Went missing after leaving a job site in Pastura." Jules typed slowly on her keyboard. "He was reported missing on March 26th."

Four missing wolves in the area and now one has turned up dead. Not just dead, but halfway through the wolf transformation without a full moon. Alex had no leads other than the mobile clinic. She tossed the file folder on the desk. Jules grabbed it before the fan attacked it.

"I am going to keep an eye on that lab and the source of their blood donations. They have to return sometime." Alex nodded and stood. She turned towards the door and Jules stopped her.

"Hey, Alex." She started. "I know you came out here to live in isolation, but if you ever want to join Carmen and I for dinner we will keep a chair open for you."

Alex looked down at her boots, dust caked into worn leather. She exhaled quietly. She deserved the solitude, the punishment. No dinners with friends. Most definitely, no stolen kisses with that attractive scientist. An image that has fluttered through her mind since yesterday.

"I don't eat." She said low, her hand resting on the doorknob. Ready to flee.

Jules spoke to her back. "You can drink a blood bag

in front of us. I've seen it before. I just - I just thought maybe you would want company instead of drinking yourself into a stupor every night."

"I also drink during the day." Alex said flatly. Jules's sighed. "Thanks for the offer, but I don't need company."

Alex opened the door quickly and moved through the police station before Jules could respond. She was outside on her bike in a blink.

She pinched her eyes shut.

The sun was moving too slow. She needed it to be night. Needed to be surrounded by darkness.

Her phone buzzed in her pocket. She pulled up the live stream. Mariana was exiting the lab towards her small tan sedan. *Not working late tonight*. Alex thought. She tucked the phone into her pocket and turned towards Santa Rosa. Towards Mariana's apartment.

Alex stood on the hardware store roof, the warm desert breeze gently tickling the shaved undercut of her scalp. She had always loved watching people from above. Whether it was perched on a limestone roof in Greece or slate shingles in Chicago, the view from up high always felt like home.

Mariana did not go straight home. She stopped by the grocery store first and emerged with a paper bag filled with food. Including a large baguette sticking out of the top. Alex watched her unload the groceries from the hardware store roof. Mariana cut up celery, carrots, and broccoli. She put them on a plate with a container of hummus in the center.

She was humming a tune, but Alex could not make it out from where she was. She moved across the street and up the fire escapes like before. The sun had dipped below the horizon. Alex stood on her balcony, grateful for the darkness concealing her body. She watched Mariana dance in her kitchen while pouring a glass of red wine. Swaying her round hips.

She had replaced the lab attire with black leggings and a purple tank top. It fit snug on her curves. Lush thick curves that would prove hard for Alex to resist.

You're just horny. She told herself. *It's been too long. Well, long by your standards. Don't jump the first sexy woman you see. And don't assume every woman wants to sleep with you.*

She blinked hard. Cursing herself for not filling up her flask. When she opened her eyes, Mariana stood on the other side of the glass. Her expression was not fear. She had one hand propped up on her hip. She pointed to the locked latch and smirked.

"You think that little lock could stop me from getting in?" Alex tapped the glass with her nail. She could shatter it with one finger if she wanted to. That would go against her plan. She needed the scientist to trust her. Time to lay on the charm. Alex softened her face and smiled. "May I come in?"

Mariana looked down at Alex's motorcycle boots. Her brows scrunched together as she scanned up her body. Alex hated not knowing what she was thinking. She placed a finger on the door latch but did not move. "What do you want?"

"Just to talk."

"I want a blood sample."

Alex dropped her head back. "You know I can't do that."

Mariana groaned. A mini tantrum. Alex heard the

latch click and watched Mariana walk back into the kitchen. Slowly Alex slid open the door and shut it behind her.

Soulful music played in the background. Alex stood in the middle of the living room. Everything was grey. Grey walls. Grey couch. Grey carpet. The plants in the corner smelt of plastic with a fine layer of dust on the leaves.

Alex took up a corner spot on the couch and rested an ankle oner a knee. Balancing, a small cutting board, now filled with food on her hand and a glass of wine in the other, Mariana made her way to the couch. She placed the food on the coffee table and leaned back. Taking a long slow sip of wine.

"I'm sorry I have no- um" she paused, "ya know, blood. To offer you." Mariana's dark eyes lingered on Alex for a moment before moving back to the wine glass.

"I already ate." Alex watched her throat bob as she swallowed. No doubt wondering if her last meal was from a bag or a vein. "When's your next sample delivery scheduled for?"

Mariana reached over and grabbed a small slice of baguette and spread soft cheese on it. "They always come on Thursdays, but not every Thursday. I think it depends on how many donations they receive that qualify for my research."

"What makes them qualify?"

"Do I get to ask questions too?" Mariana flicked her long hair over her shoulder. The thick dark wave sent a river of roses towards Alex's nose. She inhaled deeply. Trying not to be too obvious that she was memorizing her scent.

"Not this time." She clenched her jaw. "What is your research looking for in samples?"

Mariana shifted her feet under her. Looking relaxed as ever.

"My project is confidential. I have told you everything I can without Gibbard coming after me. Plus, you are not FBI. You are not even Shade. I don't have to tell you anything."

Alex reached out and grabbed her wrist just as her glass hovered near her bottom lip. Mariana gasped into her wine. Alex moved her hand to cover hers and pulled the wine glass closer. She leaned over and forced Mariana to tilt the glass towards her. Alex took a slow sip. Keeping her dark red eyes piercing Mariana. The corners of Alex's lips tugged up when she heard the rapid increase of her heart. She could feel Mariana's blood pulse under her palm. After long seconds Alex moved the glass back to Mariana and released her hand.

Alex thought she looked beautiful when frightened. The rapid rise and fall of her chest. She imagined chasing her through a forest. Pressing her lips to her neck while it pulsed fast. The heat of her skin makes her perfume more intense. "I could make you tell me."

Mariana stared at her glass of wine. She tilted it towards her mouth and parted her lips. Her eyes closed as she sipped from the same side where Alex drank. Alex heard a quiet clink from the tongue piercing hitting the glass. Then Mariana turned to meet the narrow gaze of dark red eyes.

"I am not afraid of you." She kept her face flat.

Alex leaned back and spread her arms on top of the couch. "Your body tells me otherwise."

"So, you are going to threaten to hurt me if I don't break my NDA and tell you about my work." Mariana scoffed. "Haven't you heard you catch more flies with honey."

"You want me to be sweet to you like honey?" Alex flashed a sinful smile. "This is me being sweet."

She rolled her eyes. "Remind me not to get on your bad side."

"A fragile thing like you would not survive long on my bad side."

Mariana put her wine on the coffee table and turned her body to face Alex. She tucked her legs underneath. A position that gave the illusion they were friends about to gossip and share bad date horror stories.

"See." She wagged her finger. "You say things like that and why would I want to help. You bounce between flirting and threatening to eat me."

"Sometimes that's the same thing." Alex said, which made Mariana toss her head back and sigh over dramatically. Alex shifted in her seat. "Did you forget I am a fucking vampire? Every second around humans we are thinking of killing or-" Alex clenched her jaw. Swallowing the rest of her sentence.

"Or what?" Mariana tilted her head.

Or fucking.

"Can we just get back to my question? You may want to be loyal to your company, but there is a chance your company is responsible for the death of an innocent man. Not to mention, all the missing wolves. Wolves with families and lives and all that shit you humans value so much."

Mariana looked around the room. Everything was a reminder why she was in Santa Rosa. Gibbard furnished this apartment. They moved her to this town. She narrowed her dark eyes on Alex. Parting her lips only to pause for a few seconds before speaking.

"What do you value, Alex?" Mariana's question was too close to something Adonis would ask her at every stage of her life. A mantra, what moves you forward, what moves you forward. Alex feared if she said it three times in a mirror, her father would appear. Alex had to stop the instinct to yell "nothing" when images of all she has lost flashed in her mind. Memories of a packed audience glues to their seats and swaying to the melody. A sultry jazz number that bounces off the back wall where Alex stood to watch. The image was immediately followed by a blade slicing through Anita's neck. Alex was still haunted by the feel of her tight curls as she held her severed head. Her body echoes the pain of hitting the concrete so hard it broke her kneecaps. She rubbed her knees just thinking about it now. She had sobbed for the first time in centuries after that assignment. In truth, Anita was not the only one that died that day.

"I care about peace and quiet. This case is kicking up shit in my back yard and I need it over." Alex should have brought blood whiskey. The film of memories projecting in her mind made her dizzy. She longed to feel numb.

Alex focused on the couch underneath her and the rose scent surrounding her. She let the soft microfiber ground her. Remind her what's real. Where she was. When she was. Living as long as she had it is common for your mind to get stuck in another time.

She took a slow breath and repeated her question. "What makes a blood sample qualify for your research?"

By the time Mariana was on her third glass of wine, Alex did not have to pry information out of her. Details about the lab's day-to-day operations flowed out of her. Alex also noticed she played with the barbell in her tongue when she was thinking. An adorable habit that Alex found extremely distracting.

It turns out, Mariana does not know much about Gibbard. Being that she was new to the company and hired by a recruiter online. The email address she corresponded with didn't even have a name attached. Just the generic HR@GibbardGRC.com. This was a tactic that many secretive organizations used. Keep the employees in the dark as much as possible. It prevents information leaks.

Alex should move on from Mariana. Find another

way into Gibbard. Find a new lead. But she didn't want to move from the couch, let alone never see this woman again.

Mariana.

She said the name in her head.

Mariana.

Alex tried to hide how restless her legs were. The longer she sat next to Mariana the lighter the pressure in her chest felt. The constant burning ache was pushed to the back burner. Still burning, but Mariana's presence required her attention. Alex was glad to give it.

Mariana had sunk down until she was partially lying. The bottoms of her feet were pressed against Alex's outer thigh. The palm of her feet kneaded her muscles as she talked. Alex's body went rigid. It didn't help that Mariana's toenails were painted blood red. A delicious color.

What would Mariana do if I grabbed them and rubbed them? The way a lover would when their partner had a long day. Or what if I lifted a foot and sucked on a big toe.

Alex shot up from the couch and moved to the kitchen.

"Do you have any whiskey?" She paced with a hand rubbing the back of her neck.

Mariana looked over her shoulder. "No. I have tequila. Just the regular kind, not the vampire kind."

"That's fine." Alex said through her teeth. She needed something to take the edge off. This is why she avoids people. They make her feel things. Anger. Regret. And the worst feeling of them all. Hope. Hope that she can be happy again. That she deserves to be happy again. Alex failed Adonis. Failed as an agent. Failed as a wife. She deserves to be hollow. The only good she can do now is help find the missing wolves for Jules, and she was doing a fucking terrible job at that.

Her mind was wandering in this apartment. Allowing Mariana to distract her from the task at hand. She's on a case. People are relying on her.

Mariana pointed to the cupboard above the sink. Alex pulled out a mostly full bottle of Vito's tequila. She didn't bother getting a glass. Alex tilted the bottle bottom up towards the ceiling and instantly relaxed at the burn as she swallowed.

When she lowered the tequila, she found Mariana watching with a look of concern.

"What?" Alex snapped.

"Can vampires get drunk?"

Alex walked back to the couch and sat on the arm rest. Away from Mariana's feet. Close enough to still smell roses. She hasn't determined if it is her shampoo, lotion, or perfume. She took another gulp of tequila. Pushing down the urge to press her face into her hair or lick her skin to learn the source of the scent.

"Not really. Our mind goes a million miles a minute. With our heightened senses and all. Alcohol," she tipped the bottle towards Mariana. "It slows it down. Quiets the thoughts."

"Were you having loud thoughts just now?"

Alex took a step back as if distance would save her from the question. From having to explain the static that has lived in her head for thirty years.

"What are you, my therapist?"

Mariana tucked her legs into a crossed position.

"You seem on edge. And I don't feel like you are really motivated to solve this case. You have that look of someone floating in a river waiting to drown."

Alex blinked slowly and placed the tequila bottle, now mostly empty, on the coffee table. "Well fuck doctor. Give me your full analysis."

Her lips were a firm line. Mariana straightened her shoulders. Alex dropped back into the corner of the couch. She placed her feet on the coffee table and hands behind her head. Indicating she was ready to be torn apart.

"Well, I have nothing to compare this conversation to. This is my first chance to talk with a vampire. The media gives the impression vampires have no fear-"

"I have no fear." Alex interrupted.

Mariana ignored her and continued. "No shame, no regrets. You seem tormented with shame and regret. I can see it in your eyes. When I ask anything personal you deflect. You are afraid to be open. To be honest. I just wonder why. What thoughts are you trying to drown with alcohol?"

Mariana's heartbeat matched the slow melodic rhythm of the music playing at a low volume. Alex made the mistake of looking into the dark pools of her eyes. She felt a wave of emotions rise in her. Alex did fear. She feared saying something to the woman sitting next to her. She feared confessing the truth. In the short time she spent around this Dr. a spark ignited within her that was dormant for years. Alex wasn't sure if it was lust or the desire to make Mariana into a new obsession. Alex determined Mariana was a dead end an hour ago. When it came to the case, yet Alex remained in her apartment.

Alex chugged the last of the tequila and set it on the table. It was a bit too rough, and the loud thump made Mariana flinch.

"Thanks for the drink." She stood. "And the information on Gibbard."

Mariana stood after her, but Alex was too fast. She was already on the balcony, ready to jump. Mariana's hand stayed suspended in the air after trying to grab Alex by the arm.

"Wait."

"Goodnight, Dr. Nava." Alex leaped off the balcony and landed with knees bent. She began walking to the alley where she parked her bike. The tequila may have numbed the images of Anita, but everything Mariana said was fresh. Running circles in her mind. It was too loud, and she needed the rumble of her motorcycle to drown out the thoughts.

You seem tormented with shame and regret.

You are afraid to be open.

To be honest.

What thoughts are you trying to drown with alcohol?

She did not look back to see Mariana watching from the balcony. The rose scent followed her in a breeze. Alex sprinted the last half block, needing to be on the open road.

Alex took a long drive after her time with Mariana, partly to clear her head but also to follow the trails leading away from Lake Sumner. She drove slowly, eyes scanning the landscape for any sign, until she found a road with fresh asphalt. Parking her motorcycle, the warm desert wind tugging at her clothes. She began walking in wide, deliberate spirals, studying the ground for anything unusual. Her boots crunched over the gritty earth as she crouched, examining faint impressions where the sand had been disturbed. The wind had swept away much of the evidence, filling the cracks with fine grains, but there were remnants of tracks. The subtle indentation from a werewolf's paws, half-erased by the shifting sands. She traced the path with her eyes, knowing the trail would be faint, but she was getting closer.

She searched for clues as long as she could before the sun began to rise. Placing dark sunglasses on her face, she headed back to her motorcycle and headed home.

There was a large truck waiting in her driveway when she returned. Desert Moon Construction was painted on the side faded by the harsh sun. Alex saw the silhouette of a person sitting on her porch. Broad shoulders and wide steel tow boots digging into the dirt. She took her time parking her bike and strolling up to him at snails' speed.

All she wanted after the visit with Mariana was an empty house and now there was a prying wolf blocking her front door.

"James."

"Alex." Streaks lined his arms from where sweat had dripped through dirt. "Some partner you are. I haven't gotten a single update."

Alex sat next to him on the porch, leaving as much space between them as possible without falling off the edge.

"We are not partners. I was given a case by the sheriff, and you are just an Oxpecker." Alex smirked.

"Ox- what?"

Alex leaned on her knees. "An Oxpecker. Ya know, the birds that hitch rides on the backs of Rhinos."

This made him laugh low in his gut. "I like you. You're an asshole, but I like you. Do you have any leads on where my brother is?"

"Where he is, no." She looked up at the moon. It was a perfect crescent. They had a couple weeks before it would be full. Alex glanced at James from the corner of her eye. She was curious what color coat

James had. Werewolves come in many colors and sizes. It was a personal question, and she had no intention of asking. Not wanting to indicate she had an interest in getting to know him on a personal level. "I am convinced the disappearances are related to a mobile blood donation van. I'm trying to track it now. There was a body found at Lake Sumner."

"And." James's jaw clenched.

"Do you know a werewolf named Alejandro Jimenez from Pastura?" James shook his head. "He was mid transformation when they found him. The Sheriff's report says the transformation killed him. He had multiple broken bones and a fractured skull."

James's eyes went wide. "He must have been dead for weeks then."

"The coroner said he has been dead for less than 24 hours. I found a trail of footprints from highway 84 to the lake. There were no tire tracks, and his footprints ended abruptly when the new asphalt ended. He must have run down the highway for quite a while before veering off towards the lake. Most likely dehydrated. Lured towards the water.

Highway 84 goes to the lab in Santa Rosa. But I smelt no werewolves when I snuck inside the other day. Also, I am pretty sure the scientist running the lab is not that involved. Gibbard is keeping her ignorant on purpose." Alex shook her head at her feet. Disappointed in herself. She used to track anyone in the world at record speeds, yet for some reason she can't find a few kidnapped wolves.

"What's next?"

What's Next? What moves you forward?

"I need to get closer to Gibbard. Get inside somehow." She huffed. "I need to find that fucking van."

James grunted. "Thor put a word out to nearby packs not to donate blood and he implemented a curfew on the commune."

"Good." Alex placed a hand on his shoulder and pushed to her feet. He got on his feet and looked down at her. A tower blocking the moonlight from hitting her face. His biceps were attempting to tear the sleeves of his T-shirt. "I won't be nearby as I search for the van. It seems to travel from town to town. Keep an eye out on Vaughn."

"Of course."

She met his eyes in the dark. "And Sherriff Jules. She's not a pup like you, and I don't want her poking around. Pissing off the wrong people."

"Will do." He smiled. "Partner."

Alex turned her back to him. "Ugh, fuck off."

Jules had the memory of a sleep deprived goldfish. Earlier, in her office, Alex found her desk in the usual constant state of distress under layers of sticky notes and food wrappers. Some notes had unfinished grocery lists. Some had passwords. Including the password to access the New Mexico DMV records. Alex filed the information away until she was home. She thanked Jules as she logged into the DMV database.

Alex leaned over her laptop with a full glass of blood whiskey. The bottle of tequila worked its way through her hours ago. She found herself thinking about Mariana and her stinging words. Kept picturing her plump lips and the tongue piercing taunting her from inside her mouth. Then she felt guilt and pain. It overwhelmed her. If she were human the solution would be therapy or something comforting, but she was not human. She was something toxic. A kind of toxic that can only do one thing, erode.

She looked down at the red tinted whiskey.

Pathetic. She told herself. *Can't handle big emotions. Are the loud thoughts too much for you? You need to be numb to function. Pathetic.*

She emptied the glass and blinked forcefully. Then focused on the records before her.

There were no vehicles matching the van description registered to The Gibbard Center for Genetic Research. There was, however, a large mobile clinic registered to Daniel Harris in Albuquerque. He was a project manager at Gibbard. Alex smiled at his name and began to copy the address into her notebook when she realized it was the same as the Gibbard office. No home address was listed. Just the Albuquerque building filled with hundreds of employees and thousands of cameras.

She could not just walk into a multi-billion-dollar pharmaceutical company and demand answers. Past Alex would have. But past Alex was protected under Shade. Charging in now would draw attention from the local authorities who would most defiantly contact Shade.

She needs a way inside the building. Something subtle.

Alex drained another glass and poured over websites. Old building permits for the Gibbard high rise trying to find blueprints. There were dozens of newspaper articles about breakthroughs in genetic research. Praise for a pill to combat Alopecia. Even more praise for a pill that gives men a boner for only 15-20 min. Advertised for when they need it fast and quick. Alex remembers a distasteful commercial last year where a man met a woman in an airplane bathroom. Gibbard received a lot of public backlash and the FFA had to release a statement reminding the horny public that it was in fact illegal to have sex in an airplane bathroom.

Alex clicked on a link and perked up. Gibbard is having a gala Saturday in Albuquerque. What are the odds? She spots a familiar name. Listed under special guests is a General Gain. The US military contact for Shade. Alex has never met him, but she remembers Adonis mentioning him in passing. The General was eager to work with Adonis. He was impressed with the global network Shade created and how they remained hidden for so long. Adonis would not indulge him. Adonis became King because he was so skilled at keeping secrets. That, and he can persuade people with a bit of eye contact and a smooth voice.

The same method he used to convince a young Alex to be his bait and do his bidding while she was human. She stiffened at the memories and reached for the bottle of whiskey only to find it empty.

She nearly crushed the bottle when she read the small print on the bottom of the Gala information. A wide grin filled her face.

Current Gibbard employees are allotted one guest ticket.

Assuming Mariana was not planning on attending, Alex took the liberty to add her to the list. Alex had not observed her speaking with anyone on a personal level. Just a friendly conversation with the grocery store cashier. Alex took it upon herself to put her name down as the plus one. She filled out the form.

Employee: Dr. Mariana Nava

Guest: Alex Sipala

"It looks like I need a suit." Alex leaned back and grinned at the screen. "And Mariana will need a dress. Something tight, with a low back would look nice."

Alex had a black dress bag draped over her arm. She was afraid of ruining the fabric inside by climbing the fire escapes as usual. Therefore, she opted for the front door. The main entrance to Mariana's apartment building needed a key fob to open. Or a very strong hand to pull the latch clean out of the door frame. *"Oops."* Alex whispered as she walked to the elevator. It had been two days since she spoke to Mariana. Although she has been watching her come and go on the camera feed linked to her phone. Mariana has become her favorite show. Alex was grateful she had no curtains on her sliding door. It gave the camera mounted on the hardware building a direct shot into the apartment.

Every night Mariana bopped in the kitchen to music while she ate dinner far too late. Her phone would ring, and she would ignore it. Alex wondered who was on the other end. She considered hacking her phone, but spying on her with cameras was already pushing her over the line into a stalker.

Mariana arrived home from work a few hours ago. Alex let her get settled and waited until the sun went down before heading into her building. The scent of seasoned meat and oil slithered under the door.

Alex pressed her ear to the door and listened to the TV.

"Tonight, Victoria will send one man home. Leaving her to face the final decision. Who will become the vampire's lover? Find out after the break."

Alex groaned. She almost turned away. How can a brilliant woman like Mariana watch such trash. A commercial for an energy drink began to play. Alex knocked twice and stepped back.

"I should have brought flowers." She murmured to herself. "No, that's stupid."

The door swung open, and Mariana stared with eyes wide. She was barefoot with black leggings and an oversized T-Shirt. A graphic with a rocket was on the front. Instead of fire bursting from the bottom, it was rulers, microscopes, protractors, beakers, and other science related items.

"Nice shirt."

"I spoke at a children's summer camp last year." She looked down the hall before stepping to the side. "You used my front door."

Alex moved past her into the apartment. The air was filled with the remnants of cooking oil. Alex saw a single plate on the coffee table. Nothing was left but bits of lettuce and tomato. "Taco night?"

Mariana shut the door and muted the TV. She began to tidy up. Moving her plate into the sink. She turned around aggressively. "Why are you here Alex?"

"I brought you something." Alex set the dress bag on the back of a dining chair. Mariana crossed her arms and said nothing. Alex ignored the hostility and sat on the couch. The flask in her back pocket bit into her ass. She ignored it too.

Mariana brought her glass of wine with her over to the dress bag. She pulled the zipper down a few inches and blinked at the shimmery fabric. "What is this?"

"I believe they call it a dress. Although it might be considered a gown."

Mariana huffed and crossed her arms. She stepped towards the couch. Alex shifted as she approached.

"I can see that asshole." She sat in the center of the couch. Not amused with Alex showing up and expecting her to fall in line with whatever she had planned for her involving a formal dress. Alex was astonished by the steadiness of Mariana's heartbeat. Far too calm for a woman who just sat next to a vampire. "Why are you bringing be a gown?"

"Why is everyone calling me an asshole?" Alex grabbed her flask but only played with the cap. "There is a fundraiser gala, and I need a date."

"You're asking me on a date?"

"Well," Alex took a long swig of the blood whiskey. Being this close to Mariana gave her a stomachache. Or her heart ached. Alex couldn't tell what she felt it had been so long since she felt anything. Fortunately, the scent of tacos was masking the usual lingering rose water aroma on her skin. Alex was not sure she could handle it now. "Actually, I need to be *your* date. Gibbard is hosting a gala, and I need to get in."

Mariana's mouth gaped. "Fuck no. I can't bring a vampire to a work event."

"Ouch."

"No offense, but you don't have the best manners." Mariana laughed into her wine. Alex watched her throat bob as she swallowed.

"Offense taken." Alex reached over and pinched a loose strand of hair. Mariana froze. The wine glass trembled in her hand as she brought it to balance on her lap. Alex tucked the hair behind her ear. "I have excellent manners when necessary. I was raised to be a chameleon. I have been to hundreds of Soirées de galas, I have bowed before Kings and Queens," Alex dropped her hand. Mariana turned to face her. Her dark eyes trying to read Alex. "Fuck I even crashed the first Met Gala in 1948."

Mariana licked her lips slightly staining them with wine. Alex ignored the heat pulling between her legs as she caught the quick glint of silver. She tried to shift further away but was already pressed up against the armrest.

"Who raised you?" Mariana asked barely louder than a whisper.

A grin spread across Alex. Her fangs are on full display.

"Pack an overnight bag. I will pick you up tomorrow afternoon. The gala is in the evening."

"I did not agree to take you. You're a vampire. And not one of the good ones."

"Good ones?" Alex barked. "What the fuck does that mean?"

Mariana moved to the edge of the couch. Remembering the danger she let enter her apartment. She looked around the room. Alex watched her eyes flick to the kitchen where her cell phone sat out of reach.

"There are vampires that work for that organization, Shade. I see them talked about on the news. They are like vampire police, or something. They stop vampires that go off the rails. Ones that kill people."

"That is what Shade claims, yes." Alex took another swig from her flask. Mariana was nervous now. Her neck had sweat gathering under her hair. Alex wanted to lift the thick dark hair and blow on her skin. Watch the bumps form under her breath.

"Is that not what they do?"

"Listen," Alex ran a hand through her hair. "Fuck. I will promise you three things. One, you will look fucking hot in that dress. Two, I will bring you home the day after the gala in one piece. Three, I will never bite you," she winked, "unless you ask."

"Why would I ask you to bite me?" Her eyes narrowed.

"Oh, doctor, you have no idea how many people have been on their knees begging. How many waited naked on my bed offering themselves. How many became addicted to the pain caused from my bite."

Mariana's chest rose quickly with each breath. She stared at Alex's mouth as she spoke. Alex wondered if a bit of Adonis's persuasion was passed onto her. She had this Dr. eating out of the palm of her hand. They stared at each other for a moment. Alex wanted to close the gap between them. Press her body against Mariana. Run her hands down her curves. Grip her plump thighs.

"I-" Mariana started then swallowed. "I would never want that."

"Of course, doctor." She smirked. "Not a good girl like you."

Mariana looked away but Alex noticed the pink flush on her cheeks.

"I looked into your case. I found a few articles about people missing. People rumored to be werewolves. Do you really think Gibbard took them?" She set her empty wine glass down.

"If they didn't, they know who did."

She rubbed her palms on her lap. "Okay, I will take you to the gala. Just don't cause any more problems for me. I had to feed the guard a bullshit story when you showed up at my lab. This may not be my dream job, but it pays great. And will open up many doors if I don't screw it up. I gave up everything for this. I moved to New Mexico. I left-" She let her sentence die.

"I won't fuck up your job." Alex moved an inch closer, and Mariana flinched. "I won't hurt you."

Alex stood up and tucked the flask in her pocket. Mariana was staring at the coffee table. Her eyes were fixed on an unopened letter. It was handwritten. The sender's name is written in green ink. *Jordan Mackey*. From a California address. In place of Mariana's name, it said *Mi Amor*. Alex's jaw tightened.

"I will be here tomorrow afternoon. Be ready." Alex opened the sliding door to the balcony. Noticing it was unlocked. "And thanks. This will be the last thing I need your help with. After the gala I will leave you alone."

She jumped off and headed towards her truck before Mariana could respond. Why the fuck would she say that. She didn't want to leave her alone. She enjoyed popping up in her apartment. She enjoyed the way she kept trying to ask questions about her life. She wanted more of Mariana. She wanted to be sober around her. To feel every moment sharp and intense.

"Fuck." Alex said as she shut the truck door. "That woman is driving me crazy. I need to solve this fucking case for Jules quick."

18

The radio in Alex's old truck was broken, leaving them in silence except for the steady hum of the engine and the rhythmic clattering of the large duffle bag in the truck bed, filled with various weapons. Outside, the dusty highway stretched endlessly before them, an empty road with barely any passing vehicles. A haze of the afternoon heat shimmered off the pavement, making the distant horizon waver like a mirage. Inside the truck cab, the scent of Mariana's rose water clung to the air, delicate and heady, a stark contrast to the old leather of the truck seats.

Alex would've preferred her motorcycle, but space was needed. Overnight luggage, weapons, surveillance gear, and two dress bags. The practical choice was her truck, with its groaning leather steering wheel now creaking under Alex's grip. Her knuckles whitened as she gripped it tighter, mind racing. She started many conversations in her head to fill the silence, but none made it past her lips. *Mariana is just a ticket into the gala. Nothing more*, she repeated in her mind. *Get in, find who's leading the program, locate the wolves, and move on.*

Next to her, Mariana sat with her arms folded across her waist, staring out the window. The dry, desert landscape went by in a blur, as her long dark hair caught the occasional breeze from the open window. Her presence made the interior cab feel smaller than usual. Alex could feel her eyes now and then, but she didn't turn to meet them.

"Where were you born?" Mariana's voice broke the stillness.

Alex jerked slightly at the sound. She hadn't been expecting it. Turning her head, she caught Mariana's gaze, her face tilted, wide-eyed with curiosity behind dark lashes. Alex blinked hard, quickly shifting in her seat to seem more relaxed under the weight of Mariana's gaze, but her grip on the steering wheel remained firm.

"Croatia." Technically that was true. Although it had another name when she was born on its soil.

"Wow. I have never known anyone from there before. That's near Italy, right?" Alex nodded. "Why would you end up out here in the US desert?"

Alex remembered the look on Mariana's face when she accused her of not opening up. Leaving her questions unanswered. She sucked in a breath. Alex shut her eyes for a second, grateful for the straight highway. The truck cabin was filled with the scent of roses. It must be something in the shower. Her shampoo or maybe bodywash. Alex's body relaxed.

"I needed quiet. I retired from my job and wanted to put as much distance between me and my ex-employers as possible." She rested her right hand on the stick shift. "I was thinking of moving though. To an Island maybe. I miss the beach."

"What job would a vampire have that they would retire from?"

"I was one of the good ones." Alex said playfully.

Mariana unfolded her hands and gripped her legs above her knees. "You worked for Shade? As what?"

"What do you think? I was a tracker." She smirked. "I was one of their best agents. Trained by Adon- the King himself."

"So, would you say you are close to the King of Vampires?" Mariana tapped her leg like she was taking notes.

"You can say that." It does not get closer than calling him father.

Mariana leaned on the truck door but kept her body turned towards Alex. She had a huge grin on her face.

"What?" Alex asked.

"I am just starting to figure you out." Her dark eyes brightened. Alex's shoulders tensed under Mariana's gaze. She did not want to be figured out. She did not want Mariana getting close to her. Everyone who got close to her ended up hurt. Or dead. Sometimes by her hand.

Alex didn't mind the idea of being close, at least for a night. Maybe even a couple of nights. But physical closeness was one thing; emotional intimacy, the kind where she would bare her soul to Mariana, was something entirely different. Opening up, sharing the dark, tangled secrets of her past, which was a vulnerability Alex wasn't ready to face. She doubted she'd ever be ready for that again. The thought of it sent a familiar wave of anxiety through her chest.

Yet, as she glanced across the seat, her eyes lingering on Mariana, she found herself mesmerized by the warmth in those deep dark eyes. For a fleeting moment, Alex imagined what it would be like to let herself go, to let the walls fall and allow Mariana into the parts of her she kept buried. The thought was both terrifying and oddly comforting.

Maybe it could be more than just one night, she thought, before quickly dismissing the idea. Who was she kidding? She didn't even know if Mariana was attracted to women. Alex turned her gaze back to the road, pushing the thought aside, but the lingering possibility hung in the air like an unspoken question.

When she looked at Alex there was interest in her expression. Alex did not know if it was attraction or curiosity. Did she want to kiss her or get a sample of her blood? Was she a love interest or a test subject in her eyes? Either way, Alex's feelings were conflicted. She wanted to pleasure Mariana. Hear the sounds she made when she came. Just as much as she wanted to sink her teeth into her and taste her sweet blood.

They pulled into Downtown Albuquerque. The area exploded with growth a decade ago. Large buildings now shadowed the historic rooftops that were significantly shorter. They drove towards a mirrored tower. One of the only hotels in the area designed to cater to vampire clientele. It had a huge overhang that shaded the front of the building. With enough space for twelve vehicles to unload.

Alex stopped in front of the bell stand. Two men with white shirts and red vests ran to get the doors. Mariana thanked them as she stepped out of the truck. Alex opened her door and tilted her sunglasses down. Flashing her crimson eyes. The bellman at her side stopped in his tracks. He tipped his head low. Almost a bow. Alex tossed him the keys.

"Bring the bags to my room. Last name Sipala." She said the last part quietly while looking over her shoulder. Mariana was already at the bell stand looking at a map. Her posture was giddy as she bounced on her toes. The realization occurring to her that she was about to have firsthand experience around many vampires. A thrilling venture for a scientist.

Alex tapped her elbow as she walked past, nudging her forward. This hotel leans heavily into the vampire stereotypes. Black leather and red velvet furniture. Chandeliers with black crystals. Even the floor was polished black stone.

Before they reached the counter, Alex led Mariana to a leather chair. It was one of four in the lobby. The table in the center was made to look like blood. It had a glossy top that appeared to be dripping. The large drips held it up like it was frozen in time.

"Wait here."

She crossed her arms. "I am not a child."

"I am just checking us in."

"Why can't I come with you?" She took a step away from the chair, but Alex stopped her. Mariana looked down at where Alex had pressed a palm to her stomach. Her skin nearly burned to touch. Alex flexed her fingers slightly before removing her hand and tucking it behind her back.

"Please." Her red eyes softened. "I will be quick. I just need privacy."

Mariana stepped back and slid into the chair. Her arms remained crossed, but the scowl melted from her face. "Fine."

The person behind the front desk was handsomely beautiful. It was as if they stole the best features from both masculine and feminine. Alex was a bit jealous. She always felt somewhere in between. Her lean body and short stature made it easy to sneak around. Someone like James would struggle to hide in the shadows. It also gave a false assumption about her strength. Being only 5'5" in height, people always underestimate her.

"Your opponent will never suspect you were trained in a multitude of ways to kill them. Let them drop their guard, then rip their heads off." Adonis's words recited in her head.

"Checking in?" The person behind the desk asked.

Alex slid her ID over the polished wood. Shade agreed to have vampires and werewolves carry identification twenty-five years ago. Once supernatural's were exposed, the world became paranoid. They wanted a registry. Adonis was in negotiations for many years with the world leaders. He already had a registry that was very accurate, but they did not know that. They agreed to give him access to GPS satellites and other technology, if he enforced ID's. He kept the registry to himself.

The person scanned the card. It was not issued by any state or country. It was registered under Shade. With the word "Vampire" in red under her name.

"Welcome Mrs. Sipala-Creon." They said.

"Just Sipala please." Alex looked over her shoulder to see if anyone with enhanced hearing heard the desk agent.

"My apologies, Mrs. Sipala." Their fingers clacked on the keyboard. "One night, king size bed, vampire friendly suite." Alex nodded. "How many room keys would you like?"

"Two is fine."

Mariana was hunched over a magazine. Her mouth agape at whatever she was looking at on the page. Alex quietly leaned down until their cheeks were level.

"What's so interesting?" She whispered. Mariana jumped and tossed the magazine like it burst into flames. Alex laughed. The magazine cover had a vampire sitting on a throne. A woman wearing barely anything sat on the armrest. She was holding her arm in front of his face. Blood dripped down as he sunk his fangs into her. The woman was throwing her head back. But it was not pain spread across her face. It was pure pleasure. "See something you like?"

Mariana stood. She pressed the creases out of her shirt and lifted her chin. "No."

"No?" Alex smirked. "Nothing?"

"Nothing."

Alex rubbed her hand up Mariana's arm and stopped on her shoulder. "Your pulse is racing." She moved her hand to lightly caress her neck. Mariana sucked in a breath. Alex loved fear and the arousal swirling in her eyes. Mariana did not flinch from her touch. She ever so slightly leaned into Alex's hand.

"This lobby is just weirding me out." Alex's red eyes were not the only one's tracing Mariana's body. She was clocked as human the moment she walked in. Alex was glad her scent was stuck to her from the truck ride. It gave the impression she was claimed already, and no vampire would challenge her. Although, a challenge would not be necessary in a place that attracts desperate humans like moths to a flame.

Alex moved Mariana's hair behind her shoulder and grazed her skin as she moved her hand away. The lobby was kind of creepy.

"Come on. Let's go up to our room." She stepped towards the elevator.

"Our room?" Mariana's sandals slapped the marble behind Alex. "One room?"

"Yes." She smiled although Mariana could not see. "Our room."

Hotel Yeha had many suites. Alex has stayed in a few. Mariana bit her bottom lip when she entered their room. Alex heard the quietest squeal that she tried to keep in her throat. She knew Mariana would love the deep purple walls in this suite. The space was opulent and luxurious.

Mariana ran her fingers through the fringe on the bedside lamps. Her heart was racing from excitement. Alex tossed her keys on a wet bar and smiled to herself.

The mini fridge was stocked to appease a vampire. Alex taking full advantage. Blood was waiting in old-fashioned milk bottles. Alex poured half a bottle into a glass and filled the rest by opening three mini bottles of whiskey. She tossed it back in a few gulps.

Mariana was watching her while leaning on the window. The glass was a one-sided mirror with the reflective side facing out. It gave the window a deep tint. Heavy black curtains hung on the sides. Her expression was somber.

Alex licked the corner of her mouth to stop a drip of blood. "What's wrong."

Mariana took a deep breath. She walked over to the bed and touched the black satin comforter. Changing her mind, she turned and sat in a dining chair at the bistro set. Unspoken words hung in the air for a moment before Mariana could gather them.

"Will you be sober at the Gala tonight?"

Alex looked at the three empty mini bottles on the counter above the mini fridge. She tossed them in the trash. Usually she would tell someone to "fuck off" or "mind your own business" if they commented on her drinking. She heard it enough from Jules. There was a look of genuine concern on Mariana's face. Alex wanted to kiss her eyelids shut and tell her "Everything will be okay". She shifted on her feet before taking up the seat across from her.

"I will be very alert tonight. You have nothing to worry about." She looked down at the table and decided against taking Mariana's hand in hers. She was nothing to Mariana. Other than an annoyance using her employment to get into an event. Alex had the urge to protect her and relieve her stress. In most situations she would crack jokes and openly flirt. But there was nothing fake about Mariana. She was kind and curious. Alex found it utterly charming. A voice inside her mind, buried behind the memories that she drinks to numb, told her to keep an open heart.

She flexed her hand, noting how empty it felt without a glass in it. Alex needed to be on her best behavior. She needed a clear head. The last thing Alex needs is a human reporting a vampire behaving badly to Shade. "Let's go over a few things."

"Ok."

"What do you prefer to introduce me as?"

Mariana tilted her head. "What do you mean?"

"Friend?" Alex paused. "Date? Girlfriend? It needs to be believable.

A shy smile bloomed on Mariana's face. "Let's go with date."

Fuck yes! Alex screamed in her head. "Cool. I'm cool with that."

Alex heard footsteps and a squeaky cart outside the door. Moments later there was a knock. Mariana walked into the bathroom and shut the door. A pristine silver hardcase for Mariana and a tattered green duffle bag for Alex. He also hung two black dress bags in the coat closet. Alex slipped the bellman a twenty after he unloaded their luggage. The bellman was human. Most of the staff were. The population of vampires was not large enough to fill service positions. Shade has always relied heavily on a few discreet humans. Until a few decades ago. Now humans beg to work at establishments that cater to vampires.

Alex used to question why Adonis did not encourage turning more vampires. He emphasized it was a privilege not to be given out lightly. A privilege Alex used to take advantage of. These days her gifts are a waste in Adonis's eyes. He tried one time to convince her to return to Shade, but her face was unmoving except for the blood red tears pouring from her eyes. Taking Anita's life broke something in Alex. Adonis had hoped with time and seclusion she would return. Go back to being his favorite daughter and his favorite pet. They are one in the same unfortunately.

Alex unzipped a dress bag and caressed the black stretched wool fabric. The suit was tailored to fit her body. It included a black silk blend shirt with black buttons to match the suit. The two buttons at each cuff can be twisted and removed. A sharp nub was on their underside allowing her easy access to break skin. A tool commonly used by vampires in hives. She could make a small puncture on a wrist or neck. Somewhere easy to cover up. The jacket of the suit had two leather lined pockets where she could sheath a knife.

"Do you think the Gala will have metal detectors?" Alex called towards the shut bathroom door. The water from the sink turned off. Alex heard Mariana sigh before the doorknob turned slowly. Mariana stepped out with her phone grasped in her hand.

"Why? What are you trying to bring?"

"I am just wondering if I can bring my knives." Alex zipped up the dress bag and moved to the empty glass of whiskey. She considered calling room service to bring up a full-size bottle. Alex set the glass down and rolled her shoulders. "I feel naked without my knives."

"And your flask?" Mariana raised a brow.

"The invitation said, 'Open Bar'. I think I will fine without my flask." Alex flashed a sharp smile.

Mariana moved to the bed and rested her back on the red tufted headboard. She kicked off her sandals and flung her feet up. "Where do you plan on sleeping?"

Alex crossed her arms. "Next to you."

Mariana swallowed. Her eyes flicked from Alex to the luxurious bed, then back to Alex. "I don't think that's a good idea."

"You fell asleep at your apartment with me a foot away on your bed." Alex took two slippery steps towards the foot on the bed.

"That was different."

Alex stepped closer until her knees touched the mattress. "How so?"

Mariana motioned wide to the room. Waving her hands towards the lamps that only made soft light. The heavy velvet drapes. The way everything was in pairs. Two chairs at the bistro table. Two champagne flutes on the counter above the mini fridge. Two pillows on the king size bed.

"This setting is very," She swallowed.

"Sensual?" Alex added.

"Romantic." Mariana barely noticed Alex crawl onto the bed until the souls of her feet were up against her thighs. "Does it make you feel uncomfortable. Being here. With me?"

Alex knew she was crossing a line. If she were an active agent with a lieutenant to report to, she would never flirt this hard with a source in a case. The reminders to be professional blinked in and out of her mind as she looked down at Mariana's body. She was a free agent. No longer required to restrain herself, and there was no one waiting for her at home. A fact she is content with. Or she thought she was. The idea of Mariana waiting in her bed intrigues her, and she cannot help her hand wanting to explore.

Alex moved her hands down her own legs until they slipped over the tops of Mariana's feet. She gently gripped her ankles. Mariana's arms fell to her side.

"Uncomfortable? No. That's the problem."

Alex abruptly pulled her legs until Mariana was flat on her back. Before she could rise Alex was over her. Their bodies not touching. Alex looked down into her dark eyes. *Kiss her. Lick her neck.* Alex blinked away the thoughts. Anyone that can kill their lover does not deserve to love again. Even for a fleeting moment.

"Why don't you rest." Alex leaped off the bed like a startled cat landing steady on her feet across the room. "We have a few hours before we need to leave."

Mariana stared at the ceiling. Unmoving from the position Alex left her in. Her chest rose rapidly with every inhale.

"Okay." Mariana rolled over and faced away from Alex.

66 It's a good thing I don't age. My hair would go grey waiting for you." Alex tugged at the sleeves of her suit. She had been impatiently pacing in a circle. Mariana was in the bathroom for nearly two hours. She wanted to shower, shave, and curl her hair. Alex resisted the urge to break the lock on the door and peak inside. The scent of rose water slithered under the door. Teasing her. Alex wanted to lick it up.

"I haven't been this dressed up since prom." There was a plastic clacking sound hitting the floor followed by a string of curse words. Alex smirked.

She continued to pace until the bathroom door jiggled. Mariana had unlocked it. It opened in slow motion. Mariana stepped out. One black strappy foot followed by the other. She was holding up her dress and didn't let it fall until she was standing in the center of the room. A mere two feet from a frozen Alex. Mariana placed her hand on top of her hip. The gleam on the purple fabric moved along her curves when the lamplight brushed over it, giving the illusion it was wet. Every inch of her body looked fun to grab.

Alex opened her mouth, but nothing came out. Mariana turned. "You picked a good dress. How did you know my size?"

Thick wavy curls hung over the thin straps of the dress. She tossed them over her shoulder and Alex had to take a step back. Overwhelmed by her beauty.

She saw the dress on a mannequin. Nothing could have prepared her for the low back that stopped just above Mariana's ass. It had a built-in bra and was praised by the shop owner. *"This is one of the only dresses that busty women can go braless in"* she had said. It was enough to convince Alex. Seeing it on Mariana now made her regret not buying it in every color.

If she ever gives in to her desires, Alex will need a map to navigate Mariana's curves. Maybe a compass. She very well could lose the ability to find her way out of her embrace.

"Lucky guess." Her voice quaked. It was uncharacteristic to show any form of nervousness.

"It is also my favorite color. How did you know I love purple?" She moved before the floor length mirror on the back of the bathroom door.

Alex cleared her throat. "The bedspread in your apartment. It was the only thing that felt like you picked it out."

"Good observation."

"Mariana, you look stunning." Mariana responded

with a soft smile through the mirror. Alex cleared her throat. "Thank you for tonight. For letting me use you to get into Gibbard."

Mariana picked up her phone and tucked it into a black sequined clutch purse. She placed a hand on Alex's shoulder.

"I like your suit." Wearing heels, she was a few inches taller than Alex. It did not bother Alex one bit. She would love to gaze upon Mariana from every angle if allowed.

"Thanks."

"Are there hidden knives?"

"Yes."

Mariana sighed and walked towards the door leading to the hallway. "Shall we go then?"

Alex opened the door and motioned like a gentleman for Mariana to go first.

The Albuquerque branch of the Gibbard Center for Genetic Research was not just a hub for cutting-edge science, it also served as a venue for numerous high-profile conventions. Beneath its towering structure lay a sprawling conference hall, seamlessly connected to a luxury hotel. Throughout the year, the hotel bustled with the comings and goings of pharmaceutical elites, industry leaders, and researchers.

One group was never welcomed, even with the changing times: vampires. The Gibbard Center, along with most pharmaceutical companies, maintained a strict policy against employing them, unless, of course, they were willing to become test subjects. A few have asked the King for permission. Lured by wealth promised in trade of being a lab rat. It was common knowledge that Adonis had made it clear, any vampire who volunteered for scientific research would lose their head, literally.

He would threaten the company for offering and punish the vampire. Depending on the status it could be time spent in an isolated cell or losing an eye. An injury that would never heal.

Still, this didn't stop the scientists from asking. Some remained persistent, ever curious. Alex kept a mental tally of how often Mariana had made such requests. So far, Mariana had only broached the subject twice, but Alex knew the night was still young.

There was in fact not a metal detector at the entrance to the Gala. Alex strolled in, knives and all. There was a noticeable silence as they entered. Not a single shutter clicks. Most Gala's would have photographers documenting the evening. In this moment she was grateful there was no whiskey in her system. Every sound and smell painted a picture even if she were to shut her eyes.

Waiters weaved through the guests with silver trays of crab rangoons and stuffed mushrooms. Heels clacked against the polished white floor. Above all the clatter and murmuring she kept note of each step from Mariana. Memorizing the exact sound of her weight on each heel. Keeping constant awareness of her location.

Alex placed her hand on Mariana's lower back and

led her through the room. When she was greeted by smooth skin, she again thanked the shop owner for suggesting the dress. They stopped near the dance floor. A handful of couples moving around the space to the slow melodic music. Alex swiped a glass of white wine from a waiter walking by and handed it to Mariana.

"None for you?" She sipped the wine.

"I prefer red."

"Oh, me too. But I will drink white if-" Mariana paused, "Oh you meant-"

The end of the sentence hung between them. Alex just smiled and tilted her head like an animal watching prey. She noticed how Mariana's breath hitched for a moment. Her brow tugged together. It was obvious to Alex that Mariana was teetering between fear and aroused. Exactly where she liked her. Most women pull away, but Alex caught the small step or body lean every time. Her body language giving her away since they met in the lab. Or at least Alex was interpreting it that way. It could be the natural curiosity of a scientist and nothing more.

She caught a few murmurs around her. There was no hiding what she was. The crystal chandeliers made enough light for her features to be easily readable. Guests around her were noticing the hue of her eyes and the sharp elongated canines. Mariana didn't seem to care. Or perhaps she just hasn't noticed yet. Alex could have put in contacts and blush to her cheeks. She could have kept her mouth shut to hide her fangs. But she spent too many years hiding and has refused to do so for the past thirty years. And she enjoyed the rhythm of rapid heartbeats as she walked past.

"So, what's your plan?" Mariana linked an arm with Alex as she scanned the crowd.

"I am going to talk to a few people, read the room, and then I might go for a walk." Alex studied the faces. The usual Gala guests. Mostly over the age of forty. She suspected the ladies have worn their dresses to other events. This was not Manhattan. No one purchased the latest Dior dress for a fundraiser in Albuquerque.

Along the edge of the room was a group of suits, standing in a huddle. Expensive watches catching the light as they peak from under the cuff. Hundreds of colognes and perfumes blended in the air. Alex centered herself by focusing on Mariana's scent at her side. The conversation of men halted as one of them was called away by a bleach blond in a gold gown.

They shifted to accommodate the gap he left in the circle. Alex narrowed her eyes on the white-haired man now in the center. She recognized his face from the news and has heard his voice through a speaker on Adonis's desk many times.

Her feet moved on their own in his direction. She grabbed Mariana by the elbow, making sure to keep her grip light, and pulled her along. When she was standing before him, the man raised a hand to signal for the group to disband. The didn't hesitate. Dropping the conversation like their tongues were just cut out. His lips were stiff in a straight line.

"General Gain." Alex hummed.

"Princess Alexandrine" he said flatly.

Alex felt the subtle shift of energy before Mariana's head snapped in her direction. Her entire body tensed. Hoping that Mariana could maintain her composure.

If it looked like Mariana didn't know her true identity, this delicate act of pretending to be a couple, would crumble. Alex's jaw tightened as she prepared to confront the man in front of her, when someone far more intriguing caught her attention.

The familiar face drew her focus like a magnet, her gaze locking onto him with such intensity that for a brief moment, the crowded room faded into a blur. She was transfixed, memories stirring in her mind. But as she stood frozen in recognition, another figure moved from behind him, stepping to his side, and Alex's attention was jolted back to the present. Involuntarily gripping Mariana's arm.

Alex's red eyes flickered, widening ever so slightly as they took tall dark form towering over her. The knives sewn into her suit jacket felt heavy. Blazing red eyes met hers.

"Imani?"

The warrior stood a head taller over Alex. Her hair was in tight waves of braids on the sides of her head. The center braids were woven together to make a larger single weave that draped down her back. Her lean body was draped with black satin. The sheen matches the silkiness of her dark skin. Imani took pleasure in showing her flawless skin. Not adorned by a single scar or mark. Evidence she was turned before she picked up a blade in battle.

"That's Lieutenant Imani. Don't forget your place." She snapped.

Mariana gripped Alex's arm. "Did he just call you Princess?"

Alex narrowed her eyes at the pair.

"Unfortunately, yes."

Alex leaned into Mariana and whispered, "I'll explain later."

Imani and the General stood side by side across from them. The General looked annoyed to see her, but Imani had an expression of pure disappointment on her face. A reflection of the way she looked at her many years ago when leaving Shade.

"What are you doing here Alex?" Imani placed a hand on her hip and shifted her weight. She did not possess the hypnotizing curves that Mariana had. Alex ran her hand through her hair. The angled bob haircut fell back into place slightly covering one eye.

"I'm on a date."

"Sure, you are."

Mariana stuck out a hand in front of Imani. "Hi. I am Dr. Nava. I work at a lab in Santa Rosa."

Imani and the general exchanged a look. After a

moment it was clear Imani was not going to shake Mariana's hand. Alex grabbed it and laced their fingers together at her side.

"Don't mind Imani she's a bitch."

Imani hissed and Alex hissed back.

"Ladies." The general interrupted. "Tonight is a celebration to raise funds for life saving research. You can fight later. Away from Gibbard property."

Alex stared daggers at Imani, ignoring the General. "What are *you* doing here?"

Alex knew Imani would not answer, but she wanted to see what lie she would force feed her. The Lieutenant does not go anywhere without it being sanctioned by Adonis. What business does the King of vampires have with a Genetic research company? A company whose focus is pharmaceuticals. And why was she standing with General Gain as if they were here together.

"I am a consultant."

"Right." Alex's tone dripped with skepticism. Holding out the "I" for a long beat. Imani was an overseer.

"Does Adonis know you are here, Alex? Or are you still giving him an unwarranted cold shoulder."

Alex flinched and didn't realize how tight she was gripping Mariana's hand. She loosened her hold just to be met with Mariana squeezing in response.

Mariana did not seem like the type to crave conflict or drama. Her heart rate had risen since Imani appeared. As much as Alex wanted to interrogate Imani, she did not want her anywhere near Mariana. She especially did not want to talk about Adonis. Having a trained Shade agent here put a wrench in her plans to snoop around the building.

"I am sure you are aware I have not spoken to Adonis. Assuming you still receive briefs from his personal team."

Imani dropped her shoulders. The warrior in her melted away for a moment. "He would really appreciate if you called."

Would he? Would a King surrounded by vampires and humans that worship at his feet worry that one of his many sired children vanishes? That would be the case if Alex was not his intended heir. A fact known to few. Adonis could find her if he really wanted to. He had eyes everywhere. Every week in Vaughn she has expected to find a Shade agent at her door with a letter revoking her status as heir.

"I will think about it." Alex turned towards General Gain. "Are you also a consultant as well, General?"

He looked at Imani and she nodded once. His worn eyes moved over Alex's face. The skin under his eyes were loose bags. He could have retired decades ago, but this man knew nothing outside of the military. She remembered hearing his voice through the speaker in Adonis's office. Gain was part of the original negotiations. Like most military representatives, he wanted to enlist vampires. An offer given by hundreds of countries. Adonis would never have choses the United States Military over other countries if he was considering it. His heart lies in the Mediterranean. He grew an empire of olive oil and wine before becoming King. A life so long ago there are few vampires from that time who remember his human self.

"I am not here on business. I am just a guest of Imani." Gain cleared phlegm from his throat. Alex could feel Mariana holding back a physical cringe.

"She's a bit old for you General." Alex tipped her chin at Imani.

"Fuck off, Alexandrine."

Alex had already exposed herself to questions by walking up to General Gain. She was off her game by allowing Imani to surprise her. She pondered her options. Stay and aggravate them in a subtle form of interrogation. See if she can squeeze out any information on what they are working on together.

Or walk away. Lingering any longer could give them the opportunity to focus the conversation on her. She had no intention on playing catch up with a bitchy old coworker and an old as fuck military goon. If Mariana was not at her side, she would have hassled her former boss until a fight broke out between them. She always had fun getting her riled up while sparing. This elegant ballroom filled with high profile people was not the time nor the place for her antics.

Alex turned to Mariana. "Would you like to dance?" Mariana just nodded. "I will see you around, Lieutenant. General."

Alex turned on a heel and pulled Mariana behind her. She reached back and took the glass of wine from her hand and swallowed the last drop. She set it on a tray as they passed. The music was common pop songs played by a five-piece orchestra. They stopped in the center of the dance floor in the middle of swaying couples. A few of them moved around the room in a traditional waltz.

Alex kept their fingers intertwined and lifted them

to the left. She slid her arm behind Mariana's lower back until they were pressed together. Mariana lifted her dress slightly and held the purple shimmery fabric in pinched fingers.

It was Alex who led their bodies around the room. Despite her height she dominated the dance. Mariana let her muscles relax. She pressed her body firmly against Alex's chest as they spun quickly. Never breaking their connection. Alex used her strength to dip Mariana back effortlessly. Her thick dark curls hung towards the floor like a veil. Alex took the opportunity to run the tip of her nose up Mariana's neck. She smiled when a woman from the side whispered that they were about to witness a vampire bite someone in public. Another murmur groaned from behind her *"who invited vampire trash"*.

Alex longed for the days when vampires lived in hiding. The only social functions she attended only by vampires or hive members. Alex didn't like a room full of humans knowing what she was. She felt at home in the shadows. Hunting.

Mariana giggled when Alex lifted her up from a dip. The sound snapped her out of her own head much like the effects of a shot of whiskey.

Alex thought being in the light with Mariana was not that bad. If she had to be seen there was no one she would rather have in her arms. Mariana is a prize Alex does not deserve to win. According to her own judgment.

Through the crowd of eyes and voices, Alex tried to focus on the two she knew. Imani was having a conversation in the back of the room with a man and his wife. They were hanging on to her every word.

The General had moved closer to one of the catering bars. His eyes lingered on the body of a much younger woman for far too long. Alex wanted to puke thinking about what was going on in his head.

There was a pause in the music. They had danced through three songs in a row. Her body yearned for more, burning from being so close to Mariana, whose intoxicating rose scent filled the air around them.

"I need a drink." Alex led Mariana off the dance floor.

Guests people stepped out of line at the bar when they saw Alex approach. The bartender was a woman with a high ponytail. Tattoos peaked out of the top of her white collared shirt. She had a hole in her nose where a piercing was removed.

Alex winked and dropped a twenty into the tip jar. "Whiskey, neat, and a glass of your house red."

They took their drinks to a quiet corner. From there Alex could see the whole room. Networking suits and gowns making small talk. No doubt someone was casually making a deal worth millions.

Alex looked down and realized they were still holding hands. She let go and stepped away. "Sorry." She rubbed the back of her neck. "Running into Imani threw me off. I don't mean to be overprotective."

"This is a formal work event. Why would you need to protect me here?"

Imani was across the room, deep in conversation. Even though Alex could not see a place to hide a weapon on her body it changed nothing. Imani was a weapon herself. Alex thought of the last time they were in the same room.

Alex tossed back her whiskey. "Just stay close, ok."

Mariana rolled her eyes and moved closer. Keeping the illusion they were on a date. She sipped her wine and mumbled heavy with sarcasm. "Thanks for being so honest and open with me."

APRILL 22ND 1994
LONDON, ENGLAND

There was a constant drizzle that wouldn't let up until summer. Alex stood up against a half wall along the edge of the roof of an empty building. Inside was abandoned equipment that hadn't made glass in many years. She has been on the roof across the cobblestone street for hours. The sky was heavy with dark clouds that were releasing a steady drizzle. The few functional streetlights reflected off the slick stones, making pools of gold light.

Alex loved melancholy weather. She wished the reason she was in London was a vacation with Anita. *This mission is almost over.* She reminded herself. *Once all the rogue members are found she can return and enjoy the magic of the city.*

Alex's pulse thudded in her ears, in rhythm with the soft patter of rain against her jacket, as she crouched in the shadows of an old industrial block. The Abernathy Glass Works stood before her like a relic of a neighborhood long past its prime. The faded letters painted on the brick were barely legible under the moonlight, weathered from years of neglect, and the building's windows were black with grime, like deadened eyes now hollow.

Alex's mind was racing, yet her body remained still, honed by years of training. The orders back at her hotel room had given her just enough to go on, a trail that led here, to this godforsaken corner of London. She was tracking the remnants of the rogue group responsible for the attacks on world leaders last year, and they had gone underground, scattering like rats. One of the last threads to unravel was a vampire, a young one by vampire standards, turned sometime in the mid-eighties. He was linked to an old associate back in New York. Foolishly, that associate had let some information slip to a stripper, who had seen the chance to make a fortune selling his secrets. The highest bidder? Shade, of course.

Alex had almost taken the vampire out at Heathrow airport, ready to pull the trigger as he made his way toward the terminal. But then, she overheard him talking on his phone. Something about rolling out the next part of their plan. He was headed to London, not for leisure, but with the purpose of meeting someone important.

Five hours ago, he had walked into the building ahead, Abernathy Glass Works. Alex had followed, lurking in the shadows, watching, waiting. Tension coiled in her muscles as she scanned the street, her senses sharp in the quiet drizzle. For hours, nothing. Then, the echo of boots clattering against cobblestones cut through the quiet night. Three distinct pairs of footsteps, two heavy, and another with a distinct scraping noise every few steps. A woman, her narrow heel catching the cracks in the cobblestones. Alex stayed still, her breath shallow.

As they approached, a voice floated up from the alley below, one that froze Alex in place. Familiar, sultry, and unmistakable. *Anita*. Her Anita. Her songbird, the one Alex had sworn she would never leave her side. Alex's blood ran cold as she crept closer to the edge of the rooftop. Her heart raced, but her expression remained steely, betraying nothing of the shock that gripped her. In this moment she needed to be a Shade Agent and not a shocked woman in love.

Peering down from the shadows, she saw them. Anita, flanked by two other vampires. Alex's stomach twisted, and for a moment, her carefully composed mask cracked. Anita? Here, of all places, walking casually into a building linked to the same rogue group Alex had been hunting for months. The realization hit her like a punch to the gut. She had thought Anita was in California on an assignment. But now, here she was, walking into the belly of the beast.

Alex's jaw tightened as a flood of emotions hit her, betrayal, disbelief, anger. But she didn't have the luxury of letting those feelings linger. There was no time for questions or second thoughts. Whatever Anita's role in all this, Alex couldn't let it distract her. She had a mission, and the pieces were falling into place.

Alex ducked low. She did not recognize the men.

Her instinct was to jump down and steal Anita away. *What did they want from her? Why was she with them?*

The door opened from the inside. Anita greeted the vampire Alex had been tracking with open arms and a warm smile. *What the fuck?*

When their hive broke up in the mid-fifties, Adonis offered to have Anita trained within Shade. Alex never fully stopped working for them while they were living together. She would only except jobs on the east coast. Refusing to be more than a day's travel away from Anita. Afraid her heart would collapse in on itself if they were separated for too long.

Imani trained Anita herself. Tapping into investigation skills no one knew Anita possessed. Anita's brown skin also allowed her to hide in plain sight easier. When Alex is filled with adrenaline you can see her dark veins through her pale skin. Another reason she prefers to work at night.

Anita was a great spy. Charming her way into exclusive night clubs. Keeping tabs on vampires and werewolves without them even knowing a Shade agent was in the crowd.

Alex was more of a raccoon. Coming out at night to rummage through belongings. Staying in the shadows and using her advanced senses to find people. The same skills that led her to the warehouse Anita was standing in now.

Alex screamed inside her head. She didn't want to alert them to her location. After the group was out of the rain, she waited for them to move deeper into the building. Alex slid her phone out of her pocket. She flipped the phone open and held down the number one. It dialed Anita.

The call went to voicemail.

She hung up and dialed again.

This time Anita answered on the last ring. The window was nearly opaque with years of dust caked on both sides of the glass. Alex could only make out Anita's silhouette. She watched her shoulders rise as she answered the call.

"Hi babe." She sing-songed.

Anita moved away from her friends and into a corner closer to a window.

"Hi love." Alex sucked in a deep breath. "I miss you. When are you getting back from Los Angeles."

"I miss you too. I watched the sunrise at the beach yesterday. Reminded me of that month we spent in Cabo. We should do that again." Despite the words being a lie, Alex recognized the familiar tone of love in her voice. Warm and tempting.

The lie stung. Alex restrained herself from crushing the phone in her fist.

"Yea, a beach vacation sounds great."

"How's your assignment?"

She could be honest and tell her the trail led her to the warehouse Anita is currently standing in. Surprise, I am here to bring you into Shade. Apparently, you are a criminal. Or associated with criminals. Not the average criminal, but vampires that are on the world most wanted list.

"I found my target. Should be able to handle them tonight and head home tomorrow." Alex bit back a waterfall of words.

"Of course you did, you are Shades best tracker." Alex heard a shuffle through the phone and saw a shadow come up next to Anita. They placed a hand on Anita's shoulder. Alex was ready to jump through the window and rip their arm off for touching her. "I will try to finish my assignment early. I hate not having you in my bed."

"Anita?"

Dozens of conversations flowed in her mind, but the words would not come out. They couldn't. She was there to complete her duty for Shade. For Imani. For Adonis. Warning Anita would put both of them on the run. Perhaps Anita has an explanation. Alex sucked in a shaky breath. She pushed down her anger and nerves. Wishing she could numb her emotions and complete the job.

"Yes babe."

Alex swallowed. The orders from Imani must be wrong. She is going to walk into that warehouse and find nothing related to the rogue group. Maybe they are a group of old friends having a reunion. Maybe Anita had a reason to lie to her. Maybe Shade sent her to London and told her to lie to Alex. But Alex was a higher rank than Anita. Alex is the one who usually works in secret.

"I love you." Alex lulled through the phone.

She could feel the smile in her voice. "I love you too. I'll call you tomorrow babe."

"Okay love."

"Goodnight."

"Goodnight." Alex snapped the cellphone shut and watched as the two figures moved away from the window. She waited a few moments before dropping into the alley. As she rose from a crouched position, she unsheathed two knives from her thighs and moved towards the unmarked metal door.

"Here we go." She said to herself and kicked the door in.

APRILL 22ND 1994
LONDON, ENGLAND

Dust floated in the stagnant air inside the warehouse. Alex could scent mildew along the walls and modern cologne from four vampires. She did not walk into an ultramodern command center for an international operation. This was a space only suitable for someone on the run. Hiding. Ashamed.

Not a single muscle flinched when Anita saw her lover standing in the cracked door frame holding a knife in each hand. Anita stood like a statue. Her eyes stayed steady. The three vampires sitting at a table had the opposite reaction. They launched at Alex with fangs on full display and hissing sounds rising from their throats.

"Halt!" Anita commanded.

Alex had just raised her knives in a battle stance when the three men stopped a few feet from her. They at once took a step back and stood with their arms at their sides. Alex tilted her head like a curious cat.

Memories and emotions surged through her mind like waves. Years of training had conditioned her to follow the Shade leaders with unwavering precision. Yet, she had never heard Anita use such a commanding tone before. Anita, a skilled reconnaissance agent, was trained to gather intelligence and pass it on to trackers like Alex. Trackers who were also adept in combat and trained to intimidate.

Alex blinked. Still hoping her eyes were playing tricks on her and the fierce woman before her was not her seductive songbird. Even her movements seem unfamiliar. As if Alex was seeing her for the first time.

"You knew I was here when you called." Anita had her tight curls tied up into a large puff. It created the illusion of a halo with the fluorescent tube hanging behind her. Alex noticed the large cork board with clippings and string covering it behind her.

Alex nodded. She sheathed her knives. Instinct had her ready to accuse Anita of every wrongdoing, but her heart demanded evidence. Was desperate for an explanation.

"What are you doing here?"

Anita motioned the men to return to their seats at the table. She stayed standing. "I am in the middle of an investigation."

Alex dug her nails into her palms. Anita raised a brow at Alex's tense posture. They both opened their mouths to speak but Alex beat her to it.

"Does Shade know you are here?"

Anita leaned on the table. "No."

The knives itched against her thighs. "Are you part of the group responsible for the attacks?"

"Who the fuck are you?" Barked a vampire with a Leo DiCaprio haircut.

"Fuck off." Alex felt her eyes flash brightly. She sucked in a slow breath. "I'm with Shade. And-"

"My wife." Anita strolled around the table. She held out a hand to indicate a corner of the warehouse. "Let's talk alone." Alex quickly scanned the cork board. All the names of the assassinated world leaders were on there as well as a few she did not know. The years 1995 and 1996" were scribbled in red on pieces of ripped paper then tacked to the board. She didn't have time to read the items tacked under them. Reluctantly she followed Anita.

They hesitantly reached the secluded corner of the warehouse. Empty except for stacks of large wooden boxes. The three vampires were pretending to read paperwork, but each of them had an ear trained on Alex. Same as she would in their position.

"You lied on the phone."

"I couldn't tell you I was here. This is bigger than me. Bigger than us." Anita leaned in and slid a hand behind Alex's neck. The movement had been done a thousand times before. It brought Alex comfort usually. Now the action made her blood boil.

"Were you lying when you said *I love you*?" She swatted Anita's hand away.

A hurt expression filled Anita's face. She sucked in a breath slowly and kept her tone soft. "Don't do that." She places her hand on her hip. Her movements were too casual. As if they were discussing which movie to rent from Blockbuster. Alex's lips formed a thin line. She was giving into Anita's attempts to calm her. A flame was building within her chest.

"What are you involved with Anita?"

Anita leaned against a large wooden box. The faded words match the outside of the building. Alex mirrored her posture on a box across from her. She tapped her fingertips on the hilts of her knives.

"I can't tell you yet, Alex." Anita crossed her arms. "I need you to trust me. Go back home and tell Imani you lost the trail."

Alex shook her head while looking at her feet. Lying to Imani meant Lying to Adonis. She couldn't do that. One of the reasons she is a good Shade agent is that fact she does not question orders. Adonis tells her to jump, and she jumps. He says kill, and she rips a head off. He says follow Imani's orders and she is compelled to comply. Alex cannot defy him even if she tried.

Those on the outside would see her as the perfect soldier. But the truth is she is guided by a stronger bond. One created when he turned her centuries ago. Her blood would literally boil if she defied him.

"You can't give me orders. I outrank you." Alex snapped.

Anita scoffed, "Only because of nepotism."

Alex growled and held back cursing at her lover. There were only a handful of vampires that knew who turned Alex. She strived to keep the truth hidden as much as possible. Most vampires would view her as a pet to the king. She has become more than that to Adonis. Alex is an extension of him. Anita knew exactly where to strike Alex and make it cut deep. Nepotism. A word too simple to describe their relationship.

"Love, tell me what you are doing lying to Shade and why you are in a seedy warehouse with those idiots. Or I will be forced to take you all to face Imani." Alex felt the vampires turn in her direction. She placed her palms flat on her knives. On the outside Alex was calm and ready. Inside embers were threatening to rage into a blaze upon this warehouse. Her instincts, which she trusted more than her ability to heal from a blade, told her to grab Anita and run. That Anita has been lured into a situation. Perhaps they are using her to get close to Alex and by doing so have leverage against the King.

"I can't." Anita softened her expression. Her fingers twitched slightly, wanting to reach out and touch the love of her life. Alex remained cold. Running multiple scenarios in her head. Trying to find an outcome that let them walk away together and unscathed. An outcome that did not involve her killing the vampires eavesdropping.

"Anita. Please." Alex begged. She was caught between two stones. Follow Shade protocol or trust Anita. Heat in her chest bloomed and she knew it would be impossible to walk away and not tell Adonis what she saw here. He bound her to him and defiance against him is impossible. He is her maker. He is her King. And he is Shade, even when her orders come from the Lieutenant.

"I can't, babe." Anita squared her shoulders. "I need you to trust me. Walk away. I will be home in two days, and we can talk then."

Alex looked at the three men sitting at the table. Two of them had guns in their hands under the table. The third gripped a similar knife to Alex. Standard Shade issue. An eight-inch double edged dagger.

Alex tilted her head trying to read Anita. "Do you think I am the enemy?"

Anita's eyes closed for a long second before focusing on Alex. When Anita was human, she would have had dark brown eyes like most woman of color, but now they were cardinal red. They were bright. A sign of her heightened emotions. Alex prepared herself, not knowing to expect a kiss or a knife to the throat. Anita took a step towards Alex. Her hand hesitated to reach out, but eventually rested on Alex's forearm. Muscle memory had Alex lean into her touch.

"We are still learning who our enemies are."

"Who is *we*?" Anita blinked at Alex's question with no intention to answer. Alex continued. "Do you think I am the enemy?" Alex bit back a sob.

Anita swallowed. "You could be."

Alex stepped away from Anita, her jaw clenched, boots pounding against the concrete. Each step echoed, a warning in itself. The vampires watched her approach, their gazes cold, reading the violence on her face. They rose as one, tense and ready, the space between them closing to twelve feet. Anita followed just behind her, silent but resolute.

"Will you come peacefully?" Alex's voice was calm, almost mocking, as she unsheathed her knives. The vampires' response was swift. Two guns raised.

She tilted her head. "I'll take that as a no."

With a flick of her wrist, a blade flew straight into the chest of the vampire furthest away. His gun fired, but Alex was already moving, her body twisting in the air, dodging the bullet by a hair's breath. Anita was shouting commands behind her, but the words were lost to the blood pumping in her ears. Alex had no time for her lover's voice. Not now.

The vampire with the flat-top afro, a knife buried deep in his chest, staggered, a river of crimson pouring from the wound as he fumbled for a backpack. But Alex didn't slow. In seconds, she was trading blows with the other two, their guns abandoned as the fight turned to close quarters. Her quick blows kept them from getting adequate aim on her. Anita screamed at them all to stop, but no one was listening.

A sudden crack, Alex's cheek exploded in pain as the butt of a gun slammed into her face. Blood flooded her mouth. She spit it out, a bright red stain at her opponent's feet. He grinned.

"You're either leaving here unconscious or dead," she sneered. Alex rolled her neck, the tension in her muscles coiling like a spring. "What's it gonna be, Kenny G?"

"Kenny what?"

She smirked, nodding at his ponytail. "The hair."

His answer was a punch to her gut, the force of it driving the air from her lungs. Another vampire, matched with her in speed, caught her from behind, locking her arms in a vice grip. His chest pressed hard against her back.

"Rip her head off!" the one at her back snarled.

"No!" Anita's scream cut through the chaos, but it was too late.

With a savage jerk, Alex slammed her head backward into the vampire's nose. Bones cracked, and his grip loosened just enough. She twisted her body, running up his chest on the ponytail vampire and flipping back in a blur of movement. In one swift motion, she drove a knife into the base of his neck. He crumpled beneath her, limp and defeated, the fight leaving him a gurgling mess.

The room went still. All eyes were on Alex, her knee pressing down on the fallen vampire's back, her blade poised at his spine. The silence buzzed with tension, as if the air itself was holding its breath. The vampires looked to Anita for instruction.

"Now that I have your attention," Alex's voice was low, deadly. Beneath her, the vampire whimpered, his body slack against the cold concrete. Struggle would mean death. A true death.

Anita's heeled boots clicked softly as she approached Alex's side. The impaled vampire watched in horror while his skin began to stitch itself together, the last remnants of a stolen blood bag trickling from his mouth. Alex kept the knife steady, feeling the faint grind of the blade against the bone.

"Are we speaking as Alex Sipala my love, the person I want by my side for all my days. Or the obedient Shade agent?" Anita's voice was eerily calm, her hand raised in a silent command for the vampires to stand down. Kenny G retreated a few steps, his smug expression unchanged, as if daring Alex to act.

"I've always been both," Alex said, her voice unwavering.

Anita sighed. "And even now your loyalty to Shade outweighs your loyalty to me."

Alex glanced down at the vampire balancing on the edge of death below her. All sets of eyes in the warehouse were waiting for her to choose. Either the fight continues, most likely ending in multiple death. Perhaps even her own. She allowed the image of her running away with Anita to float through her mind. How long could she run from Adonis? From Shade? Shade had many trackers equal to her in skill. He would not let her remain hidden for long.

Anita took her lack of response as an answer. Alex would not fight for them. For their love. For what they built in New York. She let out a slow sigh and opened her mouth to speak.

"You forget," Alex scowled. Her tone sharp enough to cut the tension like flesh. "I was there when Adonis gave Shade a name. When it became more than just an idea from the former King. I was born into its legacy."

"You were born to a human woman." Anita snapped. "He took away your childhood. All that you could have been. He is no savior. Your loyalties lay with a legacy that festers with corruption."

The younger vampires shifted on their feet, uneasy. Alex's pulse quickened. She could feel the weight of Anitas words. They bit at her like they have gone unsaid for far too long and have grown thorns. The air in the warehouse turned suffocating.

Alex was never good at handing strong emotions. She steadied her breathing and focused on the training from Adonis. *When you're working a case, you have to set your emotions aside. Don't let the suspects get under your skin or throw you off balance. Stay focused. Always remember what Shade stands for and keep your eyes on our goal.*

Alex met Anitas gaze. Red eyes warming to the

same hue. "Did you know about the attacks?" Alex's voice was a low growl, every word laced with accusation.

The healing vampire, now back on his feet, gripped the knife Alex had thrown earlier, his eyes locked on the blade still embedded in his comrade's neck. The room was so quiet Alex could hear the faint grinding of the knife against his spine. Even Anita flinched at the sound.

"I knew," Anita admitted softly.

Alex's stomach twisted. "And you did nothing? Or did you plan it?"

Anita's face remained unreadable. The two male vampires shifted closer to her side. Alex pressed harder against the vampire beneath her, eliciting a groan of pain.

"We should be asking you that," Kenny muttered.

Alex's grip tightened on her blade; her eyes pinned on Anita. Alex was struggling to read her face. A familiar face that now feels unrecognizable. "Who are you working for, Anita?"

"I wasn't instructed to stop it," Anita said, her voice betraying no emotion. "but-It needed to happen."

Alex's world flipped upside down. "What the fuck, Anita?"

"This is bigger than you, bigger than Shade." Anita stepped forward; her voice soft but unyielding.

"Stop!" Alex barked, the blade pressing dangerously against her captive's neck. "Stay back or I'll sever his spine."

Anita raised her hands, but Alex's eyes caught on

her bare ring finger. The gold band, the garnet oval Alex had given her, gone. A symbol of their love. Their life together. Gone.

"Pledge your loyalty to us, Alex," Anita whispered. "Leave Shade behind. I can tell you everything."

"Who is *US*?"

Anita's lips formed a thin line. She shook her head in response. Alex would not get an answer.

Alex's chest tightened, her vision blurring with anger, with betrayal. She looked down. Breaking eye contact with Anita. "I can't." It came out a note higher than a whisper.

Anita dropped her hands to her sides. "Then we're at an impasse."

The room buzzed with danger. Alex could feel the shift in the air, the predatory eyes of the vampires locked on her. Her time was running out.

"Last chance, love," Alex whispered, her heart pounding. "Who are you taking orders from?"

She didn't answer, her defiance speaking louder than any words.

"Fine." Alex's voice was ice. She sliced clean through the vampire's neck, the blade severing bone and flesh in one swift motion.

The vampires lunged.

One down.

Two to go.

Alex threw the severed head at one, using the split-second distraction to leap backward. She barely dodged a blade as it grazed her stomach, her skin knitting itself back together in seconds. The vampires circled her like wolves, eyes burning red, their movements swift and deadly.

But Alex was faster.

With a roar, she leaped into the fray, her knife flashing. Blood splattered across the walls as she moved, each cut precise, calculated. She was a whirlwind of violence, her body moving in a rhythm she'd honed over centuries.

Anita's voice echoed in the background, but Alex didn't listen. This was survival. This was the line between life and death, and Alex was ready to cross it.

Alex and the vampires continued to dance around each other. They were matching each other slash for slash. Blood ran down their arms, legs, and their backs. The scene becoming gorier by the minute. Anita watched from the side. Still refusing to strike against her lover.

After enough blood spilled the other vampire joined in. He was now fully healed. Alex wondered if Anita had told them to hold back in the fight. Although it was two against one, she was holding her own quite well.

Alex flashed a cocky smirk to the ponytail vampire as he cocked his shoulders. Up to this point Alex had been holding back. Testing their abilities. Learning their habits. It was easy for her to get caught up in the fight and forget who was watching.

Anita's eyes were wide. She had never seen Alex fight like this. In the 1920's-30's she occasionally stepped in when their bouncer could not break up a brawl. But it took little effort to break up a fight between two unruly humans. Alex was moving faster than their fists and hitting hard enough to knock them back several feet with a blow. Her short frame an illusion for the strength with in her.

Alex leaped in the air. Her foot contacted the side of the knife wielding vampire's head where he had stripes shaved into his fade. He hunched over for a moment. It was long enough for Alex to grab his wrist and roll over his back. The shoulder socket popped. She landed on her feet with both knives in her hand.

"Fucking bitch." He yelled as he tried to get his limp arm back in its place. She moved on him like a surge of rage. Blood ran down his dark skin. She targeted all the important arteries causing him to lose blood quickly. It was slowing him down, but not enough to stop him. Flat top had already drunk blood earlier to heal from being stabbed in the chest. Alex watched him drain their supply before the main fight began and she scented the duffle was now empty. He would get weaker by the minute. He stumbled to his knees when she cut the tendons above his heels. He let out a stream of curse words.

Her focus moved to Kenny G. He was the smallest of the two vampires alive. If you don't include Anita. His ponytail swishing behind as he threw sloppy punches. Alex dodged and returned blows. Each movement was to gage his reflexes and skill. He lacked the training she had. The evidence was in his staggering movements. He pounded her in the stomach followed by a blow to the chin. A lucky move for him. Alex teetered back, only to use the momentum to flip back into a handstand push-up. Both her boots hammered his chest. He was thrown back several feet into a stack of wooden crates.

"Alex, enough." Anita called from the side of the room where she was preparing to pop Flat-Tops arm back into place. Alex flinched at the command and threw a knife across the space straight into his eye. His scream roared through the warehouse. "No. No. No." Anita cupped his face. "Alex you're on the wrong side!"

Alex spun away from Kenny's fist and sliced his hand clean off. He fell to his knees, grasping his bleeding stub to his chest. She yanked his ponytail. Exposing his neck to her blade. Her eyes met Anita's as she ended him.

"I am not the one who stood by knowing six world leaders were going to be assassinated. Shade is supposed to protect people. That is who we are. That is who I am." The vampire's lifeless body fell to the floor. Alex stood still with the ponytail gripped in her hand. Thick blood dripping onto her boots. Anita turned slowly to face the remaining male vampire and whispered close to his ear. Half his face was covered in blood. The skin around his eye was healing, but the eyeball would never regenerate.

In a quick movement, he ran towards a large window a moment later. Alex went to chase him, but Anita gripped her waist and pulled her back. They tumbled to the floor as he broke through the glass and onto the street. Alex flipped her onto her back and sat on her hips. The knife was shaking in her hand as she held it to Anita's throat. Her clothes were tattered with blood-soaked slashes. She was a feral animal atop Anita's graceful clean body.

Anita did not move to strike Alex. She only watched with hardened eyes.

"Enough." Anita screamed.

"Enough what? Enough lies?" Alex's voice shook. She wished it had been anyone else in the warehouse.

Anyone else under her blade. Anita swallowed and the knife pressed into her skin. A thin red line appeared. Alex sucked in a breath that felt like needles in her lungs.

"Enough violence in the name of Shade." Anita's tone had the remnants of the smooth songbird that Alex loved. The voice that stopped her from a rampage when they first met.

"You lied to me." Alex choked on her words and had to swallow the pain with an audible gulp.

Anita placed her palms gently on Alex's calves. "Yes."

Alex's jaw flexed. "You're still lying to me." It was not a question. Tonight, a wall was built between them. Built with bricks manufactured by Shade and held together with secrets and lies. Alex was too weak to break it down. She had never developed the skills for forgiveness and was raised to trust one person.

"And I will continue until you disavow Shade until I can find the source of its rot. Even if that leads me to the top." Anita moved her hand up to rest on Alex's thighs. The intimate gesture meant to coax Alex into dropping her guard. She tightened her grip on the knife in response. "Denounce Imani, denounce Adonis, denounce Shade, and I will tell you everything."

Alex looked at the blade in her hand. Covered in blood from three vampires and now a fourth. The small slit on Anita's throat heals, only to be reopened with each deep breath.

"Imani is just a lieutenant. My loyalties are not with her." Alex said through gritted teeth.

"And Adonis?" Anita tilted her head slightly and the movement caused the blade to dig deeper.

And Adonis? Adonis. Her family. Her only family. Alex swallowed a sob. She shook her head frantically. A blur of images filled her mind. Decades stacked of memories at his side. She was drowning. Over the years she has found herself in many episodes of her mind spiraling. She buried it deep inside her and used alcohol to numb. The past sixty-four years have been easier to handle with Anita at her side.

Now, firm in her convictions, pinned underneath Alex, Anita is the cause of the tidal wave flooding her inside. Alex shook.

Anita gripped her thighs and threw her off. Alex landed in a pile of shattered glass under the broken window. After catching her breath, she retrieved her twin blade from the rubble. Glass crunched beneath her as she stood to face Anita who was a few yards away. Alex flipped her knives in her hands as she walked towards Anita. The action was the final brick in the wall between them.

Anita waited. No weapons in her hands. No expression on her face. No ring on her finger.

"You are going to have to kill me." She said flatly.

Alex hissed through her fangs. "Don't fucking say that."

Anita closed her eyes. An act that made her look vulnerable. She exhaled slowly. Alex listened to her steady heartbeat. Anita was not afraid. She was calm like the eye of a storm. "If you are with Shade, you are my enemy."

"You are with Shade!" The air became sandpaper as Alex could not steady her breathing. She hyper focused on the drips of blood on Anita's neck. The slice has healed but the blood remained. She has never caused Anita pain before, but dark red evidence of what she has already done coats her skin. Alex repeated her words in a pleading whisper. "You are with Shade."

"I have not been with Shade for a long time." She lifted her hand as if ready to stroll in a park. "Leave them. Join me. I will tell you everything."

"I-" Alex gulped down air. "I can't go against him. He made me. You know that."

A war was being fought within Alex. Her mind begging her body to walk away. Her heart desperate to protect Anita. Losing against the blood vow that ties her to Adonis and everything he controls. She walks with the confidence of a free agent, but at the end of the day Alex is nothing but a bound soldier.

Anita dropped her hand and sighed. "I know. That is why it hurts to love you." Anita bolted towards the door. Alex threw her knives out of instinct. One after another impaling her calves. Anita fell forward. Alex leaped onto her back. Landing like a cat on prey.

"I am so sorry." Tears ran down Alex's face. She reached back and removed her knives. "I didn't mean to-"

Anita rolled to her back. She kicked Alex in the chest and attempted to run again. Alex was on her in a second. Pinning her back flat against her chest. Her blades making an X at Anita's throat.

"I said you would have to kill me." Anita gripped Alex's wrists. "Do it."

"No."

Alex shook, and her vision tunneled. The bond to

Adonis was too strong for her to resist. She felt the need to protect him pulsing inside her blood. Tattooed on every cell in her body.

Her thoughts were still trying to decipher who was betraying who. She could not make sense of the situation. This is the part where Anita confesses it was a misunderstanding. Anita would place a passionate kiss on her lips, ignoring the blood splattered from the fight, and they would return home. Together. Alex would learn Anita was a double agent and confess everything to Imani.

Alex growled through her teeth. Physically fighting the urge to end Anita. A desire that was not her own. A twisted side effect of unwavering loyalty towards Adonis and all he controls.

Alex knew the outcome before Anita spoke one more. Her tone staying as calm and beautiful as the day they met.

"I won't stop. Until Shade is gone." Anita paused, bracing her palms on Alex's hips. "And that includes killing Adonis."

Alex screamed. Her arms moved quickly on their own. Decapitating Anita and covering Alex in her blood.

PRESENT DAY

Overlapping voices and classical music trickled in from the grand ballroom. Alex used the importance of keeping Mariana safe as an anchor to stop her mind from wandering. Jules was patiently waiting for an update on the case. She was sending her a text every couple hours to make sure Alex has not been caught breaking into Gibbard.

Mariana leaned into Alex. Her soft lips brushing against Alex's hair. Alex swiped another alert from Jules away from the top of her phone that was hidden between their bodies. At this angle, anyone behind the camera would assume they were two lovers who snuck off into a quiet corner for privacy.

"Can you help cover the phone screen?" Alex asked.

Mariana linked her hands behind Alex's neck and

toyed with the shaved underside of her hair. Alex closed her eyes and almost dropped her phone. A shiver ran up her back. It has been a long time since someone touched her with such intimacy. She considered skipping the mission all together. Dragging Mariana back to the hotel and ripping her amethyst dress off.

Alex forced herself to focus on her phone. The software was syncing with the building's camera feed. She programed it before leaving Vaughn. It should put some of the cameras in a loop. Only the ones in the office building. It would have been too obvious to have Gala guests repeating the same dance steps over and over.

Gibbard had an impressive security system. Not good enough to keep a Shade agent out. She was trained as technology advanced. Alex was breaking into buildings when cameras were invented. Every advancement in security became an exciting challenge for her. Always wanting to be the best. To make Adonis proud.

Alex estimated they would have ten minutes to get in and find Daniel Harris's office. The directory has him on the eleventh floor.

"Let me know if I am making you uncomfortable." Mariana's breath was warm on Alex's neck. A shiver went down her spine. It was intoxicating. She wished her flask was in her pocket, despite the promise she made not to bring it.

"I'm good." Alex tapped on her screen. "It's set. Wait here. I should be less than ten minutes."

Mariana pulled back until they were face to face. "No. I'm coming with you."

Alex slid her phone into her pocket and grabbed Mariana's hand with a sigh. "Fine." Her protest was a show. She enjoyed Mariana at her side. Depending on the path of the case after tonight, this might be her last change to flirt with the Doctor and test her boundaries. She intended on taking full advantage of every second together.

They headed towards the silver elevator doors. She could feel Mariana smiling without looking back. Please she was part of the mission more than a ticket in.

No guests saw them enter the elevator. She dropped Mariana's hand when the doors closed.

The eleventh floor looked like a set for a TV show. A cross between a futuristic hospital and an office where angels worked in heaven. White tiles sparkled under their feet. Alex had dress shoes with a soft rubber sole. They kept her steps quiet. It did no good though, Mariana was clacking behind her in her heels.

Noticing how Alex's brows knit together with each sharp impact on the tile, Mariana took off her heels. She gave up trying to keep up with Alex who was jetting around the hall like a bullet train. Quickly reading the names on doors.

Alex froze at the end of the hall.

"Is this his office?" Mariana asked, finally reaching her side.

Alex pointed to the white plaque on the door with black lettering. *Sidi.*

She may have been looking for the name Harris, but this was even better. She curled her fist around the doorknob. "Locked." She mumbled.

"Whose office is this?"

Alex forced the doorknob to turn until the latch inside broke. "Imani Sidi."

"The scary vampire downstairs?"

"She's not that scary." Alex opened the door and motioned for her to enter. She followed close behind and shut the door.

A large window framed the skyline of downtown Albuquerque. In front of it was a polished white desk. Alex sat in the white leatherback chair. Mariana walked over to a tall, refrigerated cabinet. She peaked through the frosted glass. "This is filled with blood."

"She is a vampire." Alex moved the mouse. A password prompt popped up on the screen. She didn't have time to guess the password of a raging workaholic bitch. So, she moved on opening a side drawer.

Mariana had opened the refrigerator and was leaning in. Humming quietly to herself. Alex could not tell if it was boredom or a nervous habit. Judging by her pounding heart, it was nerves.

"Is it common for a vampire to categorize their food like this?" Mariana tapped her nails on a glass shelf.

Alex pulled out a stack of red file folders. There were only numbers on the tabs. No names. She wished she had trained in a Shade field office and understood the methods used. Office work was foreign to her. Her skills are best suited for the ground. Just like Imani. It was a shock to the Agents and Adonis when she requested to move to a desk job in the seventies.

"Like what? Blood type? Donor?" Alex spoke to Mariana's back.

"You usually drink from blood bags. These are labeled test tubes. Not much for a meal." Mariana bent over to look at the lower shelves. Alex glanced up from the files. Heat building in her. That dress really did look good on Mariana. Hugging every glorious curve. "Are you checking out my ass?"

"What?" Alex faked a cough and looked down at the file.

"I can see you in the reflection." Mariana smiled.

Alex met her eyes in the reflective surface at the back of the fridge. "We don't have much time. You're distracting me."

"Are you hungry? I found her meal stash. There are bags on the bottom shelf."

Alex rubbed the back of her neck and tried to focus. "I'm good." Mariana took the single empty seat on the other side of the desk. A white upholstered chair that looked like it belonged in a doctor's waiting room. "Thanks."

"I just don't want my date to get hangry." Mariana emphasized the word date. The corners of Alex's lips tugged into a short-lived smile.

Alex looked up and let herself drown in the dark pools of Mariana's eyes for a moment. Here the world was quiet.

"I meant thanks for helping me."

Mariana kicked her bare feet onto the corner of the desk and tossed her head back. "I am just the ticket. I am not much help with the investigating part. Unless you need me to run a polymerase chain reaction."

Alex's phone buzzed in her pocket. A five-minute warning. She didn't want to take the files with her. Imani will already know they were in her office by the scent. Mariana left a trail of roses everywhere she went. Alex can only hope she made the right decision by choosing to search Imani's office and end the search for Harris's. There would not be another easy opportunity to access the building. Her instincts better not fail her. Something in Imani's office must prove to be fruitful. Running into her at a Gala for Gibbard is far to coincidental.

The first file had numbers in the first column and a simple yes or no in the second column. It made no sense to her. She opened the second folder. It was more of the same. She kept her growl inside. Her phone buzzed again. Three minutes. She blinked hard looking for a pattern to appear. Frantically she shuffled through the files only looking at the labeled tab.

"Does DHIB mean anything to you?"

Mariana remained staring at the ceiling. Alex noticed her heart skipped a beat. "No."

"It's on every file, followed by a series of seven numbers." Alex grabbed her phone and began to take photos of each file. "Could be identifying test subjects. I just don't know what any of these numbers mean. Do you think these are medical codes?"

Alex held the paper towards Mariana. The door burst open, and Imani stood in the doorway with a gun aimed at Alex's head.

Stagnant air was sucked out of the room and replaced with thick tension. Built brick-by-brick over years of taking orders from the Ethiopian woman scowling before Alex. No doubt a slurry of curse words in both Amharic and Italian filling her head. Alex wished the warrior wasn't so stoic. She always found the way she blended languages entertaining. Adonis insisted all Shade agents learn English to help then blend in expanding empires. Imani always found popular American curse words to be the crudest.

"Hey bitch." Alex tucked the files back into the drawer. Mariana let her bare feet slap on the floor. Her back was to Imani. She shuffled to stand but froze when the gun came in her view.

"I should have known you were up to something

the moment I saw your slimy face." Imani moved into the room. Her black satin dress in high contrast to the sterile environment.

"I have been told I have a nice face." Alex stood.

"Why are you in my office?"

"We got lost."

Imani sucked in a breath through her teeth. Her red eyes pinned on Alex. Slowly she moved the gun to aim at Mariana.

"Why are you in my office," She cocked the gun, "Princess?"

Alex would really appreciate it if Imani stopped calling her Princess. Especially in front of Mariana. Every Princess Alex has known was a spoiled twat that coasted on their family name and never needed to learn skills. She was royalty in inheritance only. She was not born with Adonis's blood in her veins. It was given to her. Not like a gift, but in the way of a brand. Marking every cell within her with his name. It came with a title, wealth, and a hoard of weapons she needed to master.

Alex ran through multiple scenarios in her mind. How to disarm Imani before she could pull the trigger, and whether Adonis would be upset if she tossed his right hand out the window. She settled on stalling for a few minutes before making an exit.

"I am trying to figure out why a Shade Lieutenant has an office at a pharmaceutical company. Unless you are no longer with Shade. Did they offer you something more lucrative? A discount on antipsychotic medicine, perhaps?" Alex stepped around the desk. It was risky, but she was hoping Adonis still had orders for all of Shade to not harm is one favorite daughter.

Imani ground her teeth and lowered the gun. Alex moved in front of Mariana in a flash. Maraina was clutching her heels to her chest. The thumping of her heart was drumming loud enough for both vampires in the room to take notice. Alex reached behind herself and placed a hand on Mariana's hip. A gesture to mean *"I got you"*. The gentle contact had Mariana release the breath she was holding.

"You no longer have the right to know what is going on within Shade. You are not a part of us remember." Imani took her place behind the desk and put the gun in the slightly opened drawer. "Find anything interesting?" She motioned with arms wide to the room before placing them on the arm rests.

Alex shifted to keep Mariana behind her and stared down Imani. Their height difference barely noticeable with Imani sitting. The phone buzzed in her pocket. Alex squeezed Mariana's hip. She was ready to throw Mariana into the hall in an instant if Imani wanted a fight. The phone notification showed the cameras would turn back on in one minute. They were supposed to be in the elevator by now.

"Nothing interesting. This job must be boring as fuck." She nudged Mariana. Taking the cue, Mariana stepped backwards towards the door. Alex tapped the phone in her suit pocket. "Our car is here, we gotta run."

"Are you staying in town, Alex." Imani leaned back in her chair. "I would love to catch up. It's been so long."

"Another time. We are leaving tonight. Right now, actually."

Mariana crossed the threshold, her bare feet padding softly down the hall. Alex forced a smile at Imani, knowing she would be a formidable opponent. After all, Imani had trained her in many fighting techniques. It wouldn't be easy to outmaneuver her it if came to blows. The elevator dinged, and Imani raised a brow.

"Your girlfriend, Dr. Nava from Santa Rosa is waiting." A silent threat lingered in the way Imani said her name and where she lived. Alex read her face loud and clear. She had crossed a line by being in her office. Imani had long suspected Alex knew more about Anita's involvement with the 1993 attacks. The last time they stood this close was when Alex walked away from Shade. Following Anita's death.

Alex wiggled her fingers in a mocking wave of enthusiasm.

"See ya, bitch." She ran.

Mariana was holding the elevator door open. Alex sprinted inside. The door whined shut.

They stood in silence across from each other. Mariana's heart was racing faster than they were descending floors. Adrenaline pumped through them both. Something between them changed as they stared into each other's eyes. Alex's going bright red with the rise and fall of Mariana's chest peeking out of her dress.

There are moments in a relationship when something snaps. The last link tying two people together.

The moment they know it is over between them. This was not the end. It was the beginning of something possibly unbreakable.

Standing on opposite sides of the elevator Alex felt a link form. No longer blinking out of existence. There was no denying. As heat bloomed between them, filling the elevator with desperate breaths, Alex was hooked. And didn't just want Mariana, she need-ed her.

Alex opened her mouth to speak, but Mariana moved in, closing the space between them in an instant. Her shoes slipped from her hands. Abandoned to the polished floor with a sharp clack. Alex's grip tightened around her waist, fingers sinking into the curve of her hips, while her other hand tangled in Mariana's thick hair. Their mouths crashed together in a desperate, frenzied kiss. Restraint lost in the heat between them.

Alex pinned her to the mirrored wall. The glass was cool against Mariana's open back and she sucked in a breath of Alex's air. Alex slid her hand from her waist to cup her breast. The weight a reminder of their fullness that has been distracting her all night. She moaned into Mariana's mouth. The start of a fevered growl in her throat. Alex was holding herself back. Every inch of her body was begging for more. Their tongues slid against each other. Mariana arched her back and let Alex step between her legs. Her dress was too tight to allow Alex the friction she craved. The purple shimmery fabric becoming an enemy to tear apart.

Alex lost herself in the taste of red wine and the feel

of her pierced tongue. If the piercing was a lure, Alex had allowed herself to be trapped. Usually the predator, but now prey to Mariana's seduction.

Alex left her lips and trailed kisses along her jaw. Pressing her thigh against the heat between Mariana's legs. Alex nibbled her neck and felt Mariana's pulse jump. Her breath caught and her grip on Alex loosened.

Alex pulled back.

Their eyes met for a beat.

"I am not going to bite you."

Mariana's chest rose quickly under shaky breaths. Alex wanted to dive in her cleavage and suck on her nipples. Something was wrong. In Mariana's lust filled eyes there was fear. She shook her head. This was wrong. What was she doing? Alex had nothing to offer Mariana. No more than a night of pleasure. Mariana deserved more. Alex was broken. Not worthy of her title. Not worthy of friends. Not worthy to be kissed by a brilliant, gorgeous woman with an amazing life ahead of her.

"I know. I trust you." Mariana kissed Alex gently on the lips. It was slow and passionate. It was comforting. It stung. Alex thrust herself off so hard she cracked the mirror behind her. Mariana's eyes went wide at the sudden space between them.

"You shouldn't trust me." The door opened. Music and chatter filled the air. The Gala was still going strong. Alex moved quickly into the hall but paused to make sure Mariana was following. She paused to lean on the wall and put her heels back on. "I will call the driver; we need to leave tonight."

Heels clacked. Alex unlocked her phone it was still

open to the camera app. The last photo she took filled the screen. Taken right before Imani interrupted their snooping. It was Mariana with her bare feet propped up and her head thrown back. She looked carefree and fucking sexy. She swiped away and dialed the driver to return to the hotel.

Mariana was changing out of her dress in the hotel bathroom while Alex hunched over her phone. She held a half drank bag of blood in her hand. She had already drained the mini bar of tiny bottles of whiskey and was annoyed with the headache surfacing as she stared at the photos. The numbers made no sense. The columns held no clues to what they meant. Alex licked the corner of her mouth. The taste of Mariana was long gone.

She needed a drink. Alex stood and paced by the door. She didn't want to leave Mariana alone, but she was fast. Alex could make it to the hotel bar and back before she noticed she was gone. Alex turned towards the door as Mariana's phone buzzed. The phone call went unanswered. The tapping of fingers followed before it buzzed once. She could be texting the man who sent the letter Alex saw in the apartment. Ashamed that she kissed a vampire. Not a sexy famous vampire that has created a following of lust filled humans. A has-been drunk with no direction in life and a knack for fucking things up.

"I am running downstairs. I will be right back." Mariana just hummed from behind the door. "Don't leave."

"Okay, mom."

Alex ground her teeth all the way to the elevator. She smelled the lobby before she reached it. Clouds of perfume and dozens of humans. Desperate people in their best attire trying to flirt their way into the night club. The only thing stopping them was a tall dark-skinned vampire standing behind a velvet rope.

Alex came to the Velvel Vein opening weekend years ago. It was the last time she drank directly from a human. She allowed herself to get caught up in overflowing drinks and sensual dancing. She led a woman to a booth. Dipped her head back and sucked. It started out as a kiss. Hard enough to leave a mark but escalated quickly. Her body felt aflame when her fangs punctured the skin. The tight grip from her lips stopped any drops from slipping out. It had been so long. She forgot the pleasures of fresh blood still warm from the person's body.

"What will it be?"

Alex blinked at the bartender. She was lost in thought and didn't realize he was staring at her. He wore the standard red vest over a button up. His dark hair was slicked back. It was obvious he was leaning into the role working at a vampire hotel. He looked straight out of a fan made movie.

"A bottle of blood whiskey." Alex slapped a hundred-dollar bill on the black granite counter. He slipped it into his pocket.

"What kind?"

This is one part of the city she missed. Options. She smiled, "Do you have Crimson Reserve or Midnight Vice?"

"I have both."

"Fuck yes." She threw her head back thanking a God she didn't believe in. "I'll take one of each." Alex placed another hundred on the counter.

There was a slight bounce in her step as she walked down the hall towards their hotel room. The recognizance didn't go as planned, but she had her favorite whiskey in hand and a stunning woman waiting in her hotel room. She didn't expect to find Mariana lying on the bed waiting for her, but a connection has been made. Alex just needs to figure out if it was a mistake. If Mariana had regrets. If Alex was fooling herself to consider more with a woman, she clearly doesn't deserve.

The rose water scent from Mariana still lingered in the hall. It teased the memory of their kiss. She had been unsure if Mariana would even want her. Up to this point Alex had been abrasive and cold. Perhaps it was Alex's overprotective behavior at the Gala that intrigued Mariana. She is a strong independent woman. Her curiosity is one of the things Alex likes most about her. Alex had put her hand on her casually. On the low curve of her back or grabbing her hand to lead her. But it was Mariana that made the move to cross the line. Then she took those steps in the elevator. Closing the space between them. There was no denying Mariana enjoyed the kiss. Enjoyed grinding on Alex's thigh.

Was it adrenaline after being caught in Iman's office? Was it the glass of wine she had earlier? Alex felt herself spiraling. She lost her balance thirty years ago and still has not found her footing. The whiskey bottle sloshed in her hand as she reached the door. She convinced herself to save it for home and let her mind clear a bit. If she lets the effects of the alcohol fade, her thoughts will be less muted. She might be able to read Mariana better. Or she might open a flood gate of emotion and painful memories.

Alex exhaled and slipped the key card through the slot.

After opening the door, she paused. It was too quiet. There were no footsteps. No heartbeats. No water running.

She set the bottles down and checked the room. None of the furniture was disturbed. The TV was off. Alex inhaled through her nose. There were no other scents, human or vampire in the room. The only foreign object was a room service tray on the edge of the bed. It was empty.

She took off her suit jacket and reached into her duffle bag. Her dress pants were tight enough that she could fit her thigh holsters over the fabric. Her eyes scanned the room for something that looked delivered. There was no aroma of food, but there was a faint scent of black licorice.

On the open bathroom door hung the purple dress. It shimmered in the low light from a built-in night-light near the mirror making stars on the walls. Her attention went to the small white paper. Next to it sat a crystal goblet with only a drop left of green liquid.

Alex held it to her nose and tried to remember her poison training. Nothing felt nefarious, just normal hard liquor. She ran her thumb through the smear of Mariana's lipstick. Lost for a moment thinking about their kiss before she picked up the paper and read.

Meet me at Velvet Vein. I put you on the list.
Let's have some fun before we leave.
Alex

Alex hissed at the false note. She crumpled the paper in her fist and ran out the door in a flash, nearly ripping off the doorknob. Racing past the elevator, Alex threw open the door to the stairs. Her feet barely touched the concrete stairs as she sprinted. Bursting into the lobby. She was no more than a blur to the eager humans waiting to be chosen for club entry.

Alex stopped before the velvet rope and forced a grin. The vampire looked down at her knives and shook his head.

"I am Princess Alexandrine Sipala-Creon," she tilted her head to the side. "Google me if you have doubts."

His red eyes widened, and he unlatched the rope while reaching back to open the heavy black door. "No need. Your Royal Highness. I was told to expect you."

The door swung open, and she was instantly hit by a wave of aggressive bass that pounded through her head. Blood-red spotlights sliced through the dark, erratic over the writhing bodies on the dance floor. The air was suffocating, thick with the stench of sweat, alcohol, and blood. Her senses were overwhelmed, and she shook her head trying to reset herself. The layers int eh air was drowning out any hope of tracking Mariana by scent. A low growl rumbled in her throat as she pushed forward into the chaos, eyes narrowing with determination.

Mariana should have known better. Alex would never have sent that note. How could she not realize by now? A loud, flashy nightclub blaring obnoxious pop songs and serving drinks with little umbrellas was the last place Alex would ever choose. Alex wanted nothing more than to yank Mariana out of this mess and teleport them both to the dive bar in Vaughn. The whiskey at Jackalope couldn't compete with Velvet Vein, but she'd take it any day over whatever trap had lured her here. Putting Mariana in danger. She cursed herself as she moved forward.

Pushing through the thick crowd, Alex felt eyes on her from all directions. Accompanied by whispers from the humans as she passed. Despite the club's reputation as a vampire hotspot, it was still swarming with humans, twenty to every one vampire. She kept her hands close to her knives, ready for anything. Drunken idiots were bound to get bold. Sure enough, as she squeezed by, a hand brushed over her ass. Her blood boiled. Spinning around, she fixed her icy gaze on the fools, two frat boy types who looked like they'd bought their way into the club with trust fund cash. They had no idea who they'd just touched.

"Don't." She hissed.

They both put up their hands. "Sorry, master."

"I am not your master."

The men looked at each other before one stepped forward. She noticed they were holding hands. Alex rolled her eyes knowing what was coming next.

"You could be. You can have us both."

She retreated without responding. Making her way to the main bar in the back of the room. The counter was the same polished black granite as the public hotel bar. She nodded at the human bartender who was finishing making a blended drink. Blood orange by the smell of it.

Before 1994, humans didn't beg to be owned by vampires. Hives had to carefully select those without families, people no one would miss. The grim truth was humans never survived. Whether a hive relocated without them or feeding went too far, death was inevitable. Vampires aren't good, something the wannabe goths in this club seemed to forget. Alex had ended more lives than she could count, helping Adonis in Croatia, Greece, and France long before she became a vampire herself. Humans were always prey. Now, vampires just show up to a nightclub. No chase, no thrill. Boring. Alex preferred it when they ran.

"What will it be?" The bartender wore fishnet

stockings under tattered black shorts and a crop top. She approached expecting a regular customer, but her heart raced when she locked eyes with Alex. "You're-"

"Looking for someone." She cut her off. Alex was not sure if she was shocked that she was a vampire or that she recognized her face. From all the times she was on television standing behind Adonis when he gave press releases. Introducing her team as the one assigned to track down the attackers, but never announcing who she was to him.

Alex felt her eyes flare bright with impatience. The woman shut her mouth tight enough to hide her lips.

"Have you seen this woman?" Alex flashed the photo she took of Mariana at the bartender. The bartenders' eyes narrowed.

"There's like twenty women that look like that here."

Alex held in a growl. It was not her fault. Humans have feeble memories and weak senses. She turned her back to the bar and scanned the room. It was too crowded, and her viewpoint was a disadvantage. She needed to get higher.

Red carpeted stairs led up to a balcony that circled the dance floor. A white-haired man stood at the bottom with his arms crossed. When Alex approached, she almost ripped the wig off his head. He was cosplaying her father, the King. It was disgusting.

"Let me up." She barked.

"This is for VIP only." He was a foot taller than her but cowered back a step. She touched the tip of her tongue to one fang. The act had him terrified and fascinated.

"I am not going to do the whole *'Do you know who I am?'* thing." She grinned. "But if you don't let me up you will lose more than your job."

He stepped aside. His head snapping around to see if anyone was watching. She was up the stairs before he could exhale the breath he held in his stiff chest.

Booths lined the wall out of view from the main floor. As expected, vampires were feeding on willing humans. Her mouth watered at the thought of intoxicated blood. Not as strong as what she mixes at home, but enough to give a buzz when drank directly from a vein.

Alex peered into each booth, praying she didn't find Mariana.

She was too smart for that. Mariana would never be persuaded by a vampire to let them feed. She hated the thought of Alex biting her. Mariana either saw vampires as a science experiment or something repulsive. Or at least Alex thought. Mariana had kissed her. Didn't pull away when she was touching her body. Even leaned into the grasp she had on her breast.

A server walked by holding a tray of empty glasses. She flicked her hair over her shoulder and a faint wave of rose water hit Alex like the tide.

"Have you seen this woman?" Alex gripped her arm. The server struggled not to drop the tray. She looked closely at the photo on Alex's phone screen.

"Yea, maybe." She pointed to a narrow hall leading away from the balcony. "Heading to a private VIP room with a group. She must have been drunk because she almost knocked me over. They were practically holding her up."

Fire rose in Alex. Her eyes flashed bright red. The

server bit her lip and looked down where Alex was gripping her arm. She removed her hand and stepped back. Drums rumbled in her ears. "Sorry. Um thanks."

She jetted away from the server.

The walls had two tone red wallpaper with big flowers that looked soft to the touch. Alex confirmed it was velvet when she pressed her cheek to the wall and sniffed. The hint of Mariana lingered. She scanned the hall for blood. A sign of injury. The floor had too many impressions to tell her how many people waited behind each door. Alex didn't know what shoes Mariana was wearing to match the footsteps anyway.

The scent led her to the last room. Two white doors practically aglow in the sea of red and black. Alex had no intention of knocking. She unsheathed both knives and kicked the doors in. They cracked like a spine.

The black carpet stretched into the expansive room, absorbing the dim light and giving the space an eerie stillness. At the center, Mariana sat on a stark white couch, her arms folded tightly across her chest. She didn't rise or even flinch, her gaze fixed on Alex. Flanking her on either side were two men, lounging far too comfortably for the situation. Their postures oozed confidence, as if oblivious to the fact that a knife-wielding vampire had just stormed in. No tension, no alarm. They looked more like they were waiting for a show than bracing for a threat. In unison they turned their heads to the woman standing on the other side of the room. Alex followed their gaze to her right.

"Seventeen minutes and thirty-four seconds." Imani stood leaning against a white tufted bar stool. "Tsk, tsk. You're losing your touch, Alexandrine."

"Let her go."

Imani swung her braids off her shoulder. They hit the stool like a whip. "She is free to go. I told her she needed to wait for you. And poof. You showed up. Proving just how important she is to you. I can see why. The doctor is quite lovely."

Alex spoke through clenched teeth. "What do you want Imani." The handles of her knives bit into her palms.

"Relax. I just wanted to play." Imani reached back and grabbed a wine glass from the bar. It was filled to the top with blood. Fresh blood by the smell of it. Alex's attention flicked on to Mariana. She floated across the room and stood at her feet. Her eyes checked every inch of Mariana. Pleading with fate that the blood was not hers. Anger boiling at the thought Imani had hurt her and jealous that she was tasting her blood.

Mariana reached out and grabbed Alex's wrist. The contact stopped her from spiraling. "Hey. I am fine." She squeezed. "Annoyed that I was used as bait, but I am unharmed."

Alex put the knives away and lifted Mariana to her feet. She giggled when Alex pulled her flush with her body. She had changed out of the gown and was wearing black leggings with a cropped t-shirt. A faded graphic of a 90's pop star on the front. Alex leaned in and tilted her nose towards Mariana's mouth.

She flinched and glared at Imani.

"You gave her Absinthe!"

Mariana giggled again. "You. Well not you, left a full glass with a note to meet here. It was the prettiest shade of green. I do love green, but it's not my favorite color." Mariana flicked Alex's nose. "You know my favorite color. Don't you? This club is very cool, but some of the vampires are dicks." She flipped off the man to her right. Alex grabbed her wrist and forced her hand down.

"Not cool, Imani."

She looked at her fingernails. "My bad. I forget humans can't handle liquor like us. You would think I would be better at remembering their weaknesses. I am around them so much. You would know what that's like. You are working with them now aren't you."

Alex slid her hand into Mariana's, locking their fingers. She tugged her away from the couch. The two men did not try to stop her. They stared patiently at Imani waiting for orders. Only one was a vampire. Head to toe muscles with scars on his knuckles. He must have been a boxer before he was turned. The human had bruising healing on his hands and under an eye. There were no visible bite marks on him. Imani must be recruiting him. Adonis has always allowed her to keep a few humans in training. Doing whatever she asks for the sliver of a chance she turns them. Most disappear after a few years.

Imani's vanilla sweet perfume was all over both. Alex was not surprised Imani was blurring the line between teacher and student. She tried centuries ago with Alex. Adonis put a stop to it when it was only flirting. She preferred her women with hearts.

Alex stood before the door with Mariana at her back. The door latch was broken, and one side hung at an angle from a single hinge.

"I am not working for anyone."

"I said with." Imani gulped down blood. It collected at the corners of her mouth. "Rodrick reported back weeks ago after I sent him to a redneck town not far from here. The police officers had the weirdest things to say. Rumors were circulating in the department that the Sherrif was friends with a vampire who occasionally helped on cases."

"I am not the only vampire in New Mexico."

Imani hummed. She took up the spot on the couch that was vacated by Mariana.

"They said the vampire had dark hair and olive skin, rode a motorcycle, and had a drinking problem." She looked Alex up and down with a grin on her face. "All those things sound like you to me."

"Fuck off."

"No Alex, you fuck off." She put her hand on the thighs of both men. "This is my hotel, my club, & my city. I hope you are sincere about leaving tonight. I would hate to chase a has-been like yourself out of town for lowering the value of my establishment."

Alex hissed. Her hands flinched towards her knives.

Imani continued. "You have one hour before I call daddy and tell him I found you."

Alex squeezed Mariana's hand and tugged towards the hall. The music thudded louder as they made their way to the stairs.

"Do we have to go?" Mariana pouted. "I never went to clubs in college. Had to focus. Had to be perfect. And this is a vampire club. So, fucking cool."

She gave Alex's hand a playful tug to get her to look back at her.

How was Alex supposed to resist that smile? The sheer perfection of her face. The thick curves of her body. They stopped at the bottom of the stairs. Mariana slamming into her with a clumsy bounce. Alex was painfully aware of every inch where they were pressed together. She turned and found Imani standing up against the railing with her henchmen. The henchmen watched the dance floor while Imani kept her eyes narrowed on Alex.

"We can dance for a few songs." Mariana spoke close enough for Alex to hear the clink of the barbell over the music. Alex's eyes remained pinned on Imani. A challenge to come down and force her out of the club. As fierce as Imani was, she had always feared Adonis more. Her father was still Imani's boss, and Alex was his favorite daughter. Or she was the last time they spoke.

The crowd cheered as a smoke machine filled the air. Lasers and red spotlights flickered over the crowd to the beat.

Alex pulled Mariana to the center of the dance floor. Grinding couples surrounded them. The two trust fund boys from before were sandwiching a human with goth makeup and red contacts. A common misconception that all vampires are goths. Alex rolled her eyes.

Mariana stole her attention by linking her arms behind Alex's neck. One hand rubbed up the edge of her hair where it was shaved in the back. She swayed slowly. One leg between Alex's. Rubbing herself on her thigh. Picking up where they left off in the elevator.

If only vampires had the ability to snap their fingers and make people disappear. She would have Mariana spread on the dance floor in an instant.

Mariana's skin was hot from the Absinthe pulsing through her veins. Alex slid her hands up the back of her loose shirt and pressed their bodies closer until they were moving as one. She could feel Imani staring daggers into the back of her head. Alex was enjoying putting on a show. Acting. It was just an act. Although with each grind she was acting less and less. Just like she has been making excuses to go to Mariana's apartment. Just how she didn't really need Mariana to get into the Gala. Alex found five different ways to break into the Gibbard building when doing research. Truthfully, she wanted more time with Mariana. Found a way to trick her into a date. Alex expected nothing to come of it but that kiss. Mariana changed things with that kiss and now Alex was questioning everything.

The case. She needed to focus on the case. Find the missing wolves. Don't let herself be distracted by the burning desire building friction all over her body. She had never felt so hungry in all her years.

Over the past few weeks, she began to crave Mariana's scent. Crave the sound of her voice. It had all felt one sided until the kiss in the elevator. Now she grinds her body on Alex with her eyes full of need.

Mariana let out a quiet whimper. Alex's heightened

hearing a blessing. She wanted to reach in her leggings and see if Mariana was wet from the grinding on her thigh.

"Fuck, Mariana." She said close to her ear. "You're driving me fucking crazy."

"Can we talk about the elevator?"

"I don't want to talk." Alex captured her lips. Plump and tasting like liquor. Mariana dug her fingers into Alex's hair. They broke apart for a second.

"I want you." Mariana said onto her lips. She tilted her head back and let Mariana kiss along her jaw. The words added fuel to the fire. Alex grabbed her plump ass and pressed their bodied tighter. All reason for being in here flew from her mind.

No. She needed to focus. *Fuck*. She needed to push this until after the case was over. Make sure Mariana was safe. Find the wolves for Jules and see if Imani is involved. Thinking of Imani had her glance up in the direction of the balcony.

Imani and her henchmen were gone. Alex whipped her head around and saw the back of them leaving out a side door.

She hung her head low. "I gotta follow them."

"What?" Mariana said breathlessly.

"Go to our hotel room. Pack up everything. Take my truck to the Albuquerque Amtrak station and wait in the parking lot. Text me when you are there." She pulled Mariana out of the crowd.

"Seriously Alex?" Mariana placed a hand on her hip.

"I will make it up to you." She placed a kiss on her cheek. "I promise. Now go."

Alex didn't move until Mariana passed through the main door that led to the lobby. Then she raced after Imani.

Alex adjusted her suit. The fabric suddenly felt too tight on her body as she was left with an ache in her core. Desperate for relief after dancing with Mariana.

They kissed again. With as much heat as the first time. Mariana did not pull away. She melted into Alex like they were the only ones on the dance floor. Alex kept replaying it over and over in her mind. An endless carousel of bliss.

She could not help but doubt if it was a side effect from the Absinthe. The same way she suspected the elevator kiss was caused by an adrenaline rush. Mariana spent most of her days alone in a lab or alone in an apartment. Perhaps it was a combination of the rush and proximity of working with Alex on this case that is guiding them together.

Alex had no whiskey to push the rising thoughts

from her mind. She had to rely on her own ability to focus. A skill she admittedly has let go limp after years of letting liquor do it for her. After a slow breath and heavy blink, she remembered where she was. Watching Imani from above after she left the club.

Imani who got in the back of a black SUV. Alex's black clothes allowing her to blend into the night. She ran over roof tops and jumped across alleys. The SUV was heading away from the hotel but not in the direction of Gibbard Tower. She followed from up high until the buildings were too scattered for her to make the jump. She dropped onto the street and continued her pursuit.

The neighborhood was not as maintained as downtown. Many of the vacant buildings had graffiti covering their walls and broken windows behind planks of wood. Streetlights in her path were dark. Giving her many more shadows to hide within.

The SUV pulled into a junk yard. Rows of stacked cars filled the space. All partially crushed. On the far end was a building large enough to house a private plane. There was no runway that Alex could see. Only a path wide enough for a large vehicle.

Alex inhaled through her nose slowly. Hoping to get a clue of what lies inside. She only scented metal and oil. Followed by the sickly-sweet perfume from Imani.

She walked along a row of vehicles. Keeping her steps light. A door shut out of her view. Alex waited until there were no footsteps to move closer.

Nearing the building she scanned the wall for a place to climb. She preferred to enter through a sky light or AC ducting if possible. There was nothing to grab onto. The building was entirely corrugated steel. With a sigh she turned towards the closest row of cars. Her intentions were to jump from the stack onto the roof. When she reached up to climb a new scent had her reach for her knives. A moment too late. A body of fur and claws slammed into her.

"Fuck."

One of her knives flew from her hand. Pinging off a car door. She jumped to her feet.

Standing before her was a fully transitioned werewolf. Three times the size of a regular wolf with elongated canines that stuck out past his bottom teeth. No glimpse of a man left it in. Werewolves become beasts, void of humanity, for one night a month. Controlled by the moon for reasons unknown to those on the outside. Vampires may be good at keeping secrets, but nothing compares to the prowess needed for werewolves to stay a mystery for centuries.

The wolf growled at her whilst digging his claws into the dirt. Drool dripping off his canines. His musky scent was familiar, but she couldn't place it. He lifted onto his back legs and roared. Like a gong at the beginning of a fight between two predators. She looked up at the moon and glared. They were a week away from a full moon.

Could a werewolf kill a vampire? Absolutely. They could bite off a vampire's head or sever the spine enough that it cannot be healed. Alex had seen it happen many times. Before they accepted the protection of Shade. Vampires and werewolves would fight for territory. Population numbers on both sides dwindled. Until there was very little left in Europe. Werewolves lived mainly in the Scandinavian countries. While vampires preferred the Mediterranean and northern Africa. It wasn't until much later when Europeans were migrating to the America's that Shade discovered werewolves already existed on this land. Living by their own rules within Indigenous tribes.

They passed down traditions and believed bloodlines from werewolves were sacred.

Bloodlines that can be recognized by its scent from a vampire with a particular skill. Alex's nostrils flared when the wind blew his scent in her direction.

"Paul?" Alex asked the roaring werewolf.

He lunged at her. The phone buzzed in her pocket, but she had no time to check if it was Mariana, confirming she was safe. Alex leaped out of his grasp. Long nails ripped at her shirt. She sucked in a breath through her teeth.

The half-illuminated moon cast an eerie glow over the maze of vehicles. She pushed her body off a dented red sedan and landed on his back. He propelled them backwards until she was slammed against rusting metal.

"Paul, stop." She groaned as he slammed her again. "James sent me to find you."

There was no recognition in his eyes of his brother's name. She struggled to keep a hold on her remaining knife. At this angle she could easily plunge it into his throat or chest. The image of James's face appeared. James would never forgive Alex if she killed his brother. "Fuck." She grunted. Why is this stupid case complicated with emotions and relationships?

She should not give a shit about what James thinks of her. This is a fight. A fight that she is barely paying attention to and allowing herself to be torn to shreds. James was not her friend. Not really. Alex has tried very hard to avoid building friendships.

Paul slammed her against a car, and it snapped her back into the present.

When he leaned forward before slamming her back again, she lifted her legs back as if standing on the broken car. Running backwards up she flipped in front of him. Alex moved away with inhuman speed. Paul snarled. Saliva dripped from his mouth. He dropped onto all fours and stared up at her.

"I really don't want to kill you."

He pounced in her direction. She moved quickly, but he caught her arm in his snapping snout. Alex bit her bottom lip to hold in a scream. Blood dripped from her mouth. She struck the wolf in his eye with the butt of her knife. He released her. Taking a chunk of her flesh with him.

Alex hauled herself to the top of the rusted stack of cars, her breath ragged, each movement leaving a smear of her blood on the metal beneath her. The sharp pain in her arm burned hotter with every step, but she couldn't stop. Her body was healing at a painfully slow rate.

In the distance, the black SUV sped away. Imani had no business in this fucking junkyard. She lured Alex here deliberately, knowing full well Alex would follow, knowing it was the perfect place for a fight. No witnesses, and an angry werewolf waiting to greet her.

Perfect, everything was perfect.

Alex's heart pounded as the realization hit. If Imani had led her here, it meant she was controlling the wolves. She had to be. Their kidnappings, the disappearances. They all led back to Gibbard, and the bitch had a luxury office in their building. But Alex needed proof. Without it, Jules could never go against a powerful company. With Iman's involvement, Alex was unsure Shade was also involved. She really wished her Shade security clearance was current. For the first time she doubted walking away thirty years ago. She could have been on the inside watching whatever is going on.

She limped on the jagged metal, her body trembling from both pain and the weight of the truth. If she didn't find a way to expose Imani soon, more wolves would vanish. And now Imani knows about Mariana. An innocent person dragged into this mess because Alex was denying her loneliness. Time was running out.

Claws scraped at the cars as Paul tried to climb after her. Werewolves can only focus on two things when they transform. Hunt for food & protect the pack. Still able to recognize voices and scents, even though they are unable to speak themselves. His claws dug into the metal like small ice picks. He hauled his body up towards her.

Alex wished James was here. He could step in and control his brother. Paul jumped next to her causing the stack to sway. She swung her leg at his head, straining against the tight fabric of her dress pants as her muscles contract beneath. Not the ideal fighting attire. She was grunting with her movements. Her small frame was comical against him. He did not seem to stray and showed no signs of getting tired.

It is no wonder militaries have been obsessed with

finding a way to make an army of them. The only thing standing in their way is Adonis, and a deal he made with powerful alphas over a century ago.

Alex and Paul moved in a series of dance moves. Her avoiding his slashing claws, while landing blows to his ribcage. Paul tackled her. They both fell from the top of the car stack, nearly twelve feet to the hard dirt below.

Alex's vision tunneled. The impact pushing all the air from her lungs. She dropped her remaining knife as she fell. Her tongue felt like sandpaper. With a raspy cough she rolled over. The blade landed just out of reach, and she stretched to grab it. A tear in her flesh above her breast gapped in the process. She opened her mouth to scream. Paul latched onto her arm. His long canines piecing deep into her muscle. Her scream turned into a painful cry.

"Ah fuck." She yelled.

Alex rolled onto her back. Lightning spreading throughout her body. Paul was moments away from ripping a huge chunk of her flesh off. She tightened her grip on the knife. She was out of options. With a quick strike, Alex hit the side of his head. One, two, three times. His jaw finally released. As soon as she was free from his hold, she pulled her mangled arm back and impaled his lashing paw to the ground. Alex spun to grab the other knife and put it through his other paw. Pinning him in place. He screamed a gravely howl.

Alex stood over him and kicked his head with all her remaining strength. His body went limp.

"Sorry Paul." She looked down at the blood dripping from both her arms, stomach, and her back was killing her. "It was either knock you out or kill you."

She hissed, taking her phone from her pocket. The movement pointing out every torn muscle in her body. Alex dialed Mariana while she searched the junkyard for rope or chain.

"Mariana. I just sent you my location. Bring the truck."

"Are you sure you don't want me to drive?" Mariana stared with horror at the gashes healing slower than usual covering Alex. The excessive amount of blood loss showing its effects. Alex took her eyes off the road for a second to glance down at the skin knitting together. It itched like a scab and tugged at her newly forming muscles. Mariana watched with a twisted fascination. Her fingers twitched to reach out and touch it. Even though it was horrific.

"Nah, I'm good." Alex smiled. The cuts on her face were already healed, only red lines of dried blood remained. "I'll get blood when we stop, and it will be like this never happened."

"What *did* happen? Did Imani do this?

Alex suspected Imani was responsible for unleashing Paul on her, but she had no evidence. She also had no idea how Imani could get him to turn when there wasn't a full moon. Rumors and ideas of their trans-formation have circled the globe. No one, not even the werewolves who wanted it, found ways to control their transformation.

It is one week from the next full moon, and there was a fully transformed injured werewolf in the back of her truck. As she feared, the paranormal are test subjects. The deformed body found at Lake Sumner an unfortunate side effect of scientific curiosity.

"I think Imani is involved, but I am not sure how yet." Alex swallowed. Her throat is like sandpaper. Her body was using all remaining blood and energy to heal her wounds. She was becoming weak. Alex straightened her shoulders. Trying to give Mariana a sense that she was safe. That Alex could protect her still. Despite her condition. "I know the unconscious werewolf's brother. I should take him to the com-mune."

"There are children on communes. What if he doesn't change back? What if he attacks them." Mar-iana opened her phone and began to tap on the screen. Alex pondered the possibility that Paul was not close to anyone on the commune in a way that could stop him from attacking them. He has been living on his own for a few years. Anyone who is not family would be at risk. She shifted in her seat. Dried blood made her ripped dress pants stick to her body uncomfort-ably.

"Well, I can't take a rabid wolf to the police station with a bunch of humans. It's better on the commune."

"Take him to my lab." She flashed her phone screen at Alex. Then read an email out loud. "The scientist I share the lab with is out of town. I just sent a message to the guard on duty, I told him to expect me. The guards signed a huge NDA and wont question any weird shit."

"And what are you going to do with him in your lab?" Memories flooded her mind. Vampires strapped to tables, nearly drained of blood, with limbs missing. Begging to die.

"I'll find a way to reverse the transformation." Mariana's heart rate increased with excitement. The scientist within her is anxious to get her hands on a live specimen. Alex was hesitant to let her walls down. Then she looked over at Mariana biting her bottom lip. A plump lip that Alex wanted to taste again and again.

Alex was quiet. She looked in her rear-view mirror. Paul was crammed in the back of her truck under the cab cover. His breathing sounded steady and slow. She exhaled slowly.

"Tell the guard to expect one more. A consultant named James Grady." Alex grabbed her phone from the center console and tapped his name.

It rang only once.

"It's the middle of the night, you better be calling to say you found my brother." James's voice was full of sleep and an octave deeper than usual.

"I found your brother."

Shuffling and movement muffled through the phone. "You found him? Don't fuck with me. Let me talk to him."

He stumbled through his words as if his mind was still catching up to his body after being waken suddenly.

"He can't talk right now. I had to knock him out."

Alex swallowed. She really needed blood. Her injured arm was straining to hold the phone to her ear. She tried to hide the shaking from Mariana. "He is in wolf form and not in the mood for a friendly conversation."

"Wolf? But it's not-" There was no need to finish the question. Alex heard a zipper on the other end of the line. "Where are you? I'll be right there."

"Meet me at the lab in Santa Rosa. The one I broke into. The guards know you're coming."

"No. You are not taking my brother to a lab." His voice gruff.

Alex tried to keep her tone calm. Mimicking Adonis when he persuades people with just his voice. "Trust me James."

"Trust you because the Sherriff asked you?" His words were heavy with implication that this was no more than a job for her, and she did not care about the outcome. She only wanted to please a cop.

She tilted her head towards the driver's window and whispered in the phone. She was not sure why Mariana seeing her act endearing made her fidget with fear. Alex learned firsthand that relationships, whether friendships or lovers, make you vulnerable. An easy target.

Alas, she had the urge to comfort James. "Trust me to protect your family."

There was a pause in the conversation. Alex could hear his footsteps change from wood floor to dirt. "Fine. I'm heading there now."

The room spun and was too bright. She couldn't concentrate hard enough to question why there was a large cell in the back of the lab made with multiple layers of bulletproof glass. And why there was a closet in the back that conveniently had a muzzle large enough to fit a werewolf? She had used the last of her strength to carry Paul from the elevator into Mariana's lab.

James beat them to the lab and was pacing when they walked in. His expression went grim when he saw his brother hog tied and bloody. Mariana ran to unlock the cell. James grabbed his brother from Alex's arms. She collapsed into a chair.

Her head was pounding. She needs rest to recover. Her body was burning energy to regrow flesh and heal. Alex's skin was numb, and she didn't feel Mariana place a hand on her shoulder.

"What's wrong?"

What she needed was inches from her fangs. A typical vampire would take blood and ask for forgiveness after. Or just leave them dead. She should grab Mariana and feed. Explain after that she was about to fall into a frozen statis. Some call it a vampire coma. Their bodies can heal almost anything with time. Or with large amounts of blood.

"Just-" Alex mumbled. "Hungry."

"I'll be right back." Mariana left the lab and crossed the hall. Moments later she returned with two chilled blood bags. "The researcher across the hall is working on human genomes. There's more if you need it."

Alex lifted a bag to her lips and punctured it with her fangs. Her body tingled with each gulp. She dropped it on the floor and immediately started on the second bag. When she drained the last drop, Alex looked at Mariana. Her face was flush, and her heart was racing. Alex felt the rivers of blood that had escaped the corners of her mouth. She wiped her chin on her ripped sleeve.

"Fuck. I'm sorry." Alex stood, suddenly feeling energized. "I must look like a fucking monster."

"Don't apologize. We all get food on our face when we eat." Her smile looked forced.

Alex glanced around at the clean lab and down at herself. What was left of her formal outfit was tattered and covered in blood. James was staring at her. He was unable to keep his words to himself. She looked like shit, and James had tried to ignore it, but it was like watching a slow train wreck.

"Jesus Christ!" James barked. "Did my brother do that to you?"

A one note laugh escaped her. Alex's arm mostly healed, but it was caked in blood and looked atrocious. She was going to say something sarcastic, until she saw the genuine worry on James and Mariana's faces. Her chest warmed. She tugged at her shirt, trying to hide the large slashes along her side. It was no use. There were holes and tears everywhere. A dry mixture of hers and James's blood coated the expensive fabric.

"There's a shower in the bathroom." Mariana pointed. Her look was pleading. "And I keep a change of clothes in the tall cabinet."

James was looking down at his brother. It was not enough privacy to give Mariana the kiss she craved. Alex suspected she would not want her near in her current state anyway. A grotesque scene. No longer the handsome vampire that was dancing with her hours ago.

"Thanks." Alex picked up the blood bags and tossed them in the trash. Before entering the bathroom, Alex leaned close to Mariana's ear. "Don't leave the lab."

Mariana nodded without hesitation. The backs of their hands brushed against each other as Alex walked away.

The scorching water pounded down, scalding her skin, its intensity forcing her to focus. She replayed the night in her mind, grinding her teeth at the risks she never should have taken. The Gala was supposed to be simple, just a reconnaissance mission to gather intel. Alex had not planned for it to spiral out of control, resulting in following her old boss, fighting a werewolf, and then dragging its unconscious body to a lab owned by the very organization she suspected.

She winced, almost able to hear Adonis internally scolding her for the failures. A better idea would have been a vet clinic or any place with less connection to Gibbard. But she'd ignored reason.

She knew why, and the answer unnerved her. *Mariana*. Being close to her, keeping her trust, building something between them. Alex wanted it badly, maybe too badly. Even when logic shouted that she shouldn't trust anyone associated with Gibbard, her heart pulled her in the opposite direction.

Was it years of loneliness bubbling to the surface at the first sign of affection or something deeper? The fear burned up in her chest, feeling nearly as hot as the water streaming down her skin. Her lust for Mariana was clouding her judgement. Distracting her. Distracting her from the case? She has been distracted before, and it ended in death.

Alex leaned against the wall, letting the water mask her troubled expression. Every fiber of her being wanted to surrender to that closeness, that sense of companionship in a world of enemies. But could she trust herself to walk that tightrope between loyalty and distraction, between what she wanted and what she knew was right? The inner battle raged on, the need to feel something genuine against the relentless press of her own doubts. A battle that started thirty years ago in a London warehouse. Still plaguing her instincts.

Alex fidgeted in her borrowed leggings and purple hoodie. The outfit made her look soft and approachable. Not traits she usually strives to be perceived as. James watched his brother in the cell. Bandages were wrapped around gashes from Alex's knife during the fight. Paul had woken up. He fought against the ropes before giving up. He could not even sit up and was stuck lying on his side. His golden eyes stared at James over the thick leather muzzle.

"Tell me again why you have a shatterproof box and muzzle in your lab?" James placed his palm on the glass and looked at Mariana without turning his head. She was sorting equipment and moving her fingers in the air like there was an invisible checklist. They spoke without facing each other. Alex observed from her place on a cold stool.

"I would tell you if I had answers. Gibbard had this lab set up when I got here." She snapped fresh latex gloves on her hands. Observing Mariana, Alex had concluded that she was in fact innocent. Too trusting and optimistic. The perfect hire for a company with nefarious goals. She was relieved the case wouldn't lead to her having to once again take down someone she had feelings for. Because there was no more denying. Alex was falling for her.

Mariana moved fluidly around the room. Setting up tests and jotting down numbers. Alex propped her chin up with her fist and watched. Hours ago, Mariana was dancing in a seedy nightclub and taking shots of Absinthe. Now, she wore a lab coat and used this equipment like it was second nature. She scribbled notes in a shorthand that was a foreign language to Alex.

"What are you doing now?" Alex asked.

Mariana put her eyes on the lenses of a microscope and adjusted the dial. Drops of Paul's blood sat on the slide. "I already discovered the gene that reacts to the full moon. It was my biggest break though in my research, so far. My research focuses on gene editing. I plan to use a technique known as CRISPR-Cas9, a powerful tool for editing genes. I already Identified the mutation. I just need to-" Her sentence trailed off.

Mariana looked up from the microscope to see if Alex was listening. Alex was staring at her lips. She was not sure why hearing Mariana talk about gene editing with so much passion was turning her on. The heat in her body being a confirmation of her arousal. Could she delay this project for a few hours? Would

James mind if his brother was hog tied in a cell for a bit longer? Alex wanted to pull Mariana onto a table and lick every inch of her body.

She cleared her throat. "And how does one do that exactly?"

Mariana blushed under the heavy gaze of Alex's red eyes.

"Well, first I design a CRISPR system to target this specific genetic sequence. The CRISPR system consists of two main components: the Cas9 protein, which acts like a pair of molecular scissors, and a guide RNA, gRNA, which directs Cas9 to the exact location of the mutation." Mariana moved to another table and began placing small tubes into a centrifuge.

"All I heard was *scissors*." Alex winked.

"Jesus, Alex!" James grumbled from across the room. "Go take a cold shower. You look like you are about to pounce, and I need the science lady to focus."

"Science lady? What is this 1950?" Mariana snapped. "That's Dr. Nava."

"Sorry." He glared at Alex. "I need Dr. Nava to focus."

Alex smirked and raised her eyebrows in a taunting gesture at James. Mariana ignored both and marked something down in her notebook. She worked in silence for about an hour. Alex moved to the floor and leaned back against a metal cabinet. Her eyes were growing heavy. She shut them for a long moment. Preserving her strength in case someone unwelcome showed up to the lab. James found a book about werewolves. He was deep into the facts scientists believe they have gathered. Occasionally he would snort when they got something wrong but had no intention of correcting it when Mariana asked.

The lab was quiet. Calm before Mariana snapped her fingers. An invisible light bulb going on above her head.

"I need some of James blood." She announced.

Alex stood quickly. Grateful her muscles were no longer sore. "I'll make him bleed." She clacked her teeth.

His brows knit together. James shut the book so hard his brother flinched against the ropes. He rose to his feet and squared his shoulders.

"You wanna fight me, vamps? You're the size of a teenager. I can throw you across a football field." To emphasize his size, James crossed his arms and flexed his pecks. Alex mimicked the movement, and her size was comical compared to him. But her eyes blazed with a fire that would cause most men to run and hide.

"Should we settle this with an arm-wrestling match?" She beamed a smile at him. Full of deadly teeth. Yet it was playful.

James towered over Alex with a sinister smile. "I would love that."

Alex hissed and James responded with a growl. Neither one of them moving an inch.

"Geeze how long have you been friends? You act like siblings." Mariana stomped her foot.

James pointed at Alex. "She started it."

"You are proving my point." Mariana opened a

drawer with supplies to draw blood. "I prefer the sample to not be contaminated with vampire saliva." Alex backed off and returned to the empty stool.

"Don't you have a fridge full of werewolf samples?" James raised an eyebrow at Mariana.

"He's a relative. The process is more likely to succeed." Mariana moved towards him. She had on fresh gloves and held up a syringe in one hand. It was connected to a test tube by a thin rubber hose.

"What is this process?"

Mariana spoke as she gently took his arm and led him to a stool across from Alex. "Using the CRISPR-Cas9 system, I can make a precise cut at the site of the mutation in the werewolf's, Paul's, DNA. This effectively removes the defective DNA sequence. After cutting out the mutated DNA, I will introduce a healthy version of the gene—sourced from you—into the genome." She placed his arm on the counter and tied a piece of rubber over his bicep. James's heartbeat was steady. His body at ease under Mariana's touch. "Allowing the cell's natural repair mechanisms to incorporate your healthy DNA."

Alex turned away as the blood filled the tube. She was hungry again. And thirsty. And horny. And her clothes were terrible. Alex was ready to burst out of this lab. Her skin itched as she looked around the sterile room.

"I am going to check in with the sheriff. James, will you stay by her side?" Alex stood from the stool. She looked ridiculous in loungewear and dress shoes.

James held a nub of cotton to the inside of his elbow. Mariana was already splitting the blood into multiple smaller tubes at a workstation.

"She's trying to save my brother. I will protect her with my life." Their eyes met and she could have let the conversation die. They were on the same page, but Alex had the need to voice aloud a claim of protection. She needed Mariana to know that Alex was not done with her. Needed her to understand Mariana has become more than just a lead in a case. Unfortunately, Alex is not great with words.

Alex stopped in the doorway and looked over her shoulder. "Good. Cause if anything happens to her, your commune will pay the price."

As she walked down the hall she caught a faint mumble from James. "Crazy bitch."

It brought a huge smile to her face.

Alex requested James text her updates every twenty minutes. She went home first. Drank another bag of blood that she chased with a whiskey double. The leggings and oversized sweatshirt came off as soon as she walked through the door. Dark grey jeans and faded band tee have become a second skin to her. She is already more relaxed. Most importantly, healed from the fight with Paul.

It wasn't even 4:00am yet. Jules would not be happy if Alex showed up now. Out of courtesy, she opened her laptop and decided to let the sun catch up. Transferring the photos from her phone was a tedious task. She tapped her nails on the whiskey bottle. Her head was surprisingly quiet. All she could think of was what could have happened if she took Mariana back to the hotel room instead of chasing Imani.

A desperation to finish the case is growing within

Alex. For the wrong reasons. She only cares about the missing wolves because Jules asked her to help. When she first helped Jules, it was to preserve herself. It kept Shade out of Vaughn by lending her skills for a few days to the Sheriff's office.

The driving force for her has become Mariana. Alex craves more time with her. Time to figure out if there is something blooming between them or if Mariana is being seduced by the adventure and not by Alex. Alex wanted so desperately to seduce her.

She licked her lips. No longer tasting like Mariana. Alex pushed aside her thoughts and tried to focus on the documents in front of her.

Nonsense. The files were all nonsense. Searching the internet supplied no leads. She refilled her glass with smokey amber liquid and held it to her temple.

"Think Alex. Think. What is Imani up to and why is she hanging around General Old-As-Fuck Gain. And why would Adonis let her have an office at a pharmaceutical company." She considered calling Adonis. It would save time. Get answers faster.

Alex swiped through the contacts on her phone and paused at his name. The last time she spoke to him was seven years ago. It was brief. He invited her to a family gathering in Prague. She declined and asked him to give her space. He promised to wait until she contacted him and has respected her wishes.

Imani has probably already contacted him. She would claim Alex is interfering with her assignment. Whatever that may be.

Gibbard wants to control the transformation of werewolves. *Why?* They cannot be recruited into the military. Every member of the United Nations and

King Adonis have agreed to keep supernatural's out of armed forces. Every few years it gets brought up again just to have Shade end the debate quickly.

Unless Imani is not working for Shade anymore. She could be building an army for the private sector. But then why is she with General Gain.

Alex typed an internet search: *US private military contractors*

She was given a list of a dozen companies with current contracts. One name jumped off the screen. DHIB. She saw this on the files in Imani's office.

"Fuck." She placed her glass on the table with enough force to splash a bit of whiskey on her hand.

Licking her hand she stumbled to grab her phone. Alex inhaled deeply before pressing the call button. She tossed back the remaining whiskey before it rang for the third time. Needing liquid courage. Halfway through the fifth ring a young female voice answered.

"Hello."

"Give the phone to Adonis."

Was it a rude response? Yes. Did Alex care? No. People floated around Adonis his entire existence. Hoping to be given wealth, eternal life, or other plea-sures. She rolled her eyes.

"Who is this?" The woman sounded young. Early twenties if Alex had to guess. "How did you get the Kings number?

"I am Princess Alexandrine. Daughter to King Adonis." The title soured in her mouth. "Give the phone to Adonis."

The young woman sucked in a breath. Her tone immediately changed. Sweet and smooth like honey. "I can't. He is in a meeting. I could take a message for you."

Alex had not figured out what to say or how to put it in a short message. Imani could have eyes everywhere. A wall flew up and Alex ground her teeth. Her fangs digging into the inside of her bottom lip.

"No." She already regretted calling. "Just tell him-tell him I called."

Alex ended the call before the woman could respond. Her fingers glided across the keyboard. Adonis had many houses around the world. She needed to find him.

The first place she checked was vampire fan sites. Full of paparazzi images of well-known vampires. They had a tab dedicated to the King. His long white hair looks perfect in every picture. Hitting a few inches below his shoulders. He still wore a black Victorian coat but paired it with a t-shirt and jeans.

He was last seen in London two days ago. A young red headed woman latched on his arm. She wore a tight red dress and a gold dog collar. *A fucking dog collar*. Adonis proudly held the end of a gold leash. She cringed. No daughter should have to see her father's kinks displayed in public. *Gross*.

Alex shut her laptop and tucked a gun into the back of her pants. She strapped two knives to her thighs. Freshly cleaned from being covered in Paul's blood.

She paused at her motorcycle. Debating on one helmet or two. What if she takes Mariana for a ride and the sun is out? Mariana must wear a helmet. She needs protection. She is fragile. Precious.

Alex kicked a leg over the seat and lowered herself

down. Sunlight was peaking over the horizon. A new day. The machine roared to life as she headed down the road. Towards Jules's house with an extra helmet strapped behind her.

Alex sat on a saffron colored kitchen counter. Her legs dangle off the edge like a child. Jules sauntered down her hallway recovering from a sleepy haze. With hair still damp from a morning shower. Her wife was shouting a grocery list from the back bedroom. White rice. Black beans. Oreos. Alex flashed a fang filled grin when Jules came into view.

"What the fuck!" She reached for her hip, finding her holster empty. "How the hell did you get in here?"

"You'll never know."

"The kitchen window?" Jules looked over Alex's shoulder at the window seeing the latch in the unlocked position.

"The kitchen window." She hopped off the counter.

Jules's wife Carmen came around the corner. She was tilting her head to put in an earring. Her brown hair was swept up away from her face. The highlights in her hair catching the morning light. She was elegant and classy. But carried an aura that could instill fear in those around her. Carmen yawned, "Who are you talking to babe?"

Jules narrowed her eyes at her intruding friend. "Alex."

"Alex!" She rushed over and embraced Alex. Pinning her arms to her sides. "I am so happy to finally meet Jules's vampire friend. She talks about you all the time."

"Is that so." Alex said through a breath as Carmen released her. She stood next to Jules and placed a hand on one shoulder to steady herself. Carmen stepped gracefully into tall black pumps.

"She worries about you." Carmen's smile was warm. Like they were instant friends.

"Don't listen to Carmen. I hardly care." Jules retrieved the top of her sheriff uniform from the back of a chair. It smelled like it was freshly ironed with starch to make the collar lay flat.

"Oh, you love me." Alex could not help but watch Carmen. She reminded her of Mariana. Both have thick black hair and warm tan skin. She let her mind wander for a moment. Imagining a life with Mariana as a wife. An alternate reality where Alex was getting ready to work a case for Shade while Mariana put on a lab coat. They lived together like a family. Like lovers. Committed to each other.

"Alex." Jules snapped in front of Alex's face. "Earth to vamp."

She shook the thoughts from her head.

"I'm late to show a house in Duran." She kissed Jules quickly on the lips and waved at Alex. "So good to finally see your face. Come over for dinner soon."

There was an awkward pause after the door shut behind Carmen.

"Does she know I don't eat?" Alex raised an eyebrow.

Jules finished buttoning her shirt and was tucking it in. "She's being polite. You should try it."

"Speak for yourself." Alex walked into the living room. There was a large wedding photo above the fireplace. Jules was kissing Carmen on a beach with the sun setting behind them. "You asked me to find a few missing people. A favor. You told me if I took care of it then you wouldn't have to contact Shade. Well guess what Jules, Shade are the fuckers who took them. Or someone that works for Shade. Or did, I'm not sure yet."

"What?" She paused, putting her gun in the holster. "A government organization is kidnapping were-wolves."

"Technically they are not government." Jules opened her mouth to speak but nothing came out. Alex continued. "I have not confirmed that it's Shade exactly. But I do know a Shade Lieutenant is involved. She is working with Gibbard Center for Genetic Research. I think they are trying to find a way to control the transformation in werewolves."

"So, werewolves wouldn't transform anymore. Making them pretty much human."

Alex shifted on her feet. "I don't think their goals are that noble. If I had to guess by the presence of General Gain, they are trying to control it to use them as weapons. Imagine a soldier hiding in plain sight before they transform info a deadly beast. No need to wait on a full moon."

"I thought the United Nations agreed not to recruit werewolves and vampires into the military. That would be a war crime."

She crossed her arms across her chest. "Yea, and no one has ever committed war crimes before."

"Fair point." Jules paced in her living room. "Did you say General Gain?"

"Yea."

"From the Pentagon?"

Alex nodded.

"He's gotta be like," Jules tapped on her phone. "Eighty-nine years old. How is he not retired."

Gain was very alert for his age. He was even dancing with much younger women at the Gala. Either he has amazing health or-

"Fuck." Alex mumbled. Having a conversation with herself in her head. Conspiracy theories with General Gain and Imani. Different ways Shade could be involved. Her brows scrunched as she stared into the room.

"What?" Jules followed her sightline to realize she was not focused on anything. Alex shook her head. Resetting her thoughts. Jules lifted her hands waiting for a response, but Alex was already moving towards the front door.

She spoke with her back facing the living room. "I really need to get ahold of Adonis."

"The vampire King?" Jules said with a puff of air in her voice.

"Call me if anyone from Shade or Gibbard or the

fucking military shows up." She opened the door. "Call me immediately, then get Carmen and leave town. Just in case shit hits the fan. I don't want you in the cross hairs."

Before Jules could object, Alex sprinted to her motorcycle. She kept her eyes mostly closed until the helmet was secured on her head. Alex took off towards Mariana's lab. A trail of desert dust in her wake.

J ames tapped on the edge of a glass beaker. He was teetering between impatience and grate-fulness.

"How much longer?" He asked for the third time this hour. His response was a long sigh from Mariana. She did not look up from the pages of notes scattered around her lab equipment.

Mariana subdued Paul an hour ago and began the blood transfusion. He was no longer in the glass cell. In case the process didn't work Mariana had him strapped to a table. When she took this job with Gib-bard, she was told there would be no live test subjects. Just blood samples. She was so eager in the beginning that she didn't notice how many modifications had been made to allow live test subjects. Now the cell, restraints, and muzzle make sense. They were always intending for her research to expand. It was already past that point in another lab. Paul was proof of that.

"This is my first attempt at editing a genetic mutation and replacing it with a healthy sequence. It could be hours before he comes out of wolf form." She swallowed. Mariana kept her face down as she typed notes onto her laptop. "If successful, I cannot promise he will regain his ability to transform between human and wolf forms. Even with a full moon."

"You mean he might not be werewolf anymore."

"It's a possibility." The elevator buzzed in the hallway. Alex appeared but went into the lab across the hall instead. "She must be hungry. Going right to the blood stash."

James watched Mariana stare longingly into the hall. "That was fast?"

Mariana shifted her eyes from the hall to James. "What was?"

"You and Alex." He bounced his eyebrows annoyingly. "I see what's going on between you two."

Mariana hesitated before responding. Wondering how good a vampire hearing is and if Alex was hanging on her words. She swallowed and whispered. "I am not sure what is going on between us."

"But something is definitely going on." He hummed.

Mariana nodded. "I am open to figuring it out."

"But you like her, I can tell."

"She has a hard shell, and I am finding it difficult to crack. I want to. I–there's–" Mariana closed her laptop. "There's something she's not telling me."

"Look what I fucking found!" Alex burst into the lab holding a blood bag over her head. "Vampire blood."

"Where?" Mariana stood.

"You lab neighbor. He has dozens of bags filled with vampire blood in a second fridge." Alex threw it into the sink and punctured it with a nail. The red liquid seeped down the stainless-steel basin. "Stashed behind an impressive lock. Care to tell me why he has vampire blood?"

"I don't know." Mariana placed a hand on her chest. "We work separately. When I was hired, I was told I would be working alone. It's easier to control information leaking out if there is only one person with the information."

James had moved to his brother's side. He watched the slow rise and fall of his chest. "What's the big deal? Dr. Nava has a fridge full of werewolf blood."

Alex choked on the lump in her throat. She was about to reveal something Adonis would kill her for saying aloud. Perhaps she should call him first. Perhaps she should report her findings to Shade and let them take care of it. Imani's devious face flashed in her mind.

"Vampire blood can act as a fountain of youth in humans."

Mariana and James stared wide eyed. "You mean if a human drinks vampire blood they don't age?" Mariana asked.

"Sort of, but not by drinking it. There is a process. And it's not known by many. Most vampires don't even know. All they are told is the penalty for giving blood to a human for any reason is death. Adonis makes no exceptions." Alex pulled up an article on her phone. "Did you know General Gain was diagnosed with stomach cancer twenty years ago? Then seemingly overnight it was gone. Photos of him with a particular bitchy vampire became more frequent until last year when it was confirmed they were working together. Imani then took up a consulting position at a pharmaceutical company. And guess who has stocks in that company?"

"General Gain." James answered.

"Smart pup." Alex slid her phone into her pocket. James growled quietly at the jab. "See, Imani is using Shade as a cover to move around and make deals. She is going against Shade by letting Gibbard use vampire blood, and she found a way to get them werewolves to test on. She is behind all of it. And I would bet my left tit Adonis has no clue. He hates the military. No matter who they serve."

Marianna blinked, "We should probably call the authorities or at least your Sherrif friend."

"It's just a theory right now. I need evidence." Alex ran her fingers through her hair.

"Can you call the King?" Mariana asked while checking Paul's vitals and taking notes.

"I have been trying."

James was looking at his phone screen. His brows knit together. "According to paparazzi your King hasn't been seen in months."

"What do you mean? There are pictures of him all over the internet."

"Fans think he is using a body double. His face hasn't been photographed since February 22nd." James handed his phone to Alex.

She scrolled through the images and read the article. There were dozens of comments from fans. They analyzed his walk and the length of his white hair. Claiming he has been switched. Some believed he was taking a much-needed vacation from the public eye. Others speculated he was dead. That Shade was waiting to announce who his heir was. A secret known to less than ten vampires. One is currently standing in this lab.

Her hands wanted to shake but she stiffened against the urge. "I have been calling, but I can't get through. This means he hasn't been seen since the werewolves started going missing."

"You think that's related?" James looked down at her. His posture ready to go to war. All he needed was to have her aim him at the enemy.

"I think Imani needed him out of the way."

Their conversation was interrupted with moans and cracking bones. Paul's body was convulsing. Blood caked fur disappeared into his skin. Leaving behind flakes of red. His jaw popped and morphed back into human form. Mariana was diligently watching his vitals. His claws retracted under his nails.

James held his breath as the room waited for a sign of life from Paul. Red lacerations striped his skin. Mariana tossed a spare lab coat over his lower half. He was broad like his brother. With a thick neck and long black hair. Alex clamped her mouth shut. Hoping she had not injured him past survival. James went to work untying him and removing the straps.

The cracking of bones stopped, and the room went silent for two breaths.

The restraints falling from his much smaller form.

Paul suddenly sat up and latched onto James's arm. His voice was course. "James."

James grabbed him back. They held each other's forearms and pressed their foreheads together.

"I am here brother."

Alex felt Mariana's hand slide into hers. She gripped it softly. Warmth bloomed in her chest. The love between the brothers had her longing for a connection she used to have. The soft hand woven with hers had her thinking there is space to build a new one. New friendships and even new love.

The tiny steel trash can in the lab was nearly overflowing with food wrappers. Paul woke up incredibly hungry. Alex sped away on her motorcycle to the closest drive through. Mariana ate a chicken tostada with extra guacamole. The wolf brothers finished off twelve tacos. Alex helped herself to another blood bag from the lab across the hall. After destroying his entire stash of vampire blood.

While she was sipping on a corner of the bag, Alex snooped through the scientist's metal filing cabinet. The lock broke easily with a quick yank. If Alex was in her prime, she would have searched the entire lab weeks ago. Imani was right, she was losing her touch. This investigation has been sloppy from the start. Partly from her head being foggy most of the time and partly from Mariana being a distraction. Only one of those would she consider giving, and it was not the scientist in the lab next door.

The files confirmed he has been trying to use vampire blood to create an anti-aging drug. It appears his goal is to get it ready for the market in three years. He has had positive results with frequent injections. There are no patient names on the files. But one is described as an eighty-nine-year-old male.

The thought that vampire blood was pulsing through General Gain made her queasy. She slammed the cabinet shut and kicked the desk. Mariana rushed in. Alex's head was throbbing. She cursed herself for not bringing a full bottle of whiskey. If only people knew the true reason Adonis forbids vampires to donate blood. The reason why Shade spends half its resources squashing records pertaining to their blood. The almost magical effects it has on a human body. Slowly healing and stunting their cells from aging.

"Are you okay?" Mariana placed a gentle hand on her arm. Alex backed her against the desk. She pushed the pen holder aside and sat her on the edge. Alex positioned herself between her legs and stroked up her thighs before resting them on her waist.

"Nothing is okay." Alex inhaled. "This was supposed to be an easy missing person case. Wham bam, ya know. Now I am either hunting or hiding from my old boss. I am pretty sure Imani is working with Gibbard to create a werewolf super soldier and also an anti-aging drug. And now there is a chance my- "

The word paused like a lump in her throat. She swallowed. The lack of saliva had her thinking of whiskey again. Mariana leaned in and placed the softest kiss on her lips. She lingered long enough for Alex's body to relax. This was not like Anita. Time with Anita was filled with blood lust and adventurous sex. Anita had no problem sharing. She often invited vampires and humans into their bed.

When Mariana kisses her, it begs the question "will you be mine?" or maybe it is a declaration of "I am yours". Whatever Mariana means with this kiss it soothes a part of Alex that has been splintered for thirty years. An ache she has learned to live with. The pain she believes is deserved. Alex has been wrong in the past. Perhaps she is wrong about what she deserves now.

"Continue." Mariana said softly.

Alex leaned back and let herself drown in Mariana's eyes for a moment. "My father. There is a chance he is dead or missing. I hope I am overexaggerating and he is hold up in a mansion somewhere. Hiding from the media."

"Sounds like you need a plan."

Alex nodded.

"I am great at making plans. First, what have we observed? This lab we are standing in currently is doing research on both vampire and werewolf blood. We know Gibbard owns the lab. We also know they are working with a high-ranking Shade agent and a General from the US Military." Alex could not help staring at her lips as she spoke. They are plump and her breath smelled like sweet cinnamon from the Horchata she drank. "Are you listening to me?"

"Absolutely." Alex kissed her jaw and neck. "Can we have this conversation without clothes?"

"Focus."

"How can I?" Alex reached for a button on her lab coat, but Mariana swatted her hand away. "You have been talking sciencey all day and it's fucking sexy."

"I will remember that for a later date." Alex pushed herself off with a grunt and leaned against the broken filing cabinet. "I suspect we don't have much time now that Shade knows you are involved."

"Imani. Not Shade. We don't know if she is working alone or under orders." Alex crossed her arms hoping to block the heat ruminating off her body. If she can wrap up this case tonight, she could drag Mariana to bed by morning. And the next day. And the next week.

"Theres our question." Mariana exclaimed and Alex just blinked. "Is Imani working with the US Military on her own accord or under orders? She seems shady. Pun intended."

"An excellent judge of character you are." Alex mocked tipping the brim on a hat and winked. Mariana smiled quickly before changing her expression to look serious.

"You have known her for a long time." A question hid in her statement. Alex considered how much to reveal about herself. It took decades to lose any trace of an Croation accent. Always adapting to dress and speak in the modern ways.

"Centuries." She said after a long pause. Mariana had little reaction. Alex could almost see the thoughts fluttering in Mariana's head. Her brilliant, gorgeous head. She licked her lips.

"We can't just call up Gibbard or the US Military and ask if Scary Vampire Lady is on their payroll." Mariana played with the end of her ponytail. She tied it up when they arrived at the lab. It made her neck extremely distracting to Alex. She had been sipping on blood all night to suppress urges. It's been ages since she has sunk her teeth into flesh. The last several humans were all males. Willing volunteers at establishments like Velvet Vein. She chose males because it was easier for her to ignore any sexual sparks. Alex knew from a young age which direction her attention swayed. She would often lure men over women into dark alleys where Adonis waited. Not wanting to waste a beautiful face and perfect breasts to a feeding. Adonis was happy to oblige. Believing the sort of man that follows a child into a dark alley deserves a bloody fate.

"Alex?" Mariana snapped her fingers. "Are you listening to me."

"No. I mean, yes. Sorry I have a lot to think about." She shuffled her feet awkwardly.

"I asked if you had cameras we could set up and catch Imani in the act of something."

Alex held back a smile. If she only knew how many cameras had been watching her for the past couple weeks. "Yea, I got cameras."

"Great. They could lead to the rest of the missing wolves." She hopped off the desk. "I bet they are near that junk yard."

"That's what I think too. Paul popped up out of nowhere. He must have emerged close by, or I would have scented him earlier."

James popped his head in the lab. "We are leaving."

Mariana moved towards the doorway and Alex followed. Grateful of her ponytail swishing behind her causing a light wave of the rose water scent to guide her like breadcrumbs. "Leaving? I should probably do more tests. Alex should interview him. See if he remembers anything."

"He's pretty shaken. He'll talk more at home. With the pack nearby." He rubbed the back of his neck. "I will get him talking and text you with anything useful."

Alex can only relate the concept of a pack to a vampire hive. A place of security and belonging. Not as family friendly as a pack. Hives are a deadly place for monogamy.

"Alex and I are leaving to get some equipment. Please call if he shows any, um, medical issues." Mariana brushed her hand down Alex's arm, and the motion did not go unnoticed. James met Alex's eyes and smirked.

"Will do." James turned his head to watch Mariana walk back into her lab across the hall. He straightened his body filling the doorframe and looked Alex up and down. Words went unsaid for a long moment. They both stood with arms at their sides and somber expressions. "Alex, I owe you."

"You owe Sheriff Jules. She is the one who told me to find him." She slipped her hands into the front pockets of her jeans. James stepped closer.

"I will thank the Sheriff also, but you found him." He punched her arm causing her to step back. "You may be an asshole."

"Thanks. I guess." She gave him a dramatic scowl. "But you're-"

"Please don't say *my asshole*." Alex forced a frown.

James rolled his eyes and inhaled. He spoke, letting out the air from his lungs. "I was going to say, you are also a hero."

She has been called many names in her long life. Held many titles and filled many rolls for people. Human and vampire. Yet, this one was new. And he spoke it with sincerity. Her chest ached.

"Vampires can't be heroes James. Trust me."

"Look around." He motioned to the lab. "Nothing is impossible.

66 I am not getting on that thing." Mariana held her feet firm and pointed at the motorcycle. Alex was already sitting on it with a helmet snug and visor down over her eyes. The sky did not favor her with a single cloud. They were nearing midday. She held the spare helmet out to Mariana. If she had time, Alex would have gone to the closest bike shop and got her a purple helmet. The kind that sparkles in the sunlight. She would like that.

"I am not leaving it here." Alex shook the helmet at her.

"I can drive separately."

"Absolutely not." She softened her voice. The same way Adonis does when he wants to persuade people. "I'm not letting you out of my sight until I remove Imani's head from her body."

Mariana dropped her shoulders. She fought against the smile threatening her face. "How romantic."

"Plus, with your car here, anyone looking for you will think you are inside. You gotta think two steps ahead." Alex tapped her temple with two fingers. She let out her breath when Mariana took the helmet from her grasp.

"I'm a scientist. I always think ahead." Alex patiently waited for her to slip behind her on the motorcycle and find the pegs for her feet. Mariana's movements were jerky. Not at all like the way she moved around the dance floor or in her lab. Every muscle in her body was tense. "Don't let me fall. I haven't slept and my body is exhausted."

"I would never let you fall. We can nap at my place. Plus, I would rather set up the cameras when the sun is down anyway." Alex grabbed Mariana's thighs and pulled her against her body. Mariana let out a quiet whimper and she almost threw her off the bike and ripped off her clothes in this dirt parking lot. "Hold on tight."

Mariana wrapped her hands around Alex's waist. Touching has become so natural for them. Both falling into a rhythm. A push and pull. Every cell in Alex's body is being rightfully teased in the presence of her.

It is possible that Alex lurched the motorcycle forwards rougher than she usually would. She wanted to revel in the tight squeeze from Mariana. It was successful. Not only did she tighten her grip, but she also let out the cutest squeal.

"Your place is, um, nice." Mariana looked down at the dirty boots by the door and the piles of papers covering the coffee table. She clasped her hand tight in front of her body and walked slowly into the room.

Alex tossed both helmets onto the dining table. They clanked against a glass stained with a sliver of dried whiskey and a mostly empty bottle. She propped a leg on the edge of the couch and began to unbuckle her knife holsters.

"I don't get much company." Alex ran a hand through her hair. "Theres no food in my fridge. I can go get something if you are hungry."

Mariana shook her head. "I'm fine." She moved a stack of magazines to read the titles. They were all motorcycle related except one. The latest issue of National Geographic. "You subscribe to National geographic."

"I don't." Alex paused for a beat. "An archelogy team recently dug up an area of interest."

Mariana raised her eyebrows and crossed her arms. She was drawing a line for Alex. Either open up to me or I am walking away. The tension thickened in the air. Mariana cleared her throat and Alex continued. "There was a mine collapse in 1948. The Istrian Coal Mines. I am from that region originally."

"You mean, before you were a vampire?"

"I have lived in many places before I was a vampire. I have had many names and many homes. I've only had one anchor for as long as I can remember.

Adonis. He found me in my mother's arms when I was very small. My mother had already passed away from disease. I wouldn't have lasted the night."

"Wow, a vampire showing an act of mercy."

Alex laughed and fell onto the couch. "Mercy? No. Adonis saw an opportunity. He kept me fed and educated, but he also trained me to lure humans for him to feed on. Vampires were few back then and scattered around the world. Working individually to cover their tracks until Adonis teamed up with the previous King to expand Shade. It was more of a gang in the beginning. He had the vision to make it global."

Mariana paced the room. She took her hair out of the ponytail and moaned with relief.

"How did Adonis become King?"

"I can't tell you that story." Alex became hypnotized by the swish of Mariana's hips.

"Can't or won't?" She smiled over her shoulder as she fluffed out the kink in her hair.

"It is not my story to tell. You would have to ask Adonis himself.

"Can I take a shower before I crash on your bed? I smell like werewolf." Mariana sniffed her arm.

She smelled like fur, and dried sweat, and the strong hand soap she kept in her lab. Alex nodded. Words died on her tongue as she led Mariana towards the shower. Every time their eyes met; Alex wondered if it was an invitation to join her. Mariana took the towel from Alex's hand and shut the door. Alex did not hear the lock click. She stood frozen outside the door.

Is this one of those moments that she should have courage? Is Mariana testing her to see if she will make a move? Did Mariana want her to make a move?

Alex scrubbed her hands over her face. The water was running, and she could hear her feet padding on the wet tile.

Alex decided to test the waters.

She opened the door and announced herself. "I just need to brush my teeth." Mariana hummed in response. She was leaning back shampooing her hair. Alex approached the vanity cautiously. One would think her toothbrush might bite her with the way she moved. Her hand moved robotically as she looked in the mirror. White suds ran down Mariana's back and over the curve of her ass.

"Do you like what you see?"

Mariana's question had Alex stumble when spitting in the sink. "Fuck yes."

Mariana laughed.

Alex cleaned the toothpaste from the corners of her mouth. She turned to the shower. It was large enough for two although Alex has never tested that theory. Any partner she has had for the past thirty years has been in a hotel and the occasional alley behind a bar. Mariana turned her body to face Alex.

Water ran down her full breast and over her soft stomach. Mapping the most beautiful rivers Alex had ever seen. She wanted to live and die on those curves.

"Join me."

Alex feared it was a voice in her head. That the words were a symptom of sleep deprivation and whiskey. It wasn't until Mariana repeated the request that she took a step towards the shower.

"Join me."

Heightened speed came in handy as Alex stripped and sprung under the water.

The space between them might as well been miles long. It was filled with every unspoken word. Every awkward smile. Every stolen glance. Mariana closed her eyes and casually rinsed the suds from her hair. It was a pine scented 2-in-1 shampoo conditioner combination. Alex frowned internally at the thought of the rose water scent she had grown to obsess over being washed away.

While Mariana's arms were still on her head, pressing the water down her long hair, Alex stepped closer until their breasts touched. Without shoes Mariana was only an inch taller, but her body had all the curves that Alex lacked.

Alex moved her hands over her slick waist and clasped them behind her. Mariana lowered her arms to rest on Alex's shoulder and pressed their foreheads together. Together they sucked in a slow breath.

"Who's Jordan?"

Mariana pulled her face back and stared with wide eyes.

"You choose this moment to ask about my ex?" She narrowed her eyes. "How did you ger that name anyway?"

"I need to know if there is anyone else in the picture before I-" The words died on Alex's tongue. "Before we go any further. I know most vampires have a reputation of fucking anything and often. I prefer a connection. Commitment."

"I see." Mariana moved her hands from Alex's shoulders to her hips. The shower created a spray that was sticking to her lashes. Alex blinked and for a moment it looked like she was crying. "Jordan and I broke up when I took this job. We met years ago on the same research team. I was offered this opportunity from Gibbard and Jordan didn't want to more with me. I understood why. They have a great job in California. And it comes with better weather, and the beach."

Alex gently pushed Mariana out of the path of the water. She pressed her against the white subway tiles and let their bodies meet like puzzle pieces.

"If you hadn't taken this job, you would still be with him." Alex tucked the wet hair behind Mariana's neck and leaned in. Her lips grazed her skin that was reddened from the hot shower. She smiled as her pulse increased after a gentle kiss. Alex was uncertain if Mariana was looking for love and if there was a chance she could feel that for a vampire. Her instincts tell her Mariana was just curious. That she has been swept up in recent adventures and adrenaline was making her horny for the closest person. Even a dangerous one.

Mariana shook her head. "We had been falling apart for the last year. This job offer gave me the courage I needed to leave. I was always second to Jordan's work."

"Jordan is an idiot." Alex took this moment to collide with Mariana's lips. Their wet bodies rubbing against each other. Alex slipped a hand between them over the small triangle patch of hair between Mariana's legs. Alex slid one finger down the middle. Mariana instinctively opened her legs wider.

"She is." Mariana answered breathlessly between kisses.

Alex paused for a moment. She leaned back a few inches to scan face. Her fingers continue to explore Mariana's body. "She?"

"Don't get me wrong, Alex. You are fucking hot. I have no doubt you could seduce anyone, but you did not start a bi-awakening for me. I have dated men and women since I was 19."

"My ego will never recover." Alex said dryly.

Mariana kissed her cheek and jaw. "Let me make it feel better." She took Alex's earlobe in her mouth and rubbed it with the barbell in her tongue.

"Fuck." Alex moaned. She pressed two fingers inside Mariana before quickly pulling them out." I need you under me now."

Mariana laughed. "I am not getting on the floor of the shower."

Alex reached to the side and turned the water off. With small movements she opened the door to the shower and let it swing out. Everything felt too slow. Alex needed her now. She cupped her hands behind both thighs and lifted Mariana off her feet. She crossed her legs behind Alex's back.

"Careful, I am not exactly a small woman." Mariana blushed.

"Good thing I am fucking strong because I plan on putting you in all sorts of positions."

"Oh." Mariana's voice went higher as Alex sprinted into the bedroom carrying her. Careful not to slip with her wet feet.

Mariana yelped when thrown onto the bed. Her wet hair slapping against the unmade sheets. Alex moved quickly. Opening her legs and leaning down. She placed a single kiss above her core before looking up with blazing red eyes.

Mariana's pulse quickened. Alex grinned. The view of her fangs had Mariana holding her breath.

"I told you I would never hurt you." She winked. "I only want to cause you pleasure."

Mariana let out her breath and nodded. Alex looked between Mariana's legs and began to savor every inch of her sex until she was left shaking on the bed. When her screaming stopped, Alex gave her a moment to compose herself and started again.

The bed sheets stuck to their damp skin as they napped in a tangle of limbs. The afternoon had come and gone. Alex woke moments ago when her phone buzzed across the room. Still tucked in the back pocket of her jeans that were thrown on the floor in a frenzy earlier. She wanted to ignore it. Ignore the world outside of this room for as long as possible. Mariana was getting much needed rest after working in her lab all night. Alex was able to sleep for a solid three hours, which is plenty to keep a vampire going for a while.

Her phone buzzed again, and she flashed "piss off" with her fingers. A British hand gesture that she picked up a century ago. Followed by a quiet groan. Angrier that a phone call would wake Mariana. Or worse they could just show up at her door.

Alex moved her body like a trapped snake. First,

she slithered out from under Mariana's leg that was draped over hers. Next, she rolled her body off the bed and onto her feet. Barely making a sound. The pads of her feet moved gracefully over the rug. She grabbed a stack of clean laundry and her phone. It buzzed as she picked it up. Mariana stirred behind her but didn't wake up.

Alex shut the door behind her and threw the clothes on the couch. She swiped her phone screen on and began to get dressed. The same grey faded jeans with holes in the knees and a t shirt she got at a truck stop years ago. It had a woman in an American flag bikini riding the oil tank on the back of a big rig. She had ripped the sleeves off to make it even more trashy.

Her phone blinked as a fourth message from James came through.

"Paul thinks he was underground. All he could smell was dirt."

"And rust. Lots of rust."

"He stayed in the same location. He was kept in a concrete room with no light or windows, food came through a small opening in the door. He could smell humans, wolves, and vampires when they opened the door."

"Alex, if you don't answer I am going to find the bastards myself."

She picked up her sunglasses off the table and walked outside. Three dots appeared but she called him before another text could come through.

"You have no idea what I walked away from to call your annoying ass." She spoke through her teeth.

"Sorry to break up your honeymoon." James was

walking and the snores of his brother became quieter. "Paul was tranquilized when the van took him. He woke up in the cell and was there for weeks."

"Does he remember anything from the night they transformed him?"

"Yes. Paul thinks they drugged his food. He woke up strapped to a table. They kept a bag over his head."

James described every scent Paul noticed. A conversation humans would never have, but describing scents was as common as describing food when it came to a werewolf and vampire. Humans rarely notice if the air is bitter or sour. If a room is more humid than usual. If there is blood forty feet away.

Alex made mental notes. Stainless steel, concrete, blood, urine, fur, and rust. Rust is not common in a medical facility. Paul only scented it after hearing a heavy door open. She thought about the junkyard where they fought.

"All the wolves must be under the junkyard in Albuquerque. I am going there tonight to set up cameras." Alex heard a door shut in the house. She peaked through the window and saw the bathroom light was on and the bed empty.

"Why not just raid the place?" James clenched his fists. "Why wait?"

"Before I tear the building apart looking for the remaining wolves. I need evidence to show," she paused "The vampire King."

"For all we know the bastard is behind this. The bitch works for him after all."

Alex growled. "He would never. It goes against his code." She had to stop herself from crushing her phone. There was an involuntary urge to protect

Adonis. Protect his life and his reputation. It started weeks after he turned her. A side effect that he had not warned her about. She could never go against him. She could never harm him. Although she found a way to cause him pain by staying far away. Pushing him out of her personal life. It was the only power she had against him.

"Fine. Whatever." James grunted. The tone in his breath gave the sign the subject was far from over.

Alex knew after she freed the wolves and captured Imani she would need to find Adonis. Whether that meant saving him from wherever Imani stashed him or pulling him out of the bed from a month-long orgy, she did not know. As much as she did not want to see her father in bed with anyone, she hoped for the latter.

"I am heading to the junk yard as soon as the sun sets." Alex walked back into the house and nearly dropped her phone. Mariana was leaning against the wall with one leg up while she fastened the strap on her sandal. She had changed into an orange dress that hugged her hips. The V shaped neckline showcased her full cleavage.

"Alex?" James shouted through the speaker. "Did you hear what I said?"

"Um, no."

"I thought vampires had super hearing."

"I have to go." She licked her lips.

"I asked, do you need backup?" He blurted out.

Mariana stood straight and smiled at Alex. The possibility of happiness and love filling her face. Alex felt it rise within. When did she fall for this woman? Was it the moment she broke into her lab? The first or second time she barged into her apartment. Or was it the dance? Is it possible to fall for someone this fast? Her mind went back to when she met Anita. They both knew in an instant.

"Keep your phone close. I'll let you know if I need you to get Mariana out of the state."

"What about you?"

"Don't worry about me." Alex watched the edges of Mariana's lips turn down. She was only getting one side of the conversation, but she did not like what Alex said. "I'll check in after I clear it out. Maybe find a van or some way to transport all the wolves. I will tell you when I am ready."

"Alright."

"Now go bark at the moon or something."

"Bye, asshole."

"Bye, pup." She hung up. Mariana placed a hand on her hip and gave a crooked smile. "What?"

She was digging through a backpack that had the Gibbard logo on it. She pulled out a small perfume roller and ran it up the sides of her neck and inside her wrists.

"You guys are cute."

"Ew, what? If I wasn't very clear, he's not my type." Her eyes trailed the tight dress and stopped below her belly button.

Mariana stepped closer then stopped. Alex closed the gap between them until their bodies met. She threw her head back and closed her eyes. Alex inhaled deeply through her nose.

"I mean, you act like old friends." She placed her arms on Alex's shoulders and clasped her hands behind her neck.

"He's a new friend." Alex lowered her head. Their eyes met and the room melted away.

"Why do vampires eyes do that? Flash bright red sometimes." Her voice was soft and sultry. Alex kissed the tip of her nose playfully. She saw the bright red of her eyes reflected in the dark pools of Mariana's.

"It happens when our emotions are spiking. Anger, fear, or pain can cause it." Alex touched the tip of a fang with her tongue. Heat bloomed between them as Mariana watched the movements of her tongue. "Or hunger." She moved her tongue from her teeth to her lips. "Or lust."

"What are you feeling now?" Mariana said pushing out a slow breath.

"I'm fucking starving."

"Oh." Mariana tried to pull away, but Alex grabbed her waist and held her in place. Alex was smaller, but she had triple the strength in her and years of fighting training. Mariana could not get away if she tried. "Should I get you a blood bag?"

"That's not what I need." Alex pressed her against the wall. The kiss was rough. She struggled to control her passion. Mariana whimpered when she hit the wall then followed it with a moan as Alex slipped her tongue into her mouth. Alex needed this. How has she denied herself for so long? Although if she was fucking around like most vampires, she would not have met Mariana. The most gorgeous woman on the planet. The most brilliant. The only person she has wanted to open to since-

The thought of Anita pulled Alex out of the moment. She wanted to reach for her flask but chose to reach for Mariana instead. She was stronger than any whiskey. Alex ran her hand over her heavy breast, and everything was right again. Breaking the kiss, she licked down her jaw to her neck.

"I'm going back to the junkyard. To set up cameras and then try to lure the workers out before entering. Hopefully the missing werewolves are inside."

"Ok. When do we leave?"

Alex peeled her body off. Immediately feeling empty. She walked over to her table and grabbed her knives and a gun. Mariana watched as Alex strapped weapons all over her body.

"*We* aren't doing anything. I am leaving you at your lab. Where there are armed guards."

"Armed guards that you took out by yourself."

"Right." She rubbed the back of her neck. I will take you to James's pack. You will be safe on his commune."

"Fine. Drop me off at my car and I will drive to the pack myself."

Alex scoffed. She sheathed the twin knives at her thighs and stood straight. "No, way. Encino is on my way to Albuquerque."

"Well, I want my car. And I want to grab a few notebooks before I get shut out of Gibbard for associating with the vampire trying to ruin their project." She crossed her arms, and Alex did not appreciate the attitude but loved the way she propped up her chest. "They may view it as stealing, but I don't care. They offered me this job without telling me it was part of an illegal scheme to control supernaturals'. These breakthroughs are due to my elbow grease. I am not giving it up without a fight."

Despite being proud of Mariana's act of rebellion, she still grumbled her response. Alex was hoping Mariana could get out without a target on her back. "Fine. You get in and out of your lab in ten minutes and drive straight to the pack. Understand?"

"I love when you give orders." She winked.

Alex was used to receiving orders. From Adonis since she was a child. Followed by numerous trainers as she joined Shade. Then Imani when she was on her task force. She even took orders from Anita. Anita had always decided when to host gambling parties. Whether the hive needed a new human. Anita was the one that wanted to stay in New York City even though Alex preferred to move around.

Alex took her phone out of her pocket and texted James. "James will be expecting you. It takes one hour to drive from Santa Rosa to Encino. If I do not hear from you in ninety minutes, I am calling Sherrif Gefahr. Do you understand?"

"Yes Ma'am." Mariana saluted. Alex rolled her eyes.

"Fuck, you are going to look so hot on my bike in that dress."

"Oh, please can we take your truck?" She pressed her hands together.

"I'm just teasing. My truck is quieter, and I can fit more weapons in the back." Alex slapped Mariana's butt as she passed. The sun was dipping below the horizon. She grabbed a duffle bag of camera equipment and followed Mariana outside.

Alex hung off the side of a building. The tips of her boots rested on a small ledge as she attached the third and final camera to a gutter on a building across from the junkyard. She checked her phone for the twelfth time. No message from Mariana or James.

She hit the ground and let out a low growl. Mariana should have arrived at the commune fifteen minutes ago. Accounting for the stop Mariana made at a market to pick up snacks and a Topa Chica. If Alex was trailing her, the market would have been the perfect place to grab her. She kept that thought to herself. Fear of being an overprotective… lover? Friend? Alex was not sure where she stood with Mariana. She was afraid to screw it up.

This is the first time since Anita died, Alex has felt the desire to be close to anyone. Not just physically, but emotionally. She has fucked plenty but would slip out while they slept. Alex never exchanged phone numbers. Never went back for round two. However, with Mariana, every word out of her mouth is seducing. Even when explaining something she called Clustered Regularly Interspaced whatever it was.

Alex sent a text to James.

> One of your pups had better have swallowed Mariana's phone. What the fuck is going on?

Three text dots appeared and disappeared. Alex crouched behind a park car. The warehouse district she was in had very little traffic at night. She set the phone on the pavement between her legs. Alex took the gun off her belt clip and turned the safety off. She had one pistol, two extra clips, her twin blades strapped to her thighs, and a short blade tucked into her right boot.

Enough to take on a band of moderately trained vampires. Not enough for an army. Especially if werewolves are involved. Their movements are so animalistic when they fight. It is hard for Alex to predict. All her training is not much help.

A message popped up on her screen.

> Thor has people waiting for her at the gates. Paul is still recovering. Whatever Mariana did took away his wolf traits.

Heightened scent, sight, hearing, and strength… I am out looking for Mariana now.

Alex refrained from crushing her phone as she picked it up. A camera alert popped up and she swiped it away.

Looking? You better fucking find her James.

I will.

I'm coming back. I can watch the camera feed from there.

James responded quickly.

Stay I can find her.

"You couldn't even find your brother." Alex mumbled to herself. Another camera alert popped up. She ignored it.

I will find her.

Alex moved her thumb to hit send and felt a sharp pain in her neck followed by another in her arm. She dropped the phone and hissed. Rising to her feet, she blinked forcefully. Her vision was tunneling.

"Fuck." Imani stood down the sidewalk with a long-range gun in her hand. Alex stepped wobbly in her direction and was greeted with another sharp pain in her leg. She looked down at the silver dart sticking out of her flesh.

"Nice to see you, Alexandrine." Imani let the gun hang from a strap on her shoulder. "I thought I was going to have to track you down, but you made this so easy for me. Delivering yourself to my door."

Tranquilizers only work on vampires for a short time and require a high dose. The three darts were strong enough to take down a werewolf. She had three of them coursing through her veins.

Alex stumbled against the car. Her motor skills failing by the second.

Imani strolled casually towards her.

Alex had streams of words she wanted to say, but her mouth would not obey. The last thing she saw before everything went dark was the sharp smile of her former commander.

Zip ties are easy to break. Rope can be torn with the strength of most vampires. Steel on the other hand, requires more force than Alex possesses at this angle.

She woke up from a haze and found herself in an unfamiliar science lab. Her legs were chained to the metal legs of a chair. She struggled against the pressure pulling her arms behind her. Shackles bound her wrists and were connected to the chains from her legs behind her back. The overhead lighting was dim, as if the room was using a weak generator. Illuminating her space which was nothing but a large glass box. Surrounded by a larger box of concrete walls that create a hallway on each side. Grey windowless doors were spaced about twelve feet apart along three of the walls. The forth had a narrow set of stares that blended into the grey. There was a faint smell of fur and blood in the air. Along with the chemicals that Marina used to keep her lab sterile. But this space lacked any of the warmth in Mariana's lab.

Alex moaned. She rolled her neck. All her weapons and her phone were gone.

Imani walked into the room, flanked by the same two henchmen she had in the club.

"Good your awake." Imani's hair was braided tight against the sides of her head before forming a thick braided mohawk that hung down her back. She was wearing her usual Shade attire. Black pants with leather patches over the knees and built in holders for various weapons. On top she wore a black leather tank with a high neck. The leather looked liquid as she moved around the low light. Imani leaned against an exam table. The kind used during surgeries. It had built in shackles for limbs and one large one at the neck.

"When did you become a mad scientist, Imani?" She tugged against the chains to test how much room she had. When she pulled her arms, it made the chains on her legs go taught.

"I am hardly a scientist, Princess." Imani nodded to the large man with a crooked nose and scars covering his knuckles. Without a word he walked out of the glass room and up a set of concrete stairs. There were beeps on a keypad followed by a heavy door. "What I am, is someone who can see potential and has a vision for a greater future."

"By making werewolves into soldiers and using your own blood to keep old rich Generals alive longer." Alex wanted to spit at her feet, but her mouth was as dry as the desert outside.

"Oh child."

"I'm older than you bitch."

Imani waved a hand. "Only by a few years."

"Wait until-"

"Until what? Until dearest daddy the King hears about this." She scoffed. "I already have him. He's been in a state of near death for almost a year."

No. Alex shouted in her head. The bond ignited the urge to protect him. "What did you do?"

"Did you know if you drain a vampire of their blood until they are comatose, you can give them just enough blood to keep them alive and producing. That is the key. I need him to keep producing blood. Taking in the week human blood and infusing it with all the things that make us the better species. My blood is good, but his truly is the best. But I don't have to tell you that. It's coursing through you now. Can you feel the power? Can you feel it's control?"

"I will fucking kill you." Alex bites out.

"I have no doubt you will try. That is why your skinny ass is chained to that chair." Imani pulled a phone from her pocket and Alex's eyes went wide in recognition it was hers.

"All this for money? Power?"

"Those things and so much more." She walked behind Alex and bent over to press Alex's finger to the screen. Imani hummed in satisfaction when it unlocked the phone. Alex's chest rumbled holding in a growl. She almost smiled at the thought of how much she sounded like James at that moment. He would be snarling like a beast. "I have been working on my own organization for almost fifty years. Shade is not the future. Adonis has always been consumed with hiding and being secretive. I want us to rule."

"You're psychotic and greedy."

Imani's fingers swiped on the phone screen. A fang filled smile spread across her face. "You and the hot doctor have been chatting a lot. Why don't we give her a call? See if she wants to come hang out."

"Leave her out of this, you bitch." Alex tugged against the chains until her shoulder popped. She grunted and popped it back into place. Imani dialed Mariana. Silence filled the air. Thick and cold. The door at the top of the stairs opened.

First, Alex heard the ringing of a phone echoing off the stairway. Then, she smelt woody pine from her own bodywash. Alex hissed and pressed with her feet until she moved off the ground a few inches. The chair hit at an odd angle and knocked her to the ground. Her head hit the hard floor, and she grunted again. Her arms pinned painfully under the cold chair. Imani snapped her fingers at the human man in the room. He went to lift Alex up and she chomped her teeth by his forearm.

"The bitch is trying to bite me."

Imani rolled her eyes. "Pick her up from behind. Stay clear of her teeth."

Alex was brought upright in the chair just as Mariana stepped down the stairs and into the glass room. Her hands were bound behind her back. Grey tape covered her mouth.

"You don't need her. Let her go." Alex growled.

"Because of you, the Sherrif, and pretty doctor here, we need to move our operation. But I can't have you two running your mouths." Imani dropped Alex's phone on the ground and stomped it with the heel of her boot. She pulled another phone out and typed a message. "Killing you won't be a waste. I am going to drain your blood and use it to keep an old rich man alive while he pads my pockets with obscene amounts of wealth."

While Imani talks, Alex moves her fingers to cradle the large lock holding the chains together. The pads of her fingertips trace a keyhole. A plan forming inside her head.

A scream was born and died behind the tape over Mariana's mouth. She was struggling against the large vampire, but his body didn't budge.

Imani slithered to stand before her. Mariana's eyes were glossy. Tears pooling in the corners. She flinched and screamed again as Imani traced her neck with two fingers. Imani paused her touch over the pulsing vein. Marking the perfect spot with two taps.

"Don't touch her." Alex threatened through her teeth.

Mariana's eyes pleaded for Alex to do something. Anything. Alex had promised to keep her safe. All she wanted was to solve a case for a friend and keep Mariana out of the crossfire. Caring for people has always been a distraction. A weakness. But now, having Mariana, Jules, and even James in her life is driving her forward. Building a wildfire inside her that she refuses to let Imani put out.

"I am going to do far more than that." Imani pointed to a grey door across from the glass room. The vampire yanked Mariana. Her feet dragged on the concrete as he threw her into the dark room. "I am late for a client meeting. When I get back. I am going to drain you dry and then turn your girlfriend into my newest pet. Imagine that. Your woman, loyal to me, forever."

"I am going to rip your head off."

Alex saw no evidence in her long lifetime that Hell existed. She imagined it would be this. Her blood drained to the near point of death. Hanging on by the thread that makes them immortal. While knowing the woman she loves is bound to a vile vampire that she hates. Forever. Whether Imani wants her to be a lover or suicide bomber, Mariana would not be able to refuse.

Alex was straining against the chains so hard it broke her skin. She considered ripping her own hand off to get free. But she would still be stuck to the chair. If she let her anger make the plans there could be no good outcome. She would fight injured and sloppy. Solving nothing. She let out a raspy hiss at Imani who just smiled in response.

Alex did have a way out of the chains. She just needed Imani and her goons to leave.

"Maybe I will keep you alive long enough to watch her pledge herself to me." The phone in her had vibrated. She exhaled and straightened. "See you in few hours."

The vampire finished locking Mariana in the room from a keypad. There was no door handle or latch. No keyhole or window. Just a metal sheet with a slit near the floor large enough to fit a tray of food. Imani headed up the stairs. Her henchmen trailed behind.

When Alex had been a vampire for only a few years Adonis taught her a trick.

"We heal fast and without scars." He said sitting next to her on a park bench. It was just after a spring sunset in Paris. "Do you feel the space between these two tendons?" He pressed a thumb onto her forearm. Alex nodded. Adonis pulled a small paring knife from his pocket. He gripped her forearm tight underneath. Exposing her pale skin to the moon beginning illuminate. He flipped the knife in his hand and pointed the handle at her.

"You want me to cut myself?" He nodded. She hesitated for only a second before following his command and taking the knife. She would stab herself in the throat if he asked. She would survive, get up, and ask if she stabbed herself to his approval. He had not told her about the bond before he turned her. She had al-

ready grown to see him as a father by that point. The knowledge she would feel physically ill if she became disloyal would not have deterred her from wanting to be turned. He gave her a choice and she chose him. She chose a life at his side, and never questioned it. Until thirty years ago. She still needed his permission to disappear. He had told her to take all the time she needed to heal but come back to him someday.

"Cut an incision between these tendons about three inches long." He traced the spot with the tip of his sharp nail.

Alex lined up the tip of the knife. She pressed and let out a hiss. Instinct had her pull the blade away. The centimeter she cut healed before their eyes. Adonis took a white handkerchief from his pocket and wiped away the blood. "Try again. Go deeper and be quick."

Alex closed her eyes and counted.

One.

Inhale.

Two.

Exhale.

Three.

She sliced the blade into her arm. Biting her bottom lip hard enough to fill her mouth with the copper taste of her own blood. Adonis quickly pulled a small metal rod from his pocket and pressed it into her wound. She gasped. Small drops of blood dripped from her fangs.

"Good." Adonis smiled. "Now you know how to hide a lock pick on your body. I suggest putting one in the other arm too, just in case."

With each bang on the metal door from Mariana, Alex grew more heated. She rubbed her arm against the edge of the metal chair. Finding the tool hidden under her skin. "This is gonna suck." She mumbled to herself.

She had nothing sharp to dig it out, but that is why Adonis had her go through extensive training with pain tolerance. For moments like this that require mutilating oneself for a mission.

The metal chair was cold against her skin. She angled her body with one armpit on the top of the chair so her other arm could reach the edge of the back. She moved her forearm back and forth until she felt the edge catch on something long and sharp in her arm. Alex repeated the motion until her skin broke. A few drops of blood escaped before it began to mend quickly.

It was not enough. Alex needed more leverage. More sharpness.

She used all her strength to pinch the back edge of the chair back. The hallow aluminum frame flattened enough to create an angle sharp enough to work. She rubbed her forearm over it again, placing the start of the tool on the edge.

Mariana banged on the door.

Alex yelled. "I'm coming, babe."

Babe? Did I just call her babe?

The banging stopped. Either her words calmed Mariana down, or she was stunned into silence by her using a pet name.

Once Alex felt she was in the right position she pressed again. Sliding her arm across the sharp edge while applying pressure. The lock pick poked through her skin. She moved her arm down and squeezed it out. Like kneading dough. Once the metal shard was free, she caught it in her palm before it hit the floor. Alex let out a heavy breath.

Going to work on the lock at once. Praying to any God that the blood coating it will not cause it to slip from her fingers.

"Almost," She grunted. The lock clicked and fell to the ground. The chains fell from her legs and wrists. "Fuck yeah. Thanks Adonis."

Leaping out of the room she headed for a large control panel. She has seen these before in underground Shade holding facilities. Alex opened the menu to find a list of cells with names next to their numbers. All the missing wolves and a few vacant. Quickly she smashed buttons until each door popped open with a mechanical click.

She glanced up the stairs. "I'm coming Imani." She whispered then looked to the door holding Mariana and shouted. "I'm coming."

lex expected to find withering humans that were weak from poor conditions. Instead, she was greeted by three angry werewolves in their wolf forms. They prowled out of their cells with eyes ablaze. Mariana stepped one foot into the hallway and shuffled back in after hearing their growls.

Her only hope was that Imani's crew left behind tranquilizers. She moved quickly around the glass room and opened every drawer and cabinet. Time was up and she had no luck. Mariana yelled for help and Alex rushed into her dark room. Without tranquilizers, Alex would need to find another way to stop the wolves. Knowing communicating in their wolf form was not an option, and none of them would recognize her by scent.

Alex found Mariana crouched in the corner. A large

white wolf was stalking closer. It sniffed the air and whipped its neck to face Alex who stood in the doorway.

"Easy." She lifted her palm towards the wolf. "You don't want us. We let you out."

The wolf lowered its head. She noticed it was female. "Jolene? That's your name, right?"

The wolf leaped onto Alex. She was knocked into the hallway and cracked the glass wall with her back. The wolf slashed with its claws. Alex put her arms up to block her face. Her forearms took all the damage. They bled onto the floor.

"I don't have time for this Jolene." Alex pushed the werewolf off her body and kicked with all her strength on the side of the wolfs skull. Jolene flew across the room and hit the concrete wall with a loud thump. Alex cringed. Hoping the sound was normal impact and not Jolene's neck snapping. She wanted to pause long enough to hear a heartbeat, but the other wolves had other plans.

She groaned at her shredded arms, and it drew the attention of the two remaining wolves. They were at the top of the stairs sniffing loudly at the base of the door. Eager to follow the scent of their captors. The commotion behind them drew their attention. Slowly they mirrored each other and turned to face Alex. "Fuck." She murmured.

Mariana continued to cower in the dark corner of the cell. She still had tape over her mouth and her hands bound behind her back. Alex looked around for her knives. They were not in sight. She stepped slowly under the gaze of the two wolves. The gashes on her body were closing. It was using a lot of fuel and soon she would need blood to be at full strength to fight Imani.

Alex sprinted into the room with Mariana. She lifted her to her feet and ripped the tape off.

"Ouch."

"Sorry." Alex pulled at the rope until it began to tear. Within seconds she ripped it off and threw it across the room. They watched as two wolves filled the doorway. Their golden eyes glowing in the dim light. "Stay behind me."

"Duh." Mariana rolled her eyes.

Alex guided Mariana to stand behind her and she hunched lower. Reluctantly she moved her hand from Mariana's hip. Her red eyes beamed bright red. The wolves growled in unison. Slowly they moved forward with a dangerous intent behind every step. The air seemed to lack oxygen. Lacking what was necessary to stay alive. Mariana rubbed at the raw rope burns on her wrists. Quick breaths escaped her swollen lips.

Alex whispered over her shoulder. "I won't let them touch you. Do you trust me."

"More than a sane woman should." She whispered back.

"Get back in the corner and stay there." Alex didn't wait for them to lunge. She moved before one in a blink and kicked his snarling jaw. Twisting her body from the path of slashing claws on the other. Alex met them head-on, her movements a blur. She kept their focus on her and led them out of the dark room and into the hall. The concrete walls echoed the sounds of snarls and the occasional screech from their claws striking the stone. Alex had no weapons. She would hit hard enough to hear a bone crack but was not able to break their skin under the thick fur. Her body was streaked with red slashes. Adrenaline busy using all her resources to heal as quickly as possible. She jumped over an attack and her head collided with the overhead light. It hung from a white wire with the florescent rod blinking.

Alex reached up and grabbed the rod and smashed the edge against the ground. The metal cap was replaced with a sharp tip as it broke off. The space outside the glass lab darkened. She ran towards a wolf and slid on her back as he leaped up. Alex plunged the light rod into his gut. The wolf let out a haunting cry. A blend of human and animal pitch.

She staggered to her feet. The bloody light rod dripped in her hands. The single wolf left lowered his head. A growl rumbled deep in his throat.

"I don't want to hurt you." Alex tried to make her voice sound calm and soothing. Mimicking Adonis. "I am not with the vampires who-'

She stopped talking as the wolf took steps away from her direction and towards the room where Mariana was hiding. The wolf ran into the darkness. Alex's feet flew over the bleeding wolf on the ground as she sprinted after him. He had just reached Mariana when Alex grabbed the fur on his back and yanked hard. Patches of fur ripped out and she fell back on her ass. The light rod shattered. He turned from Mariana and pounced on Alex. His strong jaw clamped down on her shoulder.

A screaming grunt ricocheted off the walls.

"What do I do?" Mariana yelled.

Alex punched the wolf in the eye. He released her shoulder and snarled in her face. She reached into his mouth and grabbed his jaw. Prying his mouth wide. Drops of saliva hit her cheek. His sharp teeth bit into her hands.

"Look away!" Alex stretched his mouth until the tension pushed back. The wolf dug his claws into her sides. She felt her left lung get punctured and heard a rib crack on her right side. He pressed with all his weight until more bones inside her snapped.

The pain had her vision flashing white. If she were human, she would be dead. Lightning spread in her chest with every breath. She looked past him to see Mariana in the corner. Watching every gruesome movement and hearing every snap of bones. She did not want Mariana to see this. To see what she was about to do. Despite what Alex was doing, Mariana looked at her with hope. Hope that one day, if Alex didn't screw it up, could become something that looks like love.

Time was slipping away. The fight had gone on long enough.

Alex screamed into the face of the wolf as she tore his jaws apart. Muscles ripped. Tendons snapped. His head became a bloody gash. Blood poured onto her body, and she flung him to the side. Nothing could survive this. She had ripped his head in half. The wolf's chest rose twice slowly before it stopped mid breath.

Mariana emerged slowly from the shadowed corner. Her hands were shaking. She was biting her bottom lip with wide eyes fixated on the dead wolf.

Alex rolled onto her back with a painful grunt. "I didn't want to kill them."

Mariana knelt next to her. Alex lay in a pool of blood. Much of it hers. She attempted to sit up, but her broken body protested.

"I know." Mariana placed a hand on Alex's chest. She traced her ribs gently. "You have many broken ribs, and I think your collarbone is broken as well."

"Also, a punctured lung." Alex coughed. She shivered from the pain. "Ouch, fuck."

"Will you heal from this?"

"Yes." Alex closed her eyes. "But it will take hours." She melted into the hard ground. Unable to move her overworked muscles. She escaped from chains and fought three full grown werewolves by herself. Two of which are confirmed dead. The pack would not be happy that their violent end came from her hands.

Surges of pain spread throughout her body. Blood vessels and veins were reconnecting. Nerve ending finding their severed half. Her muscles spasmed as they replaced torn sections.

"I will wait here with you. Unless you want me to find a phone and call James or the Sherrif." Mariana scanned the trashed space. Blood, fur, and broken glass was everywhere. She watched the male vampire slip her phone into his pocket earlier and Imani smashed Alex's phone. There was no land line in sight.

Mariana's eyes softened as she looked down and found Alex staring up at her. Her eyes were a dull red. This would be the perfect moment for Alex to confess she was falling for the scientist. That after all this shit was sorted out, the only thing she wanted to do was sit on her couch and talk. Then carry her to bed. Alex closed her eyes for a long second. She pictured them in her house and at Mariana's apartment. In hotels around the world. She pictured a lifetime with her within a quick thought.

"There is no time." She sucked in a breath through her teeth. Her ribs were lining up to mend the fractures. They twisted under her skin. "I need blood. Healing will take everything I have left and could take hours. Fresh blood will speed it up."

"Ok." Mariana jumped to her feet. The rubber on the bottom of her sneakers squeaked as she darted around the central room. She cursed under her breath when she opened every cabinet and didn't find anything suitable as cold storage. She ran back to Alex. "I could leave and find the closest, um, hospital. Where do you usually get blood?"

In her mind she was screaming from the pain. Her face tried to hide the agony, but she could tell by the gentle expression that Mariana could read her. They both took slow breaths in unison. An understanding between them beginning to harmonize.

Alex eyes fixated on Mariana's throat. An unsaid answer that felt like a scream. Instinctively Mariana placed a hand on the side of her neck. Her heart raced and pulse quickened. Alex turned her head away. Not willing to say what she needed aloud. Her shoulder popped. The broken collarbone setting in place. She grunted through the pain.

"Go find a clinic, be quick." Alex pinched her eyes shut. She tried to focus on the cold concrete under her. Focus on anything but the rhythm of blood pumping through Mariana's body. Pain lit through nerves. Causing her to shake for a few seconds.

Mariana was calm. She wiped her hands down on her lap. Straightening the wrinkles of her clothes as if preparing to present herself for judgement. Gently she moved her body to hover over Alex.

"Drink me." Her voice was soft and firm.

"No."

Alex grunted as another wave of pain spread through her. The red of her eyes have faded to be void of color. Mariana scrunched her brows together and softened her eyes. Alex wants so badly to be healed and wrap her arms around her. Kiss her soft lips. Thank her for her concern and then whisk her off to safety. She opened her mouth to speak but sucked in air instead as pain blasted through her body.

Marriana wiped Alex's hair off her cheek that was stuck with a mix of sweat and wolf blood.

"You said 'I won't bite you, unless you ask'. Well, I am asking now." Mariana leaned down but was stopped by Alex. She pressed a bloody hand against Mariana's chest and forced her body to sit upright. Every movement caused her to grunt and hiss through her teeth. As quick as her body allowed, she scooted against the wall and rested her head against the rough surface. Once again, she let her arms go limp. Painfully aware of the tendons that have not reconnected. She used all her strength to move away. Any more exertion and she could fall into a comatose state. Just as Imani wanted.

"I don't want to hurt you." Every word was painful to say. "I don't want to cause you pain."

Mariana crawled across the floor. The sight made Alex's heart skip a beat. She positioned herself to staddle Alex's thighs and leaned down until their noses touched. "Watching you like this is hurting me."

Mariana kissed her lips and lingered softly. She trailed down her jaw and up to her earlobe. Alex moved her sore arms, so her hands were placed on either side of Mariana's spine.

"Is this real?" Her voice shook. It was more of a plea than a question.

"This?" She nipped at her earlobe. "It feels real. It feels like it could be more. Like we are meant to be more."

"I don't trust my judgement. If I hurt you, nothing will be the same."

"I don't want the same. I want more." Mariana held her neck an inch from Alex's lips. "Now bite me. Heal. Then go kick that bitch's ass. So, I can have you all to myself for fuck's sake, Alex."

Alex closed her eyes and inhaled her floral scent. She pressed a kiss to her neck before opening her mouth and sinking her fangs deep.

ALEX

My fangs pierced the tender flesh of Mariana's neck, a wave of euphoria washed over me. Warm, tangy blood flowed into my mouth, igniting every nerve with electric pleasure. My arms wrapped around her instinctively. Sticking to her body from the remnants of the fight that coated my skin.

She whimpered from the pain.

I should pull away. But it feels so good to press against her.

I am hurting her. I never want to hurt her.

I should not be enjoying this. I don't want to stop.

Her taste is intoxicating. Better than anything that has passed over my tongue. Mariana gripped my thighs. Her nails digging into my blood-soaked jeans. Her pinky finger slipped through a rip and the contact from her skin caused my eyes to open wide.

This is not a dream. This was real. She was real.

And I was killing her.

I forced myself off her neck and gasped towards the ceiling. My mouth was coated with her blood. She does not realize what has happened. Yes, I am healing fast. But the biggest change is not of flesh and bone.

From this moment on, she is mine. My obsession. My everything.

I will be the only one to bask in her taste.

Mariana's eyes flickered shut. Her body went limp in my arms. I stood, cradling her to my chest. Her breathing was slow but steady. Licking her from my lips, I walked towards the exit.

43

Alex could hear a car alarm miles away in the city and smelled bratwurst being cooked in caramelized onions down the street. With a bit of focus, Alex could see street signs that the average human would need binoculars for. Her hands flexed. Every gash and break in her body was healed. She was stronger than before. The first time having fresh blood from a vein in years.

A cloud crossed in front of the moon. Casting a shadow over downtown Albuquerque. In one direction was the tower full of Gibbard offices. In the opposite was the highway towards Vaughn. Would Imani go after Jules or James? Did she head into her office for a client meeting?

Alex tilted her head back and inhaled the night air.

She sifted through the scents until a familiar cologne caught her attention. A hint of vanilla mixed with its musk.

"Gotcha."

Leaping off the building she followed the trail. She needed to focus on the task at hand, and not the unconscious woman she left on the steps of a nearby urgent care. *Mariana is safe.* She told herself. *But she will not be safe if Imani is still alive. Focus.*

The boost in her senses will only be temporary. One of the reasons vampires enjoy fucking after feeding. Everything is heightened. Every scent is stronger. Every touch is more intense.

She wove around stragglers on the sidewalks who stepped out of bars for a smoke. The cars were mere hurdles for her. She covered them in a single leap. A blur of fury to anyone watching.

Turning into an alley the scent hit her like a brick. *James.* She always teased him about smelling like a dog, but the truth is he smelled like the desert. Dirt that is rich in clay. Sweat that has dried on skin. And Agave flower. They surround the entire pack commune. The flower scent has permanently woven itself into the pack's hair. But she would never tell him that. She will continue to call him a dog.

He was trading blows with Imani's henchmen. Matched in size, but failing to keep up with the vampire's speed. He bounced between the human and the vampire, never getting out of a defensive position. Alex leaped out of a shadow and kicked one in the side. He slammed into a dumpster. James grinned like a fool.

"Where the fuck have you been?"

"Why are you here?" She caught the fist of the vampire before it struck her face and twisted out of his reach. Her focus remained on James.

"I came to help find Mariana." He grunted when a blow hit his gut. "Saw these assholes leaving the junkyard and followed them."

"Mariana is safe." Alex saw the moonlight reflect off twin blades in the humans' hands. She tilted her head. The predator awakens inside her. "Those are mine."

"Come and get them bitch."

She looked at him through her brows and smiled. He took a fighting stance that was not meant to be used in a knife fight. Confirming he was a boxer by trade. "With pleasure."

Alex moved quick enough to miss his awkward swinging of the blades. She toyed with him. Laughing on the inside as he struggled to keep up. Moving swiftly behind him when he slashed with her knife. She ran up his back and forced him to faceplant into the brick building. His nose crunched and blood gushed. The copper scent had her eyes glowing. She was still riding high from Mariana's blood. Her newly healed muscles far from being tired.

There was a faint trail of warm vanilla in the air. She could not tell if it was coming from him or if Imani was close by. He spun to face her. Alex latched herself onto his neck. She haphazardly tore his flesh. Making a wound larger than necessary to feed.

He stabbed both knives into her sides as a last attempt to get her off him. Her laugh made the blood on his neck bubble. When she felt his body weakened and his arms slack, she pulled away. Blood covered her chin. The man sunk to the ground. His back scrapping the rough wall.

Alex stood before him and pulled the knives from her flesh. The gashes healing before his eyes went still. His blood pulsed through her, knitting the wounds he inflicted. She sheathed the knives, coated in her own blood, in her thigh holsters.

"Thanks for the bump." Alex licked her lips. "Now, where's-"

A bullet ripped through her calf. Cutting off her sentence. She hissed. Blood sprayed from her mouth as she turned to face Imani.

Imani pulled the trigger again from twenty feet away. Alex dodged and it went into the chest of the man dying behind her. Alex shrugged. He was already dead. It would have been ironic if Imani had killed her own man.

James and the large vampire were still fighting behind Imani. She didn't flinch at the violent sounds behind her back. She kept her aim firm on Alex. Hand unshaking as it followed Alex's movements.

Alex's hands hovered over her knives. Itching to come out and play.

"You fucking cockroach." Imani spat. "I should have killed you when you were a child."

"Aren't you a guiding light for morality." Imani took two more shots. Alex moved in a blur. Grabbing her knives as she leaped over a dumpster. Putting a barrier between them. Fresh blood from Mariana and the dead man was coursing through her. Strengthening her muscles. She landed gracefully and rolled her neck.

"Fuck morality." Imani's steps were slow and light. She was trying to sneak around the large metal dumpster. Alex crouched low. "Adonis is the one who obeys human rules. Ask yourself, why would a predator live by the rules of their prey? Why wouldn't we control their armies? Their industries?"

Imani turned the corner with her gun drawn where Alex would be if she were standing. She slashed a knife against her leg and swept her feet. Imani hit the ground, the gun falling from her hand.

Alex moved towards her. Imani jumped to her feet in a fluid motion. She dodged Alex's attack effortlessly. Mirroring her movements with a gleam in her red eyes. Imani moved in a series of precise strikes. Alex found herself on the defense, despite the knives in her hands. Her left arm was cranked behind her back. Imani squeezed her wrist until the bone cracked. The knife fell between them.

"Fuck." Alex grunted. Imani kicked her spine, and she fell to her knees. Accidently trying to catch her body with her injured wrist. Alex rolled onto her back.

"You've gotten sloppy." Imani stood over her. Alex spat blood onto Imani's boots. Imani pressed her foot onto Alex's throat. Alex jabbed the knife into the leather. Piercing through her foot and throwing Imani to the ground.

With a deep snarl, Imani removed the knife and threw it to lodge into a wooden windowsill two stories up. Alex found herself weaponless once more.

They walked in a wide circle facing each other. Alex was waiting for the last fractures in her wrist to mend. Imani was doing the same with her leg.

"It's over Imani. Turn yourself over to Shade. The real Shade. Not your gang of greedy assholes." At the other end of the alley, James lay on his back. Covered in gashes and bruises next to a lifeless body. The vampire was face down in a pool of blood. The top of his spine protruded from his neck. Alex was proud and worried. James's heart rate was faint. She needed to end this fight. Get James to a hospital and check on Mariana.

"You may be a skilled tracker, but you are a shit detective." Imani smirked.

"I discovered what you were up to."

A sinister laugh spewed out of Imani. "Anita discovered it thirty years ago."

Alex tensed. Why was she bringing up Anita in the middle of this fight? Imani's cold stare taunted her. Her stance leveled out. No longer keeping pressure off the foot that was stabbed.

"What are you talking about?" She clenched her fists. The need for answers winning over the need to punch Imani.

"I orchestrated the attacks." Imani emphasized the word I with a fang filled grin spreading across her face.

Alex shook her head. "But you lead the task force to track down those involved. I saw the evidence myself."

She had. Using her training to track the attackers around the world and bring their heads to Imani. Imani, the one who trained her in those very skills. Her mind was spinning, and she longed for a long swig of whiskey to calm her thoughts. Then Mariana slid to the fore front. She needed to stay clear. She needed to focus. For Mariana. Because Mariana wants more from Alex and she wants nothing more than to see where things will go.

Alex narrowed her eyes at Imani and felt truly like herself for the first time in a long time. Strong and ready to fight.

Imani tossed her braids over her shoulder. "You saw what I wanted you to see. I used you to clean up my loose ends. Killing Anita was an unexpected necessity."

"She wasn't-" Alex felt her stomach rise. Rage burned red in her eyes.

"Anita was never involved." Imani stopped walking and crossed her arms. "Once I suspected she was onto me, I fed her clues that led to you and your precious King. I was hoping you would take each other out, but you killed her and then ran away like a sad puppy. You weren't dead, which was my first choice, but you no longer had the Kings ear. Thanks for that."

Alex needed something sharp. She needed to rip off her head. She needed to rampage.

"I-" Her vision tunneled. Imani in the center. "Killed her."

"Oh, I know. I remember you delivering her head like a trophy."

"For nothing." Her voice cracked.

Imani grinned. "For me."

Alex screamed like an animal.

Imani's eyes went wide as Alex charged into her chest. Pinning her against the dumpster. She bent to grab her legs and flipped her into the pile of trash. Reaching out to grab a river of braids from her head. Alex pinned her neck to the edge of the dumpster. A section she had noticed was dented into a sharp angle.

Imani could not get traction at the awkward angle. She kicked to find something to push off and only sank into the trash more. Alex reached down to grab one of her knives. The handle was sticking out next to the dumpsters wheel. She raised the blade and came down onto Imani's neck.

"For Anita." She growled through her teeth. The impact of her severing Iman's head had her crashing to the ground. Fist still tight around Imani's hair.

She let herself soak up everything that had happened. All the revelations. All the wounds. Then she sat up and tossed Imani's head into the dumpster.

Mariana. She sucked in a slow breath.

She needed to check on Mariana. A grunt from the other end of the alley reminded her she was not alone.

Alex walked down the Alley towards James. She stood over him and held out a hand.

"Can you stand?"

"I think my ankle is broken." Exhaustion filled his voice. Alex lifted him off the ground and let him use her like a crutch. Her shoulder fit tucked under his arm. They hobbled towards the street.

"Thanks for having my back." She said only loud enough for his ears to hear.

He grunted and hopped on one foot. James squeezed her close. "It was an honor to fight alongside a-"

"Asshole."

He chuckled. "A hero."

Alex was grateful dark alley hid the flush in her

cheeks at his words. She led him down the street in the direction of the Urgent Care. They walked in silence the rest of the way.

Forty-eight hours ago, chaos erupted. Alex sent every second of camera footage, every photograph of paperwork, and an intense statement from Paul to all major news organizations. She also sent it to all the Shade offices. They pulled every agent associated with Imani out of the field to be questioned.

The news was plastered with Alex's face along with the words "Vampire Princess". She was considering a change from the desert. Ontario Canada had very little population. Alex could find a secluded cabin. She could bring Mariana. Would Mariana want to hide out with her? There was no way Mariana was ready to retire. She had a passion for science and Alex had a passion for her.

Alex glanced over her shoulder into the living room. Jules and Mariana stood by the door. Mariana's hand rested atop one of two suitcases. Everything she owns resides in the two cases and a backpack resting at her feet. She left her Gibbard employee badge in the apartment with the corporate furniture. It never suited her anyway. The lab in Santa Rosa mysteriously went up in flames. James sent a photo to Alex's new phone. Pictured was the back of Paul. He was holding a red gas can. The words "Therapy for Paul" were all the text said. He was no longer a wolf, but his pack welcomed him back with a feast in his honor. He was alive, and that was all that mattered to James. Who showed great strength and courage. Traits that had his Alpha looking at him to be his replacement when he becomes too old to lead.

Alex stacked knives, two Cretan Oilstones, and enough clothes for one week into a suitcase. There is a bedroom waiting for her where they are heading. In a literal fucking castle. She cannot wait to see Mariana's face when they arrive. She smiled at her over her shoulder and pretended not to hear every word of their conversation.

"She's sober. I can tell. What did you say to her?" Jules asked.

Mariana shrugged. "After the fight with Imani, she said her head was quiet and a weight was lifted."

Jules nodded and hummed. Alex felt their eyes burning into her back. She remained turned around.

"You're going with her to London. That's exciting." Jules noticed Alex shut her luggage and zip it. "Alex never talks about her family or where she is from."

"Oh, I know." Alex strolled to Mariana's side and lifted one of her suitcases. "It's like pulling teeth.

"You would never." Alex pressed a kiss to her cheek. "You love my teeth."

Mariana swatted her arm.

Alex walked through the open door and put the suitcases in the truck bed before returning for the remaining pieces of luggage. Jules was checking the straps on Alex's motorcycle. It was on a flat trailer attached to her jeep. When everything looked secure, she stood in front of Alex. The sun was low. Creating a beautiful farewell of orange and magenta in the sky.

"You know you can't take weapons on a plane." Jules pointed to the truck.

Alex smirked. She pulled her sunglasses down to narrow her red eyes to Jules. "I have a private plane."

"Of course you do." Jules rolled her eyes. There was a pregnant pause in the conversation. Alex wanted to thank her for being a friend, but the words were lodged in her throat.

"Um, -" Alex swallowed. Jules pulled her into a hug. Her muscled arms wrapped around Alex. She looked like a teenager being crushed in her arms.

"Come back and visit." She whispered.

"I will."

"Be kind to Mariana." Alex nodded. "Don't screw it up."

"I will try." They pulled apart. Mariana came up next to Alex and locked their hands together at their sides. Alex kept a flat expression as they watched Jules drive away with her motorcycle in tow. Mariana waved vigorously.

Alex led her to the passenger side of the truck but did not close the door. She let herself savor the moment of peace. Mariana wrapped her hands around her waist and pulled her in. The sun ducked below the horizon. Alex removed her sunglasses and pressed a kiss to her lips. Mariana arched her back and melted into her embrace. Time stopped for a moment. They had no responsibilities. No one relying on them. No trauma to drown them. No alcohol to cause a haze.

Alex will never forget the death of Anita. She died at her hands. At least now she understood they were both manipulated. Pawns in Imani's plans. She had to forgive herself. Mariana deserves a whole person, not the shell of a broken vampire.

For her, Alex will move on. For her, Alex will grow.

She broke the kiss and sucked in air through her teeth. Her hands roamed Mariana's curves. Making plans in her mind to use the bedroom on her jet.

"You sure you want to come with me?" Alex bit her bottom lip.

"I have nothing here." Mariana ran her fingers through Alex's hair. "And you sorta feel like home."

Her eyes flashed red. "Home, eh?"

Mariana nodded. Alex kissed her cheek and moved out of the way to shut the door. She hopped onto the driver's side and started the truck. A steady purr vibrated under the seats. She moved the gear shift before reaching over to grab Mariana's hand.

"So, I get to meet you father." A smile bloomed on Mariana's face.

"First, I have to find him." Shade agents and countless paparazzi were looking for him. Imani had him stashed somewhere and whoever was keeping him did not want to come into the light.

"Right."

"First, we get to Europe." Slowly she let out her

breath and allowed her shoulders to drop. "Then, we save a King." Alex looked at herself in the mirror. Adoni's thick accented voice filled her head, "What moves you forward?" Alex squeezed Mariana's hand and pressed on the gas pedal.

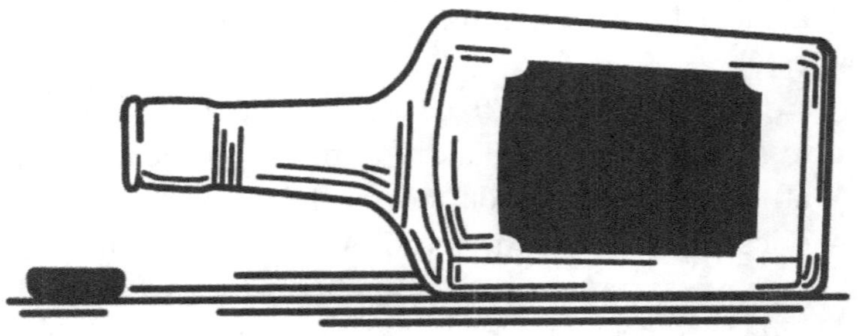

Alex raised the crystal wine glass to her lips, savoring the warm liquid within. It was freshly filled, courtesy of one of the King's loyal blood donors, a woman now resting on a couch in the next room, her pale face showing no regret of her service.

Nearby, a platter of fine cheeses and cured meats adorned the low table before Mariana, who seemed detached from the environment. The shirtless human server bowed his head low towards Alex, waiting for instructions. "Leave us." Alex flicked her hand in a lazy wave, sending him away. Mariana's rapid heart thrummed in the room.

Alex sets her glass down and studied Mariana as the door shuts. Leaving them alone in a green room. Mariana was fidgeting with the hem of her cream-colored dress. Hemmed with a lace ribbon that stopped just above her bouncing knees. Alex sighed, "Eat something."

Mariana shook her head. Eyes glued to the muted television in the corner where Adonis is addressing a packed press briefing room. "I am too nervous to eat."

"You have nothing to be nervous about. He is going to love you." Alex glanced at the TV screen. "I am afraid he will like you too much." Waves of memories went through her head. Adonis and her flirting with the same people. Placing bets to see who could seduce someone faster. Unhealthy games for a father and daughter.

Mariana stood and wiped her sweaty hands on the sides of her dress. She began to pace in front of the couch. Alex wanted nothing more than to be alone with her. They have been apart for the past six days. Alex practically grounded Mariana to a hotel room in London. She even hired security to stand outside her door. Mariana insisted it was overkill. So, Alex did not tell her she also tapped into the hotel's camera feed and was monitoring it from her phone.

All the while Alex tracked down Adonis. It took her nearly a week of following tips and trails. Eventually finding him in a secluded private estate in Brussels nearly dead. Chained to a contraption that gave him just enough blood to survive. Imani had rigged the TVs with false news reports and checked in with his captors twice a day. Other leaders in Shade were in on it. They are currently missing, but as soon as the dust settles Alex plans on smoking them out of the holes they are hiding in.

Alex moved to stand when the door peaked open. A timid female voice spoke from the other side. "King Adonis asked me to make sure you were watching the end of his statement."

The assistant shut the door before Alex could protest. She scooped an arm around Mariana's waist on her way to the tall table where the remote sat. After she clicked the sound on, Alex turned her back to the TV and nuzzled her face into Mariana's neck. She breathed in her hair and moaned.

"You're supposed to be watching." She said through a giggle as Alex sucked on her earlobe. "Alex you are wrinkling my dress."

"Then take it off."

Mariana pressed her palm on Alex's chest and pushed her off. Or rather Alex let Mariana push her off. If she wanted to, Alex could easily pin her against her will. Mariana was met with an exaggerated pout. Her cheeks flushed at the sight of a pouting vampire.

"We don't have time. Your father, the King of vampires, will be here soon, and I want to make a good impression." Mariana kissed her gently on the lips then with a hand on each shoulder and turned Alex's body to face the TV. She groaned like a child not getting her way.

On the screen, Adonis stood behind a podium. He was flanked by four large vampires. Each of them with a combination of knives and guns on their body. Alex could have been up there. He would have loved for Alex to stand by his side. Proudly for all to see. She insisted on retrieving Mariana herself and meeting up with Adonis after the press conference.

On the jet from Brussels to London, her mind finally felt at ease. Alex watched a carefree King slowly sip a blood and gin martini while reading reports about Imani's operation. Adonis will spend the next few months regaining the trust of humans, vampires, and werewolves. It is a good thing he is extraordinary when it comes to persuading people.

"You have been busy." He said with a posh Greek accent. "All this time I thought you were hiding from the world."

"I was." Alex sat with her back against the plane window, her legs spread across the seats. She has been waiting quietly for him to break the silence. Falling into a place of obedience in his presence.

The King set the papers down along with his drink. Pulling a band off his wrist he tied his white hair into a low ponytail before turning to face Alex. Their eyes were mirrors of crimson. "Why was this case so important to you that you stopped drinking long enough to solve it?"

"Who said I stopped drinking?" Alex smirked. Adonis kept his face flat and tapped his sharp nails on the armrest. "The sheriff in Vaughn is- a friend."

"Yes, the report says Sheriff Gefahr is a veteran and ex body builder. Sounds like she would make an excellent Shade-"

"You cant have her." Alex cut him off. He grinned. "She has a good life in Vaughn."

"And this James gentleman?"

"You can have him."

Adonis raised a brow. Alex scooted up straight and crossed her legs. She puffed up her chest and continued. "Actually, I wouldn't mind working on a project with him in the future. He is not completely annoying."

"There will always be a place in Shade for you, and your friend if he would like." Adonis tossed back the remaining liquid in his martini glass. "If that is what you want."

Alex glanced down at the phone in her hand. She wanted to jump through the screen and kiss Mariana. The picture she took while she slept in her bed filled the background. Alex found Adonis studying her when she raised her eyes. A pleased smiled filled his face. He looked too young to be her father, but the expression was one of pure adoration.

"Perhaps I can find something Shade adjacent. I am not ready to jump back into Shade." They stared at each other for a long moment. He tapped the stack of reports.

"I wonder what is holding you back?"

"Not holding me back," Alex paused, "Pushing me forward."

Back in the green room, Mariana stood with her arms wrapped around Alex as they watched Adonis speak. Mariana's steady heartbeat became a peaceful anchor for Alex.

"Now that I have answered your questions. I have one announcement to make. I have reigned as King for centuries. Longer than a mortal could comprehend. I have sired hundreds of vampires, each aiding to keep balance and justice. Yet only one is my true heir. Raised under my guidance, even before I made her immortal."

The room buzzed with tension. The reporters hanging on his every word.

Alex stiffened. "What the fuck!" She hissed.

"Is he talking about *you*?" Mariana asked. Alex nodded, her feet moving before her brain could catch up. She stood under the glow of the television as Adonis continued

"Princess Alexandrine will make an excellent King. In one year, I shall relinquish the title to her. At the head of Shade, she will lead us into a new era of unity and strength." The room exploded. Cameras flashed and multiple reporters stood. They were shouting questions over each other in a rumble of noise. Adonis looked at the large stationary camera with a red light on the side and winked. The gesture meant for Alex watching from the next room. She moved out of Mariana's grip and began to pace in a circle with her hands covering her face. "That is all. My team will release information as needed."

Mariana's jaw was slack and open. Her eyes wide as the TV went to the news anchors. She rushed to Alex's side, trying to stop her from spiraling.

"Why would he do this? I am not a leader." Alex said through gritted teeth. "This is so fucked up."

The door to the green room opened. One of Adonis's men filling the doorway. He scanned the room before stepping aside. Adonis floated in. His perfectly tailored suit an inky black. Alex planted her feet and flashed him a fuming glare. He ignored her and moved directly before Mariana.

"Ah," he said smoothly, his crimson eyes glinting,

"Dr. Nava. You are even more enchanting in person." He took Mariana's hand, pressing a cool kiss to her knuckles.

"Oh. Thank you. It is an honor to meet you, your highness. Um, King Adonis." She stammered, her cheeks flushing. "Um, sorry I don't know what to call you."

"You call him *ass*-hat." Alex snatched Mariana's hand away and held it at her side. "What the hell was that?" She pointed to the TV behind her.

Adonis sank gracefully onto the couch, his every movement deliberate, his demeanor maddeningly calm. "I believe it is called a press briefing."

"You announced," Alex's voice cracked with fury. "You announced to the world that I'm going to be King. In a year!"

"I would do it tomorrow," he said lightly, flashing an infuriating smile, "but these days, transitions of power require paperwork. Besides, I need time to plan the perfect coronation."

Mariana's giggle startled Alex. "Don't encourage him!" she narrowed her eyes at her.

"What?" Mariana grinned, shrugging. "He's not wrong. You'd make an amazing King."

"Stop." Alex's tone turned sharp, her eyes darting towards Adonis. "Stop influencing her thoughts in hopes it will make me go along with your crazy plan."

Adonis leaned back, arms spread casually across the couch. "Do you truly believe I need to influence her to see your worth?"

Alex gripped Mariana's chin and forced her to

make eye contact. She watched as her pupils shrink from being dilated. Adonis chuckled. "Don't make this weird."

"You stand there with ripped denim pants, protecting a human woman behind you, with my blood coursing through you. And you have the audacity to call me weird. Your father. Your King." He placed an ankle over a knee and spread his arms on the back of the couch. "Play time is over Alexandrine. Responsibility awaits. If I have to allow you to drag this human along with you, then so be it."

"You're insufferable," Alex growled, stepping protectively in front of Mariana.

"And you're *my* daughter," Adonis countered, his voice taking on an edge. "The crown awaits, Alexandrine. If you insist a mortal sits beside you on the throne, so be it."

"One year isn't enough," Alex whispered low, her voice laced with desperation. She leaned back into Mariana's arms, feeling the comfort of her embrace, the warmth of her presence.

Adonis's expression softened slightly, a flicker of something almost human crossing his face. "I gave you five hundred years," he murmured.

"One year with her, it's not enough."

"Then give her eternity," Adonis said simply, his gaze flicking between them. "If she wishes it." His words hung in the air, heavy with implication. "We leave for Monaco tonight. I'll see you on the plane." He rose in a blur, his departure leaving the room oppressive and silent.

The door clicked shut behind him.

Alex turned to Mariana, her chest tight, her hands

trembling as she cupped Mariana's face. "I can't- I won't ask you to do this," she whispered. "To give up your life. I never expected that of you."

Mariana silenced Alex with a kiss, wrapping her arms around Alex's waist, pulling her close. "You're not asking," she whispered back, her breath warm against Alex's lips. "I *want* this. I want *you*. Forever."

Alex's heart pounded as she searched Mariana's eyes for any trace of influence. Finding none, she leaned in, pressing a kiss to the delicate skin of her neck.

"You're sure?" Alex's voice was barely audible. The tone fragile.

"Forever," Mariana whispered, her voice steady, resolute.

Alex closed her eyes. Her chest inflated with hope that could pop with one harsh word from Mariana. "I love you." She whispered. "I think I loved you when I first saw you."

"I love you too, Alex." Mariana ran her hand up the shaved underside of Alex's hair. She lightly held Alex in place with her lips pressed to her neck.

"I want you Mariana."

"You have me." She said breathlessly.

"I need you to be mine." Alex opened her mouth. Her fangs rested on Mariana's skin.

"Take me." Mariana kept her grip firm on Alex's body. Bracing herself. "I am yours."

Alex had never felt clarity like this before. A breathy gasp escaped Mariana as Alex sunk her teeth into her neck. The world around them seemed to fade.

This was their beginning, The first step towards an immortal bond. Always moving forward together.

THE END

ACKNOWLEDGEMENTS

Ever since I jumped into this wild author journey, I've been blessed with the best support squad I could ask for. My husband deserves an award (or at least a cookie) for not only keeping the kids out of my office so I can focus on writing but also for creating all my book covers and artwork. I think he might secretly be my biggest fan… or maybe he just really wants to avoid seeing the laundry pile up!

Then there's my superstar friend, Toni Reeves, who has bravely read everything I've written, including the plot twists I almost regret. Her feedback and encouragement? Absolute gold. She's like my personal cheerleader, only with less pom-poms and more constructive criticism.

And, of course, my amazing community on Discord—shoutout to the Textual Tension and Best Fries Forever servers! Whether we're swapping story ideas, talking about what we're reading, or just sharing way too many memes, you all make this journey feel like a party. Our weekly chats feel like my second home, and it's honestly my favorite "place" to be.

To everyone who's read, shared, or posted about my book on social media—thank you. Seriously, you may not realize it, but each post, each comment, each share can change an author's life. You are truly amazing and so, so essential in the indie world. Cheers to all of you for making this ride so incredible

ABOUT THE AUTHOR

Rena Rene Mangold grew up in a tiny Oregon town, where she fell head over heels for theater, fashion, and writing—basically anything that would let her play dress-up and write about it. She eventually made her way to a fashion school in Los Angeles, where she filled journals with scribbles of movie plots, play ideas, and novel outlines. Finally, she decided her dreams couldn't hide in the shadows anymore, and *To Touch A Reaper* became her debut published work!

When she's not writing, Rena's likely hanging out with her husband, two kids, and her loyal hound dog in Utah. You'll find them either gaming like pros or hunting for the coolest rocks around!

MORE BOOKS BY
R.R. MANGOLD

To Touch A Reaper: A hauntingly beautiful paranormal love story (Mar 2024)

No Shade in the Desert: A Sapphic urban fantasy (Jan 2025)

To Train a Demon: A dark workplace comedy (Mar 2025)